S. L. PRATER

Court of Tricksters

Cover designed by Saint Jupiter. Edited by Erin Grey.

First edition

This book was professionally typeset on Reedsy.
Find out more at reedsy.com

Contents

Content Warning

This book is naughty and was written for adults. It contains foul language, moderate fantasy violence, sex work, off-page physical and sexual abuse, sensual dialogue, and two sexually explicit scenes between consenting adults. If you don't want spoilers about the ending, stop reading this advisory now. Court of Tricksters ends on a cliffhanger with a guaranteed series HEA.

Chapter 1

(Rain)

Night fell around Rain, and the old woods awoke in the wind, swaying lanky leafless limbs that knocked together like dried bones. She loved the gloam: the inky black, the glittering starlight, and the visitor it would bring her.

As the darkness enveloped her slight frame, the shadows glinted like the sky above, filling with the glowing, blinking eyes of wild things. Bernard, her familiar, padded after her through the autumn bramble. He'd taken the form of a small cat that evening, a scruffy creature not much bigger than her boot, with a thick fur coat the color of rain clouds. A demon, he wafted the smell of sulfur with his bushy tail.

Bernard yowled a warning to her, wary of the nearby predators, but Rain kept the dagger at her hip sheathed and pulled her woolen cloak tighter against the chill, unconcerned. The cold made her old war scars twinge.

They know better by now than to prey on us, she reminded Bernard, sending him her thoughts through their linked souls. The beasts were not hunting them. They simply watched her because they feared her the way all beings with good instincts feared a witch.

Bernard's hackles rose. He hissed at the wild things of the night, unaware of how adorable he looked in his tiny fluffy feline form. Demons feared cats. Naturally he believed himself to be at his most formidable. Biting back a smile, Rain lacked the heart to tell him otherwise.

Her thoughts traveled to the visitor she was meeting, her mystery gentleman, and her pulse surged. Despite seeing him nearly every night for the last month, she both dreaded and thrilled at the thought of sharing a space with him again. Excitement kept her returning to him, but timidity stole her voice. She'd hardly spoken to him—hadn't even asked him his name.

There were so many things she wanted to discuss with him, though. Rain stopped short to run gloved fingers through her ashen hair.

You look pleasing enough. Quit fussing, Bernard scolded. He bent to scratch behind his ear with his hindleg, creating a small whirlwind of dirt and dander in his enthusiasm.

Rain shoved her hands inside her cloak, chewing her lip. She'd taken too long sprucing up at the river Eventide, trying to rub out some of the stains on her linen shirt, and now she was running late. She usually kept silent while her gentleman gathered the offerings she'd left for him, but maybe this time would be different. Maybe this time she'd gather her courage and speak to him.

She had absolutely no idea how any of this worked. When

was it appropriate to initiate conversation with a gentleman one had an attraction to? She'd lived alone in the woods too long to have kept up with all the rules of society, and they'd changed so much over the centuries. It may still be fashionable to have family introduce her, but what was one to do when they had no family?

Her heart squeezed at the thought.

Her visitor had accepted all of her gifts and had even left some of his own: tins of sweets, rare flowers, thoughtful little mementos he'd made from folded parchment. Surely that was a good sign. Perhaps she should have shared more words with him already, but she wasn't very good at words. In his presence, her palms sweat and her tongue tied and her heart positively soared. Eloquence was impossible.

The trees rattled their limbs at her despite the absence of more wind, pulling her from her thoughts. Curious, she turned to the nearest trunk and laid the flat of her hand over the bark, sharing her warmth with it. The tree stilled. Slowly the others followed suit, and the forest fell calm once more.

She had an affinity with the woods. The trees, her friends, delivered messages to her in shared feelings. From one end of the forest to the other and beyond, they passed her communications and projections but never in words. With her palm pressed hard enough to feel the bark's ridges through her leather gloves, she *sensed* the stress and worry of a mortal she'd come to know well. An image of the woman popped into her mind, looking frazzled and worn. Susan owned the tavern not far from there, on the edges of River Row where the city met her forest.

Mortals are fragile creatures, Bernard thought, *constantly swimming in and out of the rapids, always in need of someone to save them from drowning. If you're finally tired of their antics—*

"I'm not tired of them," Rain said reprovingly. Spinning on her heels back in the direction of the Eventide, she picked up her pace, determined to reach Susan and the girls faster.

What of your visitor . . . ?

That slowed her, but only just. Tonight, he'd have to walk the woods alone. Bernard was right. Mortals were fragile, and their lives were short. Though she didn't look it, she'd lived so many centuries these mortals seemed like children to her, streetwise and world-weary though they were. They were kind and vulnerable too, offering her companionship and shelter when the ground froze over, and in exchange she promised to always come when they needed her most.

Rain's fae blood helped her navigate the trees in the dark, gave her skin its golden hue, and made her fast. Nearly faster than Bernard in his bounding cat form.

The parts of you that aren't fae are overly concerned with the weaker things of the world, Bernard mused as they ran. *You'd be better served if you listened to your immortal instincts more.*

Panting, Rain's breath fogged in front of her. *My ability to care about weaker things in this world is the only reason why you're my familiar.*

That reminder stopped his grumbling.

The trees parted—the bustling sounds of city life chasing away the quiet of the woods. The fencing was sparse here, allowing Rain to come and go easily. Susan's modest, red-brick tavern sat along a busy side street. A worn wooden sign in the shape of a red stocking hung above the front door. The words had faded long ago, so the locals simply called the tavern The Red Boot now.

Rain could hear the rush of the river Eventide in the distance, the flurry of footsteps from travelers coming and going, the clomp of horse hooves and carriage wheels, the last bell chiming before the final ferry departed. The sounds even at the edge of the Row were so different from the peaceful ambiance of the forest she called home. The energy it took to decipher it all made her pulse surge.

Hide yourself for now, she cautioned Bernard, rounding toward the side entrance. *At least until we know what's wrong.*

Bernard darkened in color and then evaporated into a puff of black smoke. The smog gathered itself into a hovering cloud and then funneled a path beneath her cloak, into her side satchel. Familiars were a type of trickster, a magical shape changer. Bernard, a particularly powerful one, could replicate any form as long as it wasn't larger than his true demon shape. She didn't know what form he'd taken once he'd settled, only that something grew solid and heavy as it weighed against her thigh.

Rain shouldered open the side door slowly, the scent of ale and excesses stinging her nose as she peered inside. Despite the traffic on the street, the front doors were shut tight and barred. Gaslights burned dully, illuminating drab wood floors and walls cluttered with paintings and hangings. There were only three patrons, which was unusual. The Boot was normally full of visitors this time of night, catching the workers as they headed home for the evening. Two men sat at the bar, and the other occupied a back table with Margot, one of the prostitutes.

Susan worked the counter, messy golden hair pinned up haphazardly, the bodice of her low-cut dress wrinkled. Rain had never seen her so untidy. Their eyes met as she slipped inside, and Susan hurried over to her in a flurry of petticoats.

"Thank the stars for you," Susan gasped, peering nervously over her shoulder. A blue vein in her forehead throbbed. "I felt like a fool shouting at that tree, but I had no other choice. The constables don't care for our lot. You're the only hope we got."

"What's the matter?" Rain matched her tone, following her anxious look to the male at the corner table. She had a better angle on him now. Four short-spiked horns sprouted from the crown of his head. His pointed ears were pierced with multiple metal loops. Bulky muscles filled out his shirt. He was a dragae, one of the Unseelie fae from the mountains.

"That one hasn't left in two days," Susan whispered. "Our regulars usually offer us protection, but they're no match for this brute. He's stayed well beyond his welcome, and he's barred the doors, only letting men inside willing to pay *him* an entrance fee, if you can believe it. Now the lot here have banded together. They've got Margot and poor Penny beyond exhausted, even with me thrown in for a break, and they won't leave. They're rough, which we tolerated for a time, but they've stopped paying my girls altogether and they steal what they want from my stock."

Rain nodded her head. She'd heard enough. The other men at the bar were human and were less of a threat to her. The dragae would pose the biggest burden with his strength and natural brutality. Descended from dragons and trickster fae, they often took whatever they wanted to add to their hoards. Tradition and power were law in the mountains, and humans were nothing to them.

Immortal Blade, Rain instructed Bernard as she crossed the room, her woolen cloak billowing at her back. The weight and shape in her satchel shifted and elongated.

Chapter 1

At the corner table, Margot laughed and tossed her head, sending her dark curls tumbling. It wasn't a true laugh. Shadows hung under her hazel eyes, and her lips were bracketed with worry lines. She carried on for the benefit of the dragae across from her.

Rain slipped into the chair beside the unwelcomed male and glanced at Margot. Relief danced in the human woman's gaze, but she refrained from breaking her composure.

"Who's this?" the dragae drawled in a bold accent.

"Oh, let me introduce my friend," Margot carried on, boisterous and playful. The frills around her bodice were torn. Bruises marred the tops of her heavy breasts. She had a warm complexion that would brown easily in the sun, and Rain suspected this careless dragae had stained her pretty skin with his rough hands.

"Keep talking," Rain told her friend, seeking cover.

The dragae sputtered, confused. Margot obeyed, laughing robustly, the perfect distraction as Rain drew Bernard—now an obsidian blade that mimicked the sort dragons feared most—out of her satchel. She wedged the sharp tip into the male's side.

The dragae yelped, then tensed. The muscles of his arms bunched.

Scooting in closer, Rain brought her lips to his tall ear, not wanting to draw the attention of the patrons at the bar. "Do you know what this is?"

"A cursed blade," the dragae spat.

"Do you understand what it can do to you . . . ? What *I* can do to you?" The scent of sulfur—the scent of hell—strengthened around her.

His eyes went wide, and his thick hands made fists on the

tabletop. "I know what a witch can do to me."

Margot babbled on, concealing their conversation from the other patrons to prevent a brawl. She made rude comments about politicians, then recited a poem about a buxom barmaid who lost her favorite ribbon and then her virginity to the man who found it for her.

Rain sunk the sharp tip through the dragae's shirt, breaking his skin, staining the linen crimson, a warning that had him groaning. "If you don't get up and leave right now," she whispered, "ride the Eventide back to your mountains, and leave these women in peace, I'm going to shove my blade between your ribs twice for good measure, then I'm going to bury it in the side of your neck so deep not even the divines will be able to dig it out for you."

The dragae bared his sharp teeth. "I leave now in exchange for my life. Do we have a bargain, witch?"

Bargains were no small thing between immortals. Failure to complete one was certain death. The source of bargain magic came from the blood and the soul, and an unfulfilled bargain had the ability to drain both should one not perform the agreed upon task. "You will leave the tavern without hurting anyone. And you will not step one foot into this place ever again. In exchange I let you live. *Now,* do we have a bargain?"

"On my life, yes," he hissed.

"On my life," Rain echoed, sealing the spell. She felt an invisible band cinch around her ribs, the pressure of the agreement-magic weighing on her. She pulled the blade back. It made a wet sound as it left his side. The dragae winced.

Margot abruptly stopped babbling. She sagged in her chair, showcasing her fatigue. The dragae took his time sliding out of his seat. He stood there for a moment, fingering the new bloody hole in his shirt, grimacing. Rain began to relive every word she'd spoken in the bargain. The longer he lingered, the sharper her uncertainty became. Perhaps she'd made a mistake. Perhaps she'd missed something, been too vague with her words.

Perhaps the bastard didn't care if he died.

In a temper, he knocked his mug off the table, and Margot jumped. The glass went clattering, spraying foam and ale in an arc across the floor. Huffing, the dragae stomped to the door and unbarred it, throwing the metal piece to the side so that it clanged like thunder against the floorboards. He glanced one last time at Margot, an unreadable expression on his twisted face. Margot made a circle with her fingers and stuck out her tongue, a crude gesture. He snarled at her, and then he was gone into the night.

And good riddance.

"I don't usually say my prayers to my ancestors like I'm supposed to," Margot panted, "but tonight I'm sending all of them a prayer of thanks for you, Rain. I wasn't going to make it another minute with that brute. And it wasn't just the bruises. His *breath*," she wheezed, chest heaving. "I'd wager my weight in gold that he's never used toothpowder before in his life."

"Penny?" Rain demanded, scanning the room for the girl.

"Upstairs in the loft. Be quick."

Rain set Bernard on the table. He transformed from a blade to smog to a little black cat. Margot watched the change with round hazel eyes.

Keep them safe, Rain insisted. Bernard groaned in her thoughts, but she trusted he'd listen. She sprinted up the stairs, taking the creaking steps two at a time. They rose into a short landing before a set of double doors.

"Please." Penny's light voice filtered through the crack. "I'm tired. No more."

Rain didn't wait for the brute to respond. She kicked the doors open. They swung wide, banging against paneled walls. Tall and coltish, Penny covered her breasts in surprise. She was naked from the waist up, her bodice and skirts draping off narrow hips. Her corset was in a torn heap on the floor beside her bare feet.

The brute glowered at Rain. His torso was bare, suspenders hanging from his trousers at his sides, his heavy brow bunched in aggravation. His nose was a bright red and veiny like he'd had too much to drink every day for the last decade.

"Who in the blazing stars are you?" he growled thickly. Rust-colored hair covered his rounded abdomen. The room stunk of sex and sweat. The tang of spirits melded strongly with an overabundance of cologne.

Rain ignored him, rushing for the window. She threw the glass up, and crisp autumn air billowed inside.

"What're you doing?" he barked.

"Putting up the window," Rain said, heat flaring in her belly. Penny looked worn and scared, and this bastard was the culprit responsible. She wanted to squeeze his neck until he turned purple. "Susan didn't like it when I broke the pane putting out the last sonofabitch who refused to listen to the word 'no.'"

"Either join in, girl," the man snapped, "or get out!"

"Pay her and leave," Rain demanded, voice as cool as the night air pouring over the sill.

"Fuck off," he grunted, putting his back to her, reaching for Penny.

"No more, please!" Penny slapped at his grabbing hands.

It was a witch's familiar that usually gave them away, as

having a familiar made one a witch—and hers was downstairs out of sight. With Rain's white-blonde hair hiding the subtle points of her ears and her slight frame, she appeared young instead of ancient, harmless instead of deadly. Rain stripped off her cloak, letting it pool on the floorboards around her boots. If he used his size, he might be able to knock her down. This was fine. When knocked down, Rain always got back up again.

She pounced, driving her knee into the man's flank, bending him in half.

He coughed and choked. "What the blue blazes—"

She grabbed the back of his neck, squeezing so hard she felt the muscles give under the leather of her gloves. He cried out, pawing at her with ineffective, pudgy mortal fingers. Rain shoved a hand into the pocket of his trousers, freed his coin purse, and tossed it at Penny's feet.

"Gah, you great cunt . . ." he spat through gritted teeth, his face purpling.

Rain jerked him toward the open window by the back of his neck and hurled him out of it. He tumbled headlong with a shrill scream, landing on his backside in the muck below. On the street, a hackney came to an abrupt halt, the horses whinnying. A lamplighter rushed to the man's side, hoisting his pole like a javelin. He glanced up at Rain and pointed. The brute rolled in the mud, whimpering.

Rain leaned out, watching the commotion grow on the street. She promptly pulled back inside, closed the window, and locked it.

Slowly, she turned to Penny. The girl sniffled, her auburn curls in tangles around her narrow face. Her slender neck was dotted in red marks, a collection of fingerprint-sized injuries. Shame and worry made Rain's insides roll together unpleasantly. She thought she should say something, but she'd never been very good at saying the right things. Rain had been a Seelie warrior once—a soldier, they called them now. Threats of violence came rather naturally, but words and feelings were another more complicated matter she rarely got right.

"Are you . . ." Rain paused, shuffling her feet anxiously. "I can have Bernard heal you . . ."

"I'm all right," Penny whimpered. She turned to her side, revealing the ridges and valleys of her ribs and the light swell of her breasts. Penny glanced down at her ruined corset, then slipped her arms into capped sleeves and swiped at her running nose.

Rain chewed her lip, struck momentarily by the girl's youth. She understood humans aged differently, but it still seemed wrong to her. Penny was only one-and-twenty and so very soft. So genteel. This wasn't the life for her.

It wasn't a good life for any of them, but a necessity if they wanted to eat and stay warm and avoid the threats of war that loomed near the borders of the province, just on the other side of the Eventide. The unfairness of it burned in her gut and made her neck hot.

Rain gathered up her cloak and left the loft to give Penny her space. As she descended the stairs, she heard Margot cooing at Bernard, "such a sweet itty bitty kitty."

The bar was empty of patrons, and two stools sat on their sides, turned over like the last of the men had left in a great hurry. Susan fetched a mop and pail and joined Margot at the corner table, smiling down at the familiar.

Why is she touching me? Bernard groused.

Rain's cheeks filled with a smile. Then the pungent scent of demon magic hit her nostrils and she grimaced. *She wants to be your friend.*

We are not friends. Tell them I am an ancient and powerful demon. Hell itself spat me out. Its fires could not hold me.

"He's happy to see you again," Rain told them, dropping her cloak over the back of the chair. They both cooed at the demon.

Bernard flexed his claws. *Fear me, mortals!*

"He likes it when you scratch behind his ears," Rain said.

Margot grabbed at him excitedly.

Unhand me, you fiend!

Bernard's grumbling in his cat form sounded a bit like purring. Encouraged, Margot petted him more enthusiastically. Then Bernard was indeed purring and through their link cursing at Rain and blaspheming the divines above colorfully, *by the moon mother's knickers . . .*

Susan lifted her chin, peering at the door to the loft. "How is she?"

Rain shook her head.

"Give Penny a moment, and she'll come around," Susan said softly.

"This one's a right hero," Margot said. Bernard was leaning into her fingers now, still cursing, but his tone had gentled. She scratched under his chin lazily. "One of those sods tried to steal from Susie again. Your boy turned into a wolf and sent them both scrambling. Now the whole place stinks like rotten eggs, but it was well worth it to see the look on their ugly faces."

I'm not a boy, Bernard hissed. *Tell them I only did it so you wouldn't lecture me.*

A growing commotion out on the street drew their eyes to the window.

A fae male had climbed down from the hackney coach with the sleek predatorial grace of a panther on the hunt, and Rain's stammering heart nearly gave out entirely.

There her nightly visitor stood, her mystery man in the flesh—in his very lovely flesh.

A small crowd gathered around the brute she'd heaved out of the window earlier, blocking traffic on the street. She'd only ever seen her gentleman visitor in traveling clothes, and rather plain ones at that. Now he called out commands to his driver, dressed in finery fit for . . . *royalty*. Her mouth dropped open.

"Ain't that . . ." Margot muttered.

"The Fae Duke of Night," Susan finished, and the air left Rain's lungs in a sharp rush. "What's the Lord of the Lunar Court doing here in the gutters with the likes of us?"

Rain flushed. Duke? Oh no, had she foolishly set her sights on the most unobtainable man in all of the Row?

The duke was beautiful like all fae were beautiful. Short curving antlers sprouted from long trimmed layers of midnight hair so blue it appeared black. His skin was a silvery gray that burned luminous in the moonlight. His cheekbones and the bridge of his nose were overly defined. He worked an angular jaw while shouting orders at the gathering men, and they heeded him without question.

Because he's a duke, for the stars' sake! Was she the biggest idiot in the province for thinking this man was interested in her? Yes! Yes, she was.

The duke was dressed like a prince in a frock coat lined in rich wolf fur, a dark silk cravat at his throat. He was so striking

Rain groaned, drawing concerned gazes from her companions. Even Bernard stopped his cursing to peer at her.

But then, why *had* he visited her and with such frequency too? *He* was the mystery. Not her. One look at Rain in her handmade leather trousers and worn woolen cloak, her demon familiar, and there was no doubt who she was—*not* a titled lady of means and grace. Not a woman who should be courting a duke. Her stomach hurt. She touched a hand to her navel hoping to calm the sensation, but it only grew.

Rain studied the duke's profile as he hovered over the brute in the mud, questioning him. Scars marred what was otherwise perfect, the skin broken near his temple and at the corner of his mouth. He wore his wounds without care, never hiding them. Never turning away even as others stared at them. It made Rain curious. She liked to keep her old scars under several layers of clothing.

Just the memory of his broken smiles as he'd looked over the paltry gifts she'd made for him in the woods took her breath. The wounds called to her fingers. She wanted to follow their jagged path with her touch. They were like a secret, one she wanted desperately to know.

And now he was here. Really here, though he looked like a vision.

Margot's next words made Rain's stomachache sharpen. "He's headed this way."

Chapter 2

(Night)

Night, the fae duke of the Lunar Province, hadn't been listening as his illegitimate brother, and estate advisor, rambled on about urban tenants and past-due rents. He sat on the bench seat across from Erikson in the tight cabin space. Their legs knocked together as the hackney coach swayed and bobbed down an ill-paved street.

His thoughts were consumed by something else again—someone else. He was thinking of his witch and the vivid dreams she'd inspired in him of late. Since he'd first glimpsed her, he'd had them every day while he slept the sun away.

For reasons he hadn't yet surmised, she'd missed their rendezvous at dusk that evening. He'd kept his brother waiting on him longer than he should have. Now they were running late, and he was left to speculate wildly about where she was. He tapped his fingers together in an anxious rhythm. His knee bobbed.

Chapter 2

His witch had left gifts for him under their tree in a basket she'd woven: soaps and scented oils she'd made herself. They smelled like her, like the little white flowers that bloomed in early fall, a fragrance not so different from vanilla. He had that fragrance on his skin now.

It both tortured and soothed him.

Night had precious little time to be spending obsessing over anything or anyone at the moment, what with war between the Seelie and Unseelie Courts looming all around his province, threatening the borders of the city of River Row. But if his instincts were right—and they usually were—he didn't just want the witch. He *needed* her. She had the potential to solve everything. Politics were like an intricate hand of Fortuity, a card game where players laid tricks and bluffed about their trump cards round after round to win the match, except here the stakes were life and death. If he played his hand correctly, his witch could save the entirety of the Lunar Court . . .

"Are you even listening to me?" Erikson broke through his reverie. "The Seelie queen sent another letter."

Just mentioning the monarch was like dumping a pail of ice water on the duke's head. "What of it?"

"She wished to encourage you, once again, to make your selection quickly and soon. The dragon king sent a similar demand from the mountains. In summary, they both expect you to take their side in the conflict, wed the woman of their choosing immediately, then sire a brood of future mages who will pledge their allegiance to them—I added that last bit after reading between the lines."

Night scoffed. "A brood? That's new. Stars, could you imagine? Me, a father?"

"Actually, I can," Erikson said.

Night pulled at his cravat, remembering uncomfortably that he'd played a role in his brother's raising centuries ago—though a majority of the credit was due to a strict nurse and a string of fae tutors. Their father had died in the first war between the Seelie and the dragon king's Unseelie. Night had stepped reluctantly into his father's place.

"Any children I make might end up just like me," the duke quipped, breaking the tension. "I wouldn't survive a brood of them."

Erikson chuckled. "Vain, bossy know-it-alls. The very picture of arrogance."

"Yes," Night said drolly, "but such a pretty picture."

The coach came to an abrupt halt. Erikson rocked forward. The duke braced himself.

"What the deuce?" his brother groused.

Night bent his head out of the hackney window. A half-naked man sprawled in the mud near the road, rolling and groaning and whimpering as a crowd of concerned citizens gathered around him.

A lamplighter stood closest to the fallen human. He pointed up at the second-story window of the nearby tavern, and Night's eyes went wide.

There she was. His witch. White hair streamed in the wind around her heart-shaped face. She leaned out into the darkness, taking in the commotion on the ground below. Her breath fogged around the delicate apples of her cheeks. His mouth went completely dry. It was like seeing her for the first time all over again.

Mate.

His very soul confirmed it, pebbling his skin, tightening his muscles. His heart jackhammered against his ribs, sending panic and pure bliss coursing through his veins. Just gazing at her was risk and reward.

Short and slight, she didn't at first appear to be the sort of woman who should be living alone in treacherous woods. But there was fire in her bottomless amber eyes, and the scent of hell followed her and the trickster familiar always at her side.

"What is it?" Erikson asked, straightening his top hat over his dark blue hair. His brother was half-fae, half-mortal: no horns or antlers or tail, and he'd grown his sideburns long to conceal the roundness of his face. Night didn't mind his mixed heritage, though his preference for mortal proprieties was trying at times. His brother peered out the window beside him. "Do you think that little woman there shoved him . . . ?"

"Wait here." Night's voice had dropped an octave.

His witch had pulled back inside and shut the window tight, then moved deeper into the room where he couldn't see her. A burst of hot frustration churned in his gut at losing sight of her. He was a calculating man, not usually so quick to aggravation, but the blooming bond instinct was a demanding thing, and its persistence grew in intensity by the minute. He shoved open the coach door and clambered out onto the street. The subtle scent of the white flowers on his skin mingled with the smell of crisp autumn air and dank river.

"Where are you going?" Erikson kept his voice low and bent to join him on the street.

"Wait here, I said," Night insisted. He wasn't accustomed to having to repeat himself, even to his brother.

Cowed, Erikson flushed. He pulled the coach door shut with a snap but continued to lean out. "You aren't going in *there*, are you?"

"It's just a tavern." Night squinted at the brick front.

"It's a cheap brothel," Erikson hissed, his breath misting in the cold. "Think what the papers will say if anyone sees you setting foot in such a low-class establishment. If you're in the mood for love, this isn't the place for that, brother. The only thing you'll get here is robbed and the pox."

"Love?" Night snorted at the notion. Love belonged in fairy stories. If it existed at all, it had no place in the real world, but he was undeterred by his brother's mortal sensibilities. More than half of River Row was human or at least partially so these days, but that seemed like a poor excuse to abandon fae traditions and duties completely in favor of nonsense like *love*.

"The whole point of hiring a hackney and leaving your guard behind in the first place," his brother grumbled, "was to conceal your presence on this particular street."

"Shall I accompany you, Your Grace?" the mortal driver offered.

Night waved him off. "No. Steady your horses. I'll be back in a moment."

"*Night*," his brother groaned, but he stayed put as the duke strolled away.

The crowd clotting the street was formed mostly of day workers headed home for the evening. They parted for the notorious duke with an echo of a humbly mumbled, "Your Grace." "My Lord," was uttered by the few fae members in the grouping. He waved them all off, closing in on the shirtless man coughing in the mud.

"You," Night said, drawing the human's gaze. "What happened here?"

"Your G-grace," he spluttered, the whites of his eyes showing in fear. The duke had a reputation, one that he'd carefully cultivated. At the moment, that reputation was a hindrance. He needed this man's tongue to wag, not to be tied up in terror.

He forced a calming smile. "Tell me what happened here," he said reassuringly.

"The wench threw me out, Your Grace," he choked. "Could have killed me! I think I broke my ass . . ."

"Someone should fetch a constable," the lamplighter murmured, leaning against his pole.

"*Why'd* she throw you out?" Night said with increasing venom, and the murmuring ceased around him. A possessive heat smoldered under his skin. The bond instinct curled in his belly, raising his blood pressure, testing his control. His hands wanted to make fists. He stopped them. "What'd you do to her?"

"Nothing, Your G-grace!" He cowered, and his eyes went big and round. "I . . . I didn't lay a hand on her, I swear it on my ancestors. I'll swear it on your divines too, if you'd like. I'll swear it on all of them!"

"You reek of spirits. Clearly, you've been deep in your cups." Night's nose wrinkled. "No man behaves well in your state."

The male sputtered denials, his voice thick. Night was done hearing from the likes of him. He ordered the lamplighter and a street cleaner to help drag him off the road so traffic could resume, then he made his way toward the entrance of the tavern, sidestepping onlookers, raising a polite hand to the men who removed their hats and the couple that bowed to him on the walkway.

He had to duck his head to avoid hitting his curved antlers on the red wooden sign shaped like a boot. The doorknob stuck a little when he twisted it. Warmth and the aroma of hops hit him as he pushed inside.

He was greeted by two scowling mortal faces, both pretty but worn, the lines near their painted mouths strained, their dresses torn and disheveled.

The dark-haired doxy rose out of her seat at the corner table. "Your Grace?" She frowned at him, a furrow of fear deepening between her black brows. Bruises stained the tops of her ample cleavage.

Night's nostrils flared. If there was so much as a mark on his witch, he was going to storm right back out of the tavern, find that drunkard, and stomp his bones into dust. He'd grind his flimsy human joints into powder between his fingers, then he'd return to his coach, retrieve the dagger his brother carried, and open up the bastard's belly. The rats could have him afterward.

The blonde nearest the door cleared her throat, her brow creased with worry. Night could only guess at how he looked with such violence on his mind. He inhaled through his nose and smoothed his expression. Once again, he needed tongues to wag, not to be tied up in fear of him.

She clutched a mop handle between her hands like it was a weapon. A bucket full of sudsy water sat beside her heeled boots. "We're closing early tonight, Your Grace. But if there's something we can help you with, of course we'll—"

"I hope you don't plan to bash me on the head with that," he said with a disarming grin.

"Er . . ." The blonde lowered the mop. "No, Your Grace. Of-of course not."

"Good." He gestured at the straight locks of his hair. "I'd never get my part right if you put a knot in my head." His spreading smile tugged at the scar tissue near his mouth. The mop dropped lower, and he continued, "I saw a fae woman in the window. It's imperative that I speak with her immediately."

Chapter 2

The dark-haired girl moved in closer. "If you're looking for the company of a woman, you've come to the right place, but there's no fae woman here, Your Grace. It's just Susie and I working now."

"As charming as your company would be, it's not the companionship I'm seeking." He kept his tone level and polite. "Lovely though you are, the two of you are several centuries too young for me, I'm afraid."

"No fae women work here. Please, Your Grace." Susie fumbled through a curtsy. "It's been an especially trying couple of days, but if there's something we can get you, some comfort or a drink perhaps . . . ?"

He met her blue eyes and read the exhaustion in her features. Her shoulders sagged. Golden hair broke free of its pins. Spilled ale stained the floor. She'd had one hell of a night for sure from the look of it. He reached into his pocket, fingering his leather purse, certain his coin would speak louder than his charms this evening. "I can pay you well just to allow me a conversation with her."

Was his poor mate a prostitute? He knew she was homeless and living in the woods, but was this how she fed and clothed herself? Bile burned the back of his throat. As he freed his full purse, he made a vow that desperation would no longer touch her.

And neither would any other man. Not ever again. She was the answer to all of his woes.

She was his.

The doors to the upstairs loft parted, and his eyes flew up to greet the new arrival. But the woman who stuck her head out wasn't his witch, and his stomach dropped. A willowy girl with auburn tresses came to lean against the banister, a curious expression on her sad face. She left the doors open at her back. Night peered around her, but the room appeared to be empty save for a collection of three small beds.

"This is all of us, Your Grace," Susie said, and Night's brows knitted. He recognized when others were lying, and neither of them were being entirely truthful. "You can pay us for that word, if you like, but if I may, please allow me to bar the door. We'd never turn Your Grace away, but we don't want more patrons tonight."

"Mother's knickers," the dark-haired one cursed. Whatever semblance of dignity she'd tried to put on in his presence, it fell away then. "The constable's coming this way, and he don't look pleased."

Susie's face went pale. She strained to peek around the duke, wielding the mop like a sword again, flicking water at him. "Which one, Margot?"

Night frowned down at the droplets of dirty water on his frock coat.

"Billingsley, it looks like." Margot jogged to the window and peered out. "Oh yes, I'd recognize his thick head anywhere."

"We can pay him off at least," Susie muttered.

"It'll be more than we can spare." Margot gathered her skirts with a sigh and turned for the stairs. "I'll get my purse."

"I'll get mine too," the auburn one called down.

"That won't be necessary," Night said, and all three women stopped to stare at him agog. The constable was in fact marching for the entrance, he noted. His brother would want him far away from this scene, not ingratiating himself further into this mess, but the duke had a higher prize on his mind. A worn cloak draped the chair at the nearby table. He recognized that cloak. The familiar smell of sulfur had found its way to his nose, over the scent of ale.

The demon familiar was close. *His witch* was close, probably hiding somewhere in this very tavern. His eyes swept the room. He had to battle down the urge to push past Susie to hunt for his mate, throwing open doors and shoving aside belongings like a dragon in heat. It was obvious these women were protecting her, which he'd appreciate more if they weren't attempting to hide her from the one male in the Row most determined to keep her safe. Now he had an opportunity to coax her out and to gain some trust.

Night wanted to scoop her up in the fae fashion and haul her away. When he'd visited her, it had taken every gallant bone in his gentry body not to simply pluck her from the forest and drag her home with him.

He'd let no one get in his way. Not these well-meaning women. Certainly not some swindling constable.

The lawman burst through the door, a mortal in a tight black cap that drew attention to the roundness of his face and ears. He filled out his dark uniform tunic with a barreled chest. "I told the lot of you . . ." His words fell away as his eyes landed on the duke and widened. "Y-your Grace? I didn't expect to find a gentleman of your caliber here of all places. Did you get lost?"

"Are you asking if I got lost in my own province?" Night straightened. Even without his antlers he towered over the stocky constable. "I was here before most of these streets were paved. I'll be here long after they're gone. Long after you're gone."

The constable blinked at him, at a loss for words. "I beg your pardon, Your Grace. I was caught off guard is all, seeing you here of all places. I hope I didn't offend." Then he turned an accusing gaze on the women.

"A drunkard caused a commotion in my place of business, and I've finally had him out," Susie said.

Billingsley scoffed. "Through a window. Yes, I've heard."

"I'm permitted as the owner of this tavern to put out them as can't behave themselves." Susie white-knuckled her broom. Margot came to stand beside her, chin lifted in challenge. The stairs creaked as the auburn female moved down them sheepishly.

"You're permitted to put them out the *door*," Billingsley said. "Not the sodding window. You stopped traffic, disturbed the peace, and injured a worker."

"But what of *our* injuries?" the auburn girl said. Her voice squeaked, and her hand went to cover her pale throat. "I'm a worker, aren't I?"

"The lout is a drunkard, Constable," Night scolded. "That pathetic excuse for a male had pickled himself so thoroughly he wouldn't know the door from the window. He belongs in a cell drying up, and these poor women should be in bed . . ." Several sets of eyes snapped to him. "Alone," he added quickly. "*Resting*."

Night watched it all unfold around him. He planned to intervene more thoroughly on their behalf, but upon inheriting the title of Lord of the Lunar Court, Duke of Night, he'd learned there were always cards that needed to be played just right. In Fortuity, he'd sacrifice a trick to reserve a trump card. The longer this went on, the more these women would trust him after he solved it for them.

The constable removed his cap as if he'd suddenly remembered his manners again. He nodded at the duke. "I understand your concern, Your Grace, and I'll see he's put in a cell, just as you say. As for these women, I know these instigators well and—"

"What's it gonna cost us?" Margot demanded. "What secret fine have we got to pay, huh?"

The constable's gaze bounced nervously from the women to Night. "I won't accept a bribe—"

"Pfft." Margot rolled her eyes. "Maybe not while the Duke of Night is staring at you like he's thinking of hurling you out the window too."

Night tapped a finger thoughtfully against a silver button on his coat, letting the cards fall as they may.

"It'll be irons for the one responsible for this mess," Billingsley shot back at Margot. Night repressed a snort. If anyone tried to put his mate in irons, he'd leave a string of dead bodies in his wake.

Susie groaned. "How long?"

"Oh no you don't," Margot said. "You sat in a rat-infested cell the last time. It's my turn." She proffered her wrists. "I did it. I shoved the bastard out the window because he smelled like shit and I was insulted by his tiny cock."

Behind her, the auburn woman bit back a smile. Night had to push down the urge to laugh. Then Billingsley reached for Margot, and finally the last card had come into play. It was time to make use of his trump.

"Don't you dare, Constable." Night's spine went rigid. The constable froze as the duke's charm melted away to be replaced by menace. He was thinking about violence again, and this time he didn't care how it made his face look.

Absolutely nothing about the duke's evening was going as planned, and he let his frustrations feed into his features. His mate had missed their meeting. He was currently abandoning another appointment he desperately needed not to abandon, his witch was hiding from him, and he was sick to death of mortal sensibilities. Fae did not treat unattached women like criminals in this way, not even courtesans. It was a ridiculous mortal belief that men were somehow superior to their women, which made absolutely no sense to Night. Only females could grow a babe in their womb. This was as close to a divine power as a mortal would ever come to know. In comparison, human males were as weak and worthless as stockings on a badger.

"Your Grace . . . ?" Billingsley stammered, his color rising.

"Leave these women be." Night was a well-practiced mage. It had been many centuries since he'd connected with elements of the Divine Night to call magic to him by accident, but he allowed it to look as though he'd let his control slip. It wasn't hard to pretend. His nerves were frayed at the edges, the night was a clear one, the moon was full, and his bond instincts simmered just below his skin, wanting to boil over. A younger fae would have lost his hold over his abilities entirely.

A nearby chair turned on its side seemingly on its own. The metal bar used to hold the door shut began to vibrate against the floorboards where it lay. Droplets of sudsy water rose out of the mop bucket to hover in the air. The scent of moon magic, a smell like incense, filled his lungs. His voice shook with restrained rage as he said, "Get out, Constable, while I'll still let you."

Chapter 3

(Rain)

He was magnificent.

Rain watched the duke in wonder. He stood so close to her, just a stride from the tavern door, she could reach out and touch him. She wanted to. She wanted to extend her hand and run her fingers over the wolf pelt that lined the lapels of his frock coat. She wanted to test the softness of the wool at his sleeves, feel his silk cravat between her fingers. She wanted to press her cooling body against his side and let him warm her up. Rain stood so close that as he called moon magic to him, his silver skin illuminating with a brilliance that rivaled the stars, she felt his power and trembled.

Moments before the duke had entered the tavern, she'd asked Bernard to cover her in his shadow form, concealing her from view.

I'll need to take more of your blood to keep this up much longer, he warned.

Do what you must, she replied, hugging her body against a chill that would not subside.

One month ago, the duke had strolled into her woods, dressed in a dark cloak and traveling clothes. The cloak hid much of him, and yet he'd still been so striking that as she watched him from her tree, she'd forgotten to ask her friend the oak to hide her. Trees made projections. The oak could have reflected an image at the duke that made it look as though the limb she perched on was empty.

He's a powerful one and a trickster, this mage, Bernard had told her in awe. *I bet he tastes delicious.*

You can't eat him, she'd retorted. Leaning in for a closer look, she'd watched the duke's long steady strides carry him across the forest floor with a bold sort of fearlessness that reminded her of a panther: a predator who knew he was unmatched, soaking up the moonlight, prowling for trouble. Then he'd seen her. Slowing his pace, he'd smiled up at her, and her stomach had swooped. There was starlight in that smile. Her want for him was so visceral, so instantaneous, she'd felt her jaw go slack.

I won't eat all of him. That'd be rude, Bernard had said. *Just a finger or two.*

You leave his fingers be! He's . . . perfect.

The duke had broken her that day. She'd thought herself reasonably content until then. Now she thought and dreamed of him constantly. What did he like? What did he eat? What did he read? What did he love? What did he think of her—how often if ever did she haunt his thoughts in return?

She'd learned so little in the last month—her fault. She spoke so infrequently to him.

Chapter 3

What could this powerful fae lord possibly want with a little forest witch like her? Rain had nothing to offer him in exchange for his attention, hadn't even the courage to speak to him. All she had was her affinity with nature and her familiar. He was a mage, a fae with a connection to the divine that allowed him to cast spells she could only dream of.

The constable planted his cap back on his head and fled. The tension in Night's body eased, but only just, as the door clapped shut behind the lawman. The duke steadied himself before he turned to face Susan and the girls. The droplets of water fell back in the bucket with an audible plop. The bar on the floor ceased vibrating.

His hand returned to his pocket. Once more, he removed the fat leather purse that bulged with coins. "If a patron wanted to ensure a companion's exclusivity for a time—"

"The price would be steep, Your Grace," Susan said, both hands clutching the mop handle. She hadn't been unaffected by the duke's show of power either. Penny had retreated to the stairs. Even Margot was speechless.

Night removed five golden crescents from his purse one at a time, making a show of them. "How many days would these assure my exclusivity with one of your employees?"

"Your Grace," Susan gasped, taking the coins in her palm. "That's more than an entire month's worth of wages for every woman at this establishment, including myself."

"Then it's more than enough to ensure exclusivity. I give you these and no one touches her. No one so much as *breathes* on her."

"I only have say over my girls here," Susan said, clutching the coins to her chest like she was frightened they'd vanish.

"The fae woman. The witch is what I want. She is dear to

me," he said thoughtfully.

"Your Grace, there's no—"

He pushed one more crescent at her. "This one is for her, and I'll give you another if you stop telling me stories. I know I saw her. I know she's the one who threw that fool out the window. You need not protect her from me. I mean her no harm. I wish only to buy her time. I *must* speak to her, and soon. Give her that message from me, and I'll return tomorrow. Unfortunately for now, I must be off."

She is dear to me. His words echoed in Rain's head.

And he thought she was a prostitute . . . She frowned. *And he wanted to buy her time.* Her cheeks heated, and her stomach fluttered.

He moved for the door, and Rain couldn't help herself. He was so close. So warm. So very beautiful. So breathtakingly potent. She stretched out a gentle hand and quickly stroked the plush fur at his lapel, gratitude infused in the stolen touch.

The duke froze for a moment. Rain jerked her hand back and slid against the wall. His gray eyes swept through her, squinting in the dull gaslights. He seemed unsure of himself.

"I'll return tomorrow," he repeated, the promise in his rich voice sinking through her skin and rooting into her marrow.

Tomorrow couldn't come fast enough.

Tomorrow needed to stay far, far away.

As always, time with him inspired both a thrill and dread, and there was no sensible reason why. That's what he did to her when he looked at her, showering her with his whole attention. He overwhelmed. His broken smile was as smothering as it was striking. His honey baritone was lush and full in her ears, leaving her so woefully out of her depths she felt like she was drowning in deep murky water.

Chapter 3

She'd lived alone in the woods much too long for courting. Especially with a lord. Why didn't he realize that? Why wasn't he off chasing a titled woman who could bring him more wealth, more power? A woman from his world, someone who knew what to say to him without falling over herself and then running away.

Margot hurried to the window, watching the duke move back up the street with his long lean strides. "He's gone."

Bernard dropped his shadows, then appeared in his cat form at Rain's feet. He yowled up at her. She squeezed her arms over her middle, seeking warmth through friction. Her breath fogged.

Your blood tastes delicious, Bernard cooed.

I'd rather you refrained from commenting on the delectability of my life source. Though minimal, the loss of blood made her lightheaded.

Bernard looked up at her with large yellow eyes and licked his muzzle. *It was meant to be a compliment, but suit yourself.*

"Rain." Susan's eyes glinted. "I didn't get a chance yet to properly thank you for earlier, before things took a turn—"

"Never mind all that," Margot said, grinning wickedly. She hurried to Rain's side and wound her arm through hers. "This girl has been holding out on us. Tell us *immediately* about your beau who won't so much as let another man *breathe* on you. I haven't heard that one before. Why the deuce did you hide yourself from him?"

Rain's face heated. Susan leaned in encouragingly. Rain knew she needed to respond with something, but she forgot momentarily how to fashion words. The duke's broken smile flashed through her mind, and a pleasant heat grew in her belly. A jab of panic quickly followed it.

"He's . . ." Rain rubbed the back of her neck.

"You've made quite the impression on him," Susan added helpfully. Then she used her mop to blot up spilled ale. "Ejecting a large man out the window and into the street will do that, though, I imagine."

"I've hardly spoken to him," Rain confessed, leaning into the heat offered by Margot's curvy frame. "We've spent time together, but . . ." She shrugged her shoulders, wondering why a duke would walk through her woods in the first place. Where did he go on his strolls? What was he up to?

"He's dashing, isn't he?" Penny said with a giggle. She'd made herself comfortable on the bottom stair, tucking her skirts beneath her.

Susan lifted a honey-colored brow. "Surely you've exchanged some words at least."

Rain worked her throat. "He does the talking usually. Mostly we go on walks . . . He reads to me sometimes. He brings me books, fairy stories mainly."

"And you don't talk to him? But isn't that dreadfully dull?" Margot frowned at her.

"Not at all." Needing something to busy her hands, Rain picked up the overturned mug from the floor and sat it on the table. "I . . ." A flush burned her cheeks. "I like the sound of his voice."

"Course you do." Margot winked at her.

Rain settled into the chair where her cloak was draped. Margot picked up Bernard who yowled in protest. She plopped into the seat across from Rain and sat the familiar on her lap. Bernard tried to jump down, but Margot stroked behind his ears, and he was purring begrudgingly soon after.

"He and I . . ." Rain began, hesitating again. "We're worlds apart. When men pass him on the street, they bow and call him 'Your Grace.' When men pass me on the street they say—"

"Fuck off?" Margot offered. She'd ceased petting Bernard.

He pawed at her to continue. *Did I say you could stop, human?*

"His intensity would give me pause too." Susan wrung the end of her mop out over the bucket. "But then fae are like that . . . and he's rich. He's got enough coin I'd forgive him for his fae bluntness."

"And so generous," Penny cooed dreamily. Rain was glad to see the sweet little glimmer had returned to her eyes. And then it made her sad again that the girl had to be so resilient.

"And he's well-endowed," Margot said. Heads shifted toward her. "What . . . ? Was I the only one looking?" She shrugged. "Professional curiosity."

She is dear to me. His words returned to Rain. Her stomach fluttered, and then like always, the warm feelings were cooled by anxious ones. "I have nothing to say to him. We're too different."

His nobility made him a different sort of trickster. Whatever he wanted from her, it would be significantly more complicated than an affair. Gentry tricksters were plotters, mages who sat at the top of society and played political games with those lesser than themselves. They didn't court those beneath them—not without great reason, a reason Rain was certain she wouldn't like.

"Don't fret too much about that," Susan said. "Men like a shy miss. A reserved woman is fun to chase, fun to warm up. Fun to *seduce*."

"Men like compliments," Margot offered. "Tell a man he's tall even if he ain't tall, and he'll be eating out of your hand. Tell him he's clever even if he's as dumb as a rock. Hmm."

She tapped her chin, using her free hand to stroke Bernard's bowed back. "Men like a young woman with little experience. A maiden."

Rain wasn't young, but she had little experience when it came to romance and seduction. One didn't get a lot of chances to seduce men when they lived alone in the woods, and she hadn't been all that interested in intimate company before now.

"Not sure anyone would believe Rain was less than thirty," Susan said, the mop hitting the floorboards wetly.

"What are you going on about?" Margot scoffed. "I'd give my left tit to have a tight little body like what she's got."

"Don't you dare do a thing to your beautiful tits. They're paying our rent." Susan paused then, propping her chin on the wooden mop handle. "Look at her eyes."

Margot peered over at Rain. Rain sunk down in her seat, feeling dissected. "I see what you mean. Too much world-weariness in those eyes. Better tell him you're thirty."

"And a widow," Penny added. "That's respectable. Then he won't think you're a spinster."

These women are fools, Bernard grumbled.

They're mine, Rain thought fondly. *Leave them be.* To the girls she added, "I might try what you've suggested."

"We can put you in a nice blouse," Margot said, straightening in her seat. "Susie's old coat is newer, and more fashionable. Leave your cloak and we'll have it cleaned. And how about a quick wash?"

"Do I smell?" Rain grabbed a lock of her white hair and sniffed.

Margot's nose wrinkled. "You smell like mud."

That made sense. She often slept on the ground. "And that's

bad . . . ?" She liked the earthy scent personally.

"Could be better, is all. We've still got a few cakes of the soap you made for us." Margot's smile was warm and convincing. "It'll be fun."

Susan attempted to hand her the gold crescent Night had left for her.

Rain shook her head. "You know I have no use for such things. The forest provides for me." She closed Susan's hand over the coin. "Keep it."

Rain was much too nervous now to fully enjoy herself, but she consented to 'the fun' all the same. The excitement of new wealth must have rejuvenated her friends. They seemed to forget about the dreadful last two days, chatting excitedly. She envied their youthful energy as they drew curtains and filled a copper tub with bucket after bucket of water from the pump sink in the scullery. They boiled more in a pot at the hearth beside the stairs, and after adding it to the cold mixture to get the temperature right, they insisted she have the honor of bathing first.

Prostitutes had a special skill for making uncomfortable things seem quite natural. Rain preferred to keep herself covered in heavy layers; her worn and scarred body was more relaxed that way. But as they helped her out of her clothes, no one stared at the jagged wound that stretched her navel or asked silly questions about her many other nicks and scrapes and gouges. Made by iron-tipped weapons in war years ago, they would never heal fully, even with magic.

Margot scrubbed Rain's hair while Penny settled in beside the tub on a bar stool.

The coltish girl regaled her with her newfound obsession: astrology. "When the moon is full and the color of brass in the sky, it means good luck—but not the sort of luck that's good for placing bets. When the moon is the color of butter, it means it's a bad time for love, and when the moon is red . . ." She tapped her chin. "Actually, I forget what that means . . . Either it means it's a bad time to breed your cows, or it's something to do with growing wheat . . . I'll have to consult my charts . . ."

Bernard did not escape the festivities. Susan was determined to rid him of his sulfur smell, and amused, Rain declined to explain that he was a demon forged in hell. No amount of hot water and rice soap would ever get the scent out.

She slept on the floor of the loft that night between their beds. The hard freeze was coming, and an old fae of Rain's ancestry wouldn't fare well in such biting cold. She was grateful for the company too. Rain couldn't remember what it was like to have a family. She remembered very little of her life before using bargain magic to share a piece of her soul with Bernard, turning him into a powerful trickster and herself into a witch.

As she stared up at the dark ceiling, the loft filled with the sound of the rise and fall of the girls' heavy breathing. Bernard curled up beside her in his cat form. She imagined that this was what it was like to be surrounded by family. She knew it couldn't be quite the same, but it made her smile anyway.

Chapter 4

(Night)

Night sighed. Erikson hadn't stopped moaning about the "gossip" and the "scandal" that was sure to follow now that the popular duke had been spotted entering such a low-class establishment.

"And on *Dimmet Street* of all places," his brother carried on.

The driver had taken the hackney back down a side alley, away from the tavern where Night had parted reluctantly from his witch. He'd sing to the divines and light a candle for the Moon Mother if his mate was still there tomorrow. Hopefully helping the women and handling their constable troubles had gotten him somewhere with her, or at least earned him a modicum of trust.

He could have sworn he'd felt something brush against him as he'd been leaving the tavern. Seated in the hackney, his head back against the rest, Night laid a hand over the lapel of his frock coat, remembering the gentle touch. It was so faint and light he could have imagined the entire event. Glancing down at his lapel, he tried to picture her golden skin, the slender fingers, her pink nails stroking down his chest, exploring his coat. Exploring him.

And then in his mind's eye, he took that hand in his and laced their fingers together . . .

". . . reputation is everything in the Row. Why do you risk sullying yours— You're not listening to me again, aren't you?" Erikson's mouth firmed into a tight line.

"I heard that last bit," Night grumped, pulled rudely from his imaginings. "And it was more than enough. We're here."

The hackney slowed to a halt. Erikson groaned. "And now you've got me doing business with the likes of—"

The coach door swung open, and Night's brother fell quiet. A narrow russet face beneath a towering felt hat leaned into the opening. Beady eyes bounced between the duke and his brother. Behind the fae, another male slouched against the corner of a brick building, a dragae with tall ears pierced with multiple loops and a bloody hole in the side of his linen shirt.

"Moon Mother bless you both," Sigurd greeted with a tip of his head. A bushy red fox tail swished at his back.

Night glowered at the dragae behind him. The lackey folded his arms dismissively over a burly chest and avoided his gaze. Dragae skin was unnaturally warm. His body steamed lightly in the crisp air.

Sigurd rubbed his gloved hands together, creating friction. "May I join you blue bloods? Or shall I remain out here, freezing my balls off in the street with my thumb in my ass?"

Erikson sneered. Night scooted over as far as the bench seat would allow. Sigurd lifted a long narrow case off the cobblestones by his feet and shoved it into Erikson's lap before climbing inside. The merchant tucked his fox tail behind him so that it pillowed at his back, then pulled the door shut. Night tapped the coach roof, and the hackney set off again, circling back toward Dimmet Street.

The curtains were pulled, sealing out the light from the gas lamps lining the road. Night had no trouble seeing, but his half-mortal brother was forced to squint down at the case in his lap.

"The price has gone up," Sigurd said.

"Highway robbery," Erikson grumbled. "And need I remind you, sir, you're speaking to the Lord of the Lunar Court."

Night raised a calming hand, and his brother quieted. He was accustomed to mage arrogance and Sigurd's crass nature, and he knew he'd get further with him by dropping pretenses and peerage nonsense. "I'll only be giving you the coin we agreed upon and no more."

Sigurd smiled at him, his teeth sharp and pearly in the shadows. "It ain't more coin I want." He scooted in closer and tapped his nose. "It's information. I'll take the coin we agreed upon, but you'll answer my questions first before we're settled."

Night shifted in the cramped space to face the business tyrant more fully. Sigurd was a mage who'd long ago set aside his studies in favor of accumulating wealth, a decision Night would never approve of. "You're testing my patience, Sigurd. I'll warn you once not to wear out your welcome. I've had a very long evening already, and I haven't been looking forward to your company."

Sigurd grabbed at his chest and pretended to be affronted. "Ack, you've hurt my feelings, My Lord. However will I recover from such a blow?"

Night was curious now exactly what it was Sigurd thought he knew. This may be yet another situation where he needed to allow things to play out a bit.

Erickson opened the latches on the sides of the case and lifted the lid. His brows came together. “It’s . . . a violin?”

“Last one crafted by Master Midnight, that is.” Sigurd ran a thick finger over the sleek scroll at the top, following the neck of the instrument down toward the heel.

Eyes on the merchant, Night fished the agreed-upon number of gold crescents and silver half-pieces out of his purse, cupping the small fortune in his large palm. “You’re already overcharging me for the damn thing, Sigurd. Your greed is bad for business.”

Sigurd cackled at that. “Not if the client is willing to pay it—then it’s very good for business. And I’ve got a hunch you’d have paid even more for the blasted thing. Now, tell me who it’s for and why, and we’ll be square.”

“I’m tempted to shove your coins in your mouth and boot you out of the coach right now,” Night drawled.

“While it’s still moving,” Erikson added.

Sigurd pushed on, undeterred, a man accustomed to threats. “You weren’t the first to ask me to acquire this piece. The original request came from a dragon familiar that reeked of brimstone. She delivered a letter from her mistress and tried to pay me with a solid gold wyvern.”

Night touched his forehead where a dull ache bloomed. When he had the information he wanted, he might just have to shove him out. “An ancient wyvern coin would be worth twice what I’m about to give you.”

“It would have been. Which made me curious, so before I accepted, I had my sniffers look into things. And you know what they found?"

"Obviously I do," Night said. "Take your money, and we'll drop you at the corner." It was the only warning he intended to give him.

Erikson was interested now. "What'd they find?"

There were a number of things Night hadn't shared with his brother, who was prone to worry, and this wasn't the time or the place. He gritted his teeth and glared at Erikson, but his brother pointedly avoided his gaze.

"Only Yaga royalty would have access to a wyvern coin." Sigurd narrowed his beady eyes at the duke. "The Yaga family keeps them secure in their magical hoards. Now then, what's a Yaga witch want with an old violin crafted by a Lunar Fae master? And why, after I refused to sell it to the familiar, is the great Lord of the Lunar Court suddenly aware I have it in my possession and now willing to overpay me for it?"

Erikson's eyes bore into the side of Night's face.

"What my plans are for my purchase are no concern of yours." The duke had just enough composure not to accidentally summon moon magic.

"It had better not be some sort of peace offering, My Lord." Sigurd's fox tail bristled. "You can't side with King Yaga in the conflict. You *can't.* Get it out of your thick head if that's what you've got in mind. The dragon king and his Unseelie fae would help themselves to more than *half* of the mortals who call River Row home. They'd enslave them. They'd shove them down into their mines and work them to death, work them harder and faster than the sods can reproduce, and—"

"Don't pretend you care for the mortals." Night rolled his eyes. "You're a man of business worried for your cheap labor and in need of more poor tenants willing to live in the slums you provide. You aren't worried for their welfare. You even employ dragae mercenaries to intimidate them, you great hypocritical prig."

"Sure I care for the human beasts." Sigurd's lip curled. "I care for them the same way I care for my coin. And I fucking love my coin."

Night pinched the bridge of his nose. The pain had expanded behind his eyes. "Sigurd, I warned you," he said quietly. He waited until the hackney slowed as it rounded the corner, then he kicked open the coach door and shoved Sigurd out into the street. The fae hit the cobblestones with a cry and rolled. Night tossed his payment out the window after him. Coins bounced and clinked against the pavers as Sigurd's curses echoed down the street. Night pulled the coach door shut with a snap.

Erikson blinked at his brother with big owlish eyes. "That could have been handled with a bit more diplomacy, I think."

Night's headache had lessened suddenly. "You were the one who suggested I boot him while the coach was still moving." His lips quirked. "See there? I listen to you sometimes."

* * *

Night's brother had wanted explanations, even demanded them with more backbone than he usually displayed. Not that Night believed Erikson didn't have a spine. He knew he did, but his younger brother had become so accustomed to the duke's bossing over the years, he usually refrained in the presence of the Lord of the Lunar Court. It was a show of Erikson's great stress over the building conflict around their borders that he dared to question him at all.

Chapter 4

But Night had to put his foot down. He'd divulge his plans when he was good and ready to and not a moment before. There were many cards at play, many things he continued to debate with himself. He didn't want to add another voice to the cacophony of opinions already cluttering his head, and the back of a small hackney was not the place for such discussions.

The coach dropped him and his new case at the edge of Dimmet Street, not far from where River Row ended in thick forest. Not far from the lesser-known path where Night had met his witch what felt like centuries and seconds ago all at once.

Erikson was forbidden from accompanying him. Once again, he'd been left to wait for his brother in the hackney.

It was nearing midnight, and the air cooled with each passing minute. The day had been a warm and clear one. Fresh dew began to form on the grass, glittering on the spider webs that clung between spindly tree limbs, gathering on the fallen leaves slicking his boots. The violin case bumped against his thigh as he stepped over tree roots and ducked under low-hanging branches. The forest was full of nocturnal predators. He saw their glowing eyes refracting the dim light cast by a yellow crescent moon overhead. The beasts recognized a greater threat when they saw one. Night slunk through the forest undisturbed.

He took the long way to his usual path, passing the old oak tree he'd come to favor. He didn't expect his witch to be there, but just in case . . . It added a half hour to his journey, and the tree was frustratingly empty.

Eventually the trees parted before a clearing crammed with tall grass and wildflowers. An arm of the river Eventide cut through the meadow. As he walked, disturbing the flora, lunar butterflies the size of sparrows burst out of their hiding places. They flapped luminescent blue wings with such force he could feel the whisper of their efforts in the air around him.

He followed the arm of the river for a time until it came to a copse of pine trees where a dilapidated hut leaned. The thatch roof was dotted in more of the nocturnal butterflies. As he neared, the hut shuddered as though it were breathing, and the scent of brimstone—the scent of a dragon familiar—filled Night's lungs. The butterflies took flight, circling the hut's single chimney, before coming to rest on its roof once again, like birds nesting.

He spotted a trickster amongst the lunar butterflies. The familiar was slightly larger than the others, with thick wings in a dark shade of purple.

"Masha," Night greeted the familiar, hefting the violin case like it was a trophy. "Please inform your mistress that I am here, I have what she wants, and I'm sincerely sorry that I'm so late. I . . ." He thought of his witch again and the choices before him, laid out like facedown playing cards, waiting to be drawn. Each selection had consequences. But every hesitation and failure to act had consequences too. "I was delayed . . ."

The trickster flapped her heavy wings, disturbing the others into another flight. Then the larger butterfly evaporated in a puff of purple smog which hovered thickly for a moment before the cloud floated toward the chimney and funneled down it.

Night set the case by his feet and waited.

And waited.

"Sora," he called, impatience flavoring the word. He glared at the front door, which remained shut up tight. "I know I'm late, but I had good reason. At least let me explain."

Chapter 4

The crooked shutters snapped closed.

With a great heaving sigh, he waited. Making himself comfortable, he perched on the edge of the case, knees bent awkwardly.

And then the hut shuddered and shook. Lunar butterflies launched into the air, a flurry of great blue wings, translucent in the moon's glow. The hut vibrated, and the wood groaned. Night jumped to his feet. The door opened and then clapped closed. The shutters did the same. And then the hut rose up on large, clawed appendages like the feet of a great chicken. The skin was dark and scaled, the legs long and as thick as tree trunks.

And it was walking away from him.

"Damn it all," Night groused. He stomped after the lumbering hut, then remembered himself. The duke spun back for the violin case, grabbed it up, and hurried after the errant building. "Sora!" he called, quickening his pace.

The claws kicked up clots of dirt at him, and the ground rumbled with each of its massive steps. The flock of lunar butterflies followed, circling above the thatch roof. The chimney coughed clouds of dark smoke.

"Gods damned witches," Night cursed. "Do you want the blasted violin or not?" he shouted, shaking the case at the stubborn house.

The hut slowed at that. It turned on its lumbering limbs so that its door faced him. The wood siding creaked, and bits of thatch fell from the roof, dusting the air. A window shutter fluttered. Then the door fell open, and the hut leaned down on its chicken feet, inching closer to the fae lord.

"Oh no you don't," Night said, moving the case behind him. "I'm not just tossing it in there for you. You'll talk to me first, or the violin stays with me. I know I'm late. I apologized."

The door sprouted teeth. Jagged bits of razor-sharp bone lined the frame, and a hot wind blew from the entrance, reeking of coal and brimstone.

Night sighed. "You've made your point, you hag."

In response, the door flopped shut and the house dropped to the ground, rumbling the earth and hiding its scaled chicken legs. It settled crookedly in the grass, canting at an odd angle. The lunar butterflies returned to the thatch roof. When the door opened again, the teeth were gone, and the hut went still.

It remained motionless and silent, the way a proper house should behave, in Night's opinion. Sora filled the shrouded doorway moments later. She wore a dress of red velvet and a straw bonnet decorated in wildflowers. The sleeves flared from her elbows to her wrists, and the fabric clung to her hips, then fell in a pool over her feet, a fashion from a time long ago. A dress for a beautiful princess now many centuries old.

"Hag?" Sora said in the bold accent of the Unseelie from the mountains. Then she grinned at him, and her mouth was full of sharp teeth. "You come inside, and be quick. You've wasted enough of my time already making me wait here on you. My house does not like to stay in one place all night long. It isn't safe for us." She waved him over and then stepped out of view.

Night hefted the violin case after her. As he entered, he eyed the door suspiciously, worried it'd sprout teeth and bite him. But it didn't, this time.

The inside of the hut was much larger and grander than it looked from the outside. The wood was a rich, red mahogany, and a crackling fire roared in a large hearth made of cut stone. Warmth touched his cheeks and nose, chasing away the autumn chill. Then he felt it through his gloves, in the tips of his fingers, and soon he was stripping out of his frock coat and hanging it on the rack by the door.

He joined Sora Yaga at a dining table made of waxed wood. She'd removed her bonnet, revealing four spiked horns sprouting from thick flaxen hair the color of ripe wheat.

"Show it to me," she insisted.

A black cat appeared then, leaping from somewhere under the table, startling Night.

"Masha," he scolded, and the cat yowled at him. The duke gathered up the case and laid it on the table, then unfastened the latches and lifted the lid.

Sora smiled. She and Masha stared at each other for a time, and Night was certain they were communicating in that mysterious way of witches. Sora reached for the violin.

Night snapped the lid back down, nearly catching her long fingers. "You owe me a boon."

Her nostrils flared. "I owe you a boon when I say I do."

"You owe me a boon," he repeated through his teeth. "I've done everything you've asked for *seven* months. You owe me."

"Perhaps," Sora said softly.

Her acquiescence immediately made Night uneasy. She was never so agreeable. Sora, the unwanted eldest daughter of King Yaga, trusted no one, a sentiment Night could relate to, in addition to sharing her deep hatred for her father. As a result, the two of them got on quite well most of the time.

Masha hissed, pacing from one side of the tabletop to the other.

"She believes," Sora interpreted, "that what you want is dangerous for me. She does not think I should help you, but rather insists you take care of the matter yourself immediately with my instruction."

Night heaved a great sigh, thinking again of cards and consequences. "I don't think she knows what I want. I hardly know it half the time." He tugged on his lip, staring at an imperfection in the wood. "But I will require your instruction."

"Then," Sora said carefully, "you no longer wish for me to advise you on how best to murder my father?"

Night chewed on the inside of his cheek. "That would solve both of our problems, I once thought. But now . . . now there's something I need more. Something a great deal more pressing."

"I will only grant you *one* boon, Night." Her golden brows lifted toward her hairline. She had large indigo eyes full of wisdom and mischief and a creamy complexion that hid her age well. "Either way, do tell. Masha and I are eager to know."

"I found my mate." He glanced at Masha, who had gone unnaturally still, before continuing. "She's a witch. A shy little thing that lives in this forest."

Sora's gaze did something he'd never seen it do before. Her eyes softened. "And you wish to bond with this witch?"

"I wish it."

Sora leaned back in her chair and exchanged a meaningful look with her familiar. "And you want me to help you how?"

"You have a true mate." It wasn't a question. There was a different energy, a contentment in a fae with a true mate. He sensed Sora had one the same way he could feel energy from the Divine Night all around him when the moon was high. "There aren't many fae with true mates available to offer me guidance, and of the ones I could inquire with, there are exactly none in my company who have bonded a witch." Night tapped on the leather case. "This is for him, isn't it? Or her? The violin is for your mate."

Chapter 4

The corner of her mouth lifted in an expression both light and youthful and not at all like the Sora he knew. "It is for my mate, yes. You do realize that because your bond is not yet complete, you could part from the witch and seek another compatible match? One who hasn't already given a piece of her soul to another, complicating matters for you."

The notion made his stomach drop, and his lips turned down. He'd felt the bond pull with other women before in his long lifetime, but their draw had been dull or barely there and easily ignored. What he felt with Rain had been like a strike of lightning: sure and compelling. Those other women were from his world, each an exact replica of the many proper and titled ladies he'd been introduced to over the centuries.

With every fiber of his being, he sensed Rain was something so much more. Whomever he true-mated, they needed to be a partner, a confidant in the coming conflict, dependable, and strong. He hadn't any practice at depending on others, but he'd always had a gift when it came to judging a person's character. It made it easier to move and motivate them in the way he needed to. Rain was a woman of excellent character. Noble. Protective. Reserved.

Innocent.

An ancient warrior who'd somehow managed to preserve an unwavering goodness through a great war. He could only imagine what sort of moral fiber it had taken to experience such wickedness, so much death and destruction, and still be so very sweet. More than anything else about her, he felt pulled toward that goodness.

Night took a moment to select his words carefully, before realizing that the pause gave far more away than he'd like. "I need her," he said finally.

Sora chuckled and Masha meowed. "Masha thinks you're a fool. She thinks you should get on with ending my father. Love and other such nonsense can wait, she says."

Love? He didn't believe such a thing existed. He understood duty. He understood responsibility. These were the weights he carried on his back. Weights that would soon crush him into the ground, long before the current conflict was over. Love was not something he'd experienced in any relationship he'd ever had. Not with any woman. Not with his father nor his mother. Not with the uncle who'd raised him. Not even with his brother. No, love was a thing from a fairy story. There was only duty and instinct and the mate bond.

And lust. He understood lust quite well.

Night canted his head to the side, considering the cat. "Masha has a grudge, if I recall."

Sora nodded. "Many, many ages ago when I was a better-behaved daughter, my father ordered me to kill Masha. She was a powerful dragon and a threat to his throne. And so I did." Her sharp grin went lopsided. "Thankfully, before her soul slipped away, she had the good sense to agree to become my familiar and make me a witch instead."

Masha hissed at that. The hair down her back rose.

"The Seelie queen and the dragon king are using their power to try to force me to pick a bride from within their relations," Night said, playing absently with the latch on the violin case. "Then they'll make use of my mages, my magic, and devastate my province. In the case of your father, if I give him what he wants, he'll enslave my people. If I side with the Seelie Tree Court, they'll stuff a sword in my people's hands and shove them onto the front lines to die in a war that has nothing to do with them. For the sake of everyone in the Lunar Province,

I'd love to kill them both and let their conflict die with them, but that's no easy task. Killing one of them will be nearly impossible, let alone the two of them, and another ruler would step into their place and take up their fight. So I've chosen another path."

"Fae laws surrounding one's true mate are still sacred even to the Seelie and Unseelie," Sora guessed.

"It would be impossible for them to force me into an alliance by marriage were I to take my true mate as my bride," he confirmed.

She reached out and stroked Masha's back. The cat stirred and yowled in an agitated fashion. "Of course, you'd need to marry and complete the bond with your witch soon. Their demands will only become harder to ignore over time. My father is not patient, and neither is the warrior queen."

At the mention of the Seelie queen, Night touched the scarred side of his mouth. "No, she isn't." His voice dropped an octave. "Were I successful, were I to bond my witch and make her my true mate, would it be—"

"With a true mate bond, you would become immune to all forms of mind-bending magic." Sora nodded, her voice passionless. Her face was without pity, another reason the duke trusted and got on with her so well. "The Seelie queen could never again compel you."

A well of relief surged inside him. He hadn't dared to hope that his theories were correct, but Sora was old and knowledgeable and honest to a fault. His hand went to the scars at his mouth again. "Finally . . ." he muttered.

"You're certain this is the boon you want from me?" Sora said. "You could ask for anything. I could grant you any number of gifts, and yet all you want is for me to be your matchmaker?"

Night scoffed. "Advise me on how to bond with my mate. It's been done before with a witch, obviously." He gestured at her. "It can be done again. Finding another suitable match, though possible, isn't a simple solution. The witch is here now. I need *her* . . . or my plan falls apart."

"You want her." Sora's sharp smile was all-knowing.

"I've tried courting," Night said with a groan, "but this woman is incredibly timid. She flees from me when I push her to speak to me, though I know she must feel the instinctive pull that I do because she's given me gifts, gifts she's made herself."

"The bond makes her timid." Sora stroked her chin in thought. Masha nudged her arm with her muzzle, demanding more affection. "Gifts are good. The compulsion to give and make gifts is a sign that the bonding instinct has started to take root."

"But it's not enough?"

Sora sighed, brushing fingers down Masha's neck. "Imagine you've been submerged in a dark pool of water, a lake. This lake is full of monsters, and there's a heavy boulder on your chest holding you in place, preventing you from rising to safety and fleeing."

Night's brows knitted. "That would be horrifying."

"Yes. Now imagine you can see your mate. She rolls the boulder off. You think she's there to help you, but then she plants a boot in your chest, keeping you pinned. She orders you to breathe. The monsters are closing in all around you. It feels like you'll both soon die. Would you do as she says?"

Night shook his head, knocking strands of dark blue hair into his eyes. He brushed them back impatiently. "No. I'm underwater."

"Convincing your witch with her broken soul to bond with you will be like convincing her to drown in that lake full of monsters. Your witch has bargained away a piece of her soul, granting her a familiar with great powers. As a consequence, a witch's soul is damaged, injured. Your blooming bond picks at this wound, inflaming it. It's scared of being broken again and will continue to bring her distress during your mating. There is no greater act of trust, no greater act of love, than to bond with your one and only true mate. She needs your help, Night. Do you understand?"

Her words had his arms flexing, his stomach clenching. "Some part of her wants to be with me. Some part of her isn't frightened of bonding. I'm certain of it . . ."

"Of course she wants to be with you. She's your mate. She's compatible, and you've triggered the blooming bond instincts in each other. But if you're determined to wait on her, hoping she'll come around on her own because she gives you gifts, you're going to be waiting forever. No witch would willingly drown themselves. Her broken soul is in panic. It's distressed by the pull of you. She needs you to be strong and unyielding to help her through it. That will require some force."

Night's nose wrinkled. "I've never forced a woman's affections in my life, and I don't plan to start with her. I'm not interested in frightening her."

Sora played absentmindedly with Masha's black tail while the cat licked her paws. "Then you're not listening to your instincts any more than she is, and you're both hopeless. If she were here right now, what would you *want* to do with her? What do your fae instincts tell you to do?"

Night didn't even have to ponder it. "If life were simpler, I'd have thrown her over my shoulder and hauled her off already like the old fae used to."

Sora dropped Masha's tail and raised a brow at the duke. "Then why haven't you? Are you a fae male, or aren't you?"

"I can't just—"

Sora wagged a finger at him. "That's a very mortal sensibility you've got tying you up. This strange fear of being impolite about bonding her will do neither of you any good. I don't know why you'd listen to mortal proprieties in this case. Humans don't have mates or witches. What wisdom could their courting practices possibly offer you here?"

Night stiffened at the idea that he, of all people, would behave like a mortal. "It's not as simple as all that. There are laws. Some of which I was responsible for enacting. Getting the fae to behave in a civilized fashion took great difficulty. If their lord suddenly set aside law and order and—"

"Do you want her or not?"

Night's jaw set. "I want her."

Sora leaned across the table. "Then go and get her."

Chapter 5

(Rain)

Rain awoke late the next morning. She'd slept well and deeply, surrounded by friends. They readied for their day lazily, then ate an expensive breakfast of fine pastries and fresh fruit, courtesy of the duke's generous coin.

They'd bought way more than all of them could eat. Rain suspected it was done on purpose. Susan shared the leftovers with the street urchins, pretending it was just to keep good food from spoiling. The girls were always doing things like that. What little they had, they often gave away to the needy of Dimmet Street, especially the children. Though they pretended otherwise for reasons Rain couldn't comprehend, hearts of gold beat in their chests.

Margot helped Rain braid her ashen hair, winding the plait into an elegant knot at the nape of her neck, leaving one lock of white hair left to curl along her shoulder. The new coat—

new to her—gifted by Susan was warm and fawn-colored and made of a soft wool with a velvet collar. Penny's blouse was a little big on Rain, but the coat hid it anyway, and the fabric was thicker and finer than the linen she'd worn down roughing it outside. It felt nice against her old war injuries.

Eager to spend more of the duke's coin, Margot and Penny went out shopping for new clothes. Susan needed to order supplies to replace what had been stolen. She asked Rain to watch over the tavern in her absence. Feeling fond of the humans, she agreed.

The girls had been gone nearly an hour. Rain pushed a broom around the tables for something useful to do. Bernard leapt up onto the windowsill in his cat form. He poked his nose at the glass, peering out at the street. *The duke is coming.*

He's coming? Her stomach dropped.

No. That couldn't be right. She hadn't even made a decision about seeing him yet. She wanted to see him, of course, but everything had gotten so much more complicated when she learned he was Lord of the Lunar Court. Already the very notion of being near him again caused her heart to squeeze in her chest. And he thought she was a prostitute. And he wanted to buy her time . . .

And exactly what did he plan to do with her time?

He's not coming. Just pulling your leg, Bernard thought, *as the humans say.*

"As the humans say," Rain huffed. Now she felt both relieved and disappointed at the same time. She leaned her broom against the wall, then made a circle with her fingers and showed him the crude gesture.

What's that even supposed to mean?

Rain glanced at her hand. "I think it's supposed to be an

asshole. Then you stick your tongue out and pretend to lick it."

Very ladylike—and he really is coming. I was joking about joking.

She rolled her eyes dismissively. The duke was nocturnal, and it was morning still. Dusk, their usual meeting time, was hours away.

And then the shuffle of boots on the walkway and the scrape of the doorknob turning caught in her sensitive ears. Her stomach dropped.

Oh, sacred stars, no, it couldn't really be . . .

The Lord of the Lunar Court ducked beneath the door lintel, filling the tavern with his presence.

Rain dropped her hands to her sides, wiping clammy palms on her trousers. She wanted both to stand there and stare at him until the end of time and to run away as fast as her legs could carry her. In the end, it was indecision that kept her rooted to the spot.

"Frey Magis," she whispered, the old fae honorific that had died out long ago. Words that meant one was as great as the Vanir, the Lunar Fae's demi-god ancestors.

His chin lifted as though he'd heard her, his gaze glittering. A hint of his broken smile tugged at his mouth. She wanted to touch that smile, feel the pillows of his lips, explore the jagged edges of his scars, test the stubble at his jaw, stroke the velvet on his curved antlers. Instead, she laced her fingers together in front of her, averting her eyes.

It took forever and an instant for him to remove his coat and gloves and cross to her, his strides long and lean. He was tall. Most people were taller than Rain, but Night positively towered in a manner that had more to do with his presence than his height. He carried himself like he was always the tallest man in the room, and in a fashion, he probably was. He smelled like old books and ink and parchment, bee's wax, and a hint of peppery cologne. He was close enough now it was time for her to make words . . . *What were words?*

"You're the Duke of Night," she said lamely. "I hadn't realized . . ."

His broken smile sent a shiver of pleasure through her that turned her skin to gooseflesh. "I am."

What should I say to him next? she asked Bernard. Her mind had stopped being helpful.

Something nice? Don't ask me what. Demons aren't nice.

The duke's eyes met hers, and the corners crinkled with mirth and warmth. Rain wetted her lips and dug for her courage. She had so many questions, but in that moment, not one of them came to her. She could think of only one thing.

"You have kind eyes," she said softly, her cheeks heating.

"They're kind because they're looking at you." He spoke in a baritone that reminded Rain of warmed honey.

"Does no one else think you're kind?"

"No," he confessed. "But don't let that trouble you. I vow *you* will always think I'm kind."

Rain couldn't reconcile the gentleman she'd met in the woods with the dark and fearsome reputation of the Lord of the Lunar Court. Fae lords were often tricksters in more than just their appearances and forms. By reputation they wore political masks and were conniving plotters. Looking at him now, Rain wondered which one was the mask. Was it the noble duke before her, or was the mask her sweet visitor in the woods?

Rain picked at the soft wood of the table, leaning her

hip against the edge, feeling sheepish. He stared at her encouragingly, and she realized, stomach churning, that he wanted her to say something else.

Stars, she was terrible at this.

Bernard jumped from the windowsill to the table, bushy tail crooking behind him. Rain was grateful for the interruption.

"Hello again, little friend," Night said with a respectful bow of his head. A significant gesture, considering he was the Duke of Night and Bernard was a . . . cat.

Inform him that I'm not little, Bernard ordered. *I'm savage and majestic in my true form.*

I'm not telling him that. But you can show him your true form and tell him yourself if you'd like.

I'd have to take a great deal of your blood first . . . Are you really that desperate for another distraction?

Yes, actually, she was. Normally he remained in smaller animal forms so taking in blood wasn't necessary.

Night slipped a hand into his pocket and removed a square of cheese covered in brown paper. Carefully he separated the paper. Bernard perked at that, extending his nose to sniff at the duke's fingers.

I accept your offering, Frey Magis of the Lunar Fae, Bernard thought. *Though I'd appreciate it more if it was dipped in your mage blood. Maybe next time?*

Night placed the piece of cheese in his flattened palm for Bernard, peering over at Rain through heavy lashes. A lock of blue-black hair tumbled over his brow as the familiar filled his greedy maw. Rain backed farther behind the table, hiding more of herself from his study. He was intoxicating, and she was once again overcome. She tugged up the soft woolen coat that had belonged to Susan, tucking it tighter around her neck and shoulders. Margot said the fawn color did lovely things to the golden hues of her skin.

She hoped that was true.

"I'll bring you an entire wheel of cheese," Night whispered to Bernard, "if you'll convince your mistress to keep talking to me."

I approve of him, Bernard said. *Talk to him.*

Of course you do. Rain rolled her eyes. *He gives you things.*

And he doesn't paw at me.

"Bernard would like you to rub his belly," Rain said, her voice breaking. *There. I talked to him.*

Bernard shouted a litany of colorful curses at her, some of them in languages that had died long ago.

"Does he now?" Night's brows rose. He reached for her familiar. "I never would have imagined that demons liked getting their bellies rubbed."

I hate you, Bernard groused. *Ugh— Oh, that's unexpectedly pleasant.* With his cheeks full of cheese, he rolled onto his back, his furry stomach covered by Night's large palm.

"And . . ." Rain said, grasping for something else, anything else to tell the duke. She'd called his gaze back to her, and her tongue seemed to swell in her mouth. "And I'm thirty winters old and a widow . . . ? Apparently . . . ?"

Night's chuckle was incredulous. He released Bernard, resting his knuckles on the table. "Are you really?"

She sighed. "No. Not at all. Not even close."

Another chortle shook his shoulders. The sound did things to her, made her skin flush, her stomach flutter. "Then why did you say you were?"

"Stars if I know." She bit her lip, glad for his good humor. "Apparently men prefer young women and I shouldn't just come out and tell you that I'm a tired old spinster."

"I've seen five hundred and thirty-two winters," he said, "And I've been tired for all of them. I'm not concerned that you're too old for me."

Turning to Bernard she asked, "How long have we been together now?" She couldn't quite recall. He told her through their link, and Rain interpreted for the duke. "Five hundred and two years, he says. Before Bernard I'm afraid I don't remember much. Suffice it to say, I'm rather ancient."

"That so?" His voice was gentle and encouraging. "You lived through the Seelie and Unseelie wars, then?"

These were the most words she'd ever dared to share with him. Each one she spoke got a little easier than the last, though the muscles in her arms, legs, and stomach were so tense they'd begun to ache. "My memories of the war are hazy at best, and probably for good reason." Rain pointed behind her in the direction of the forest. "I nearly died back in those trees. In the oldest memory I have, I'm alone in the dirt, wearing Seelie armor, with an iron dagger in my stomach . . ."

Night's eyes rounded. "It's a miracle you survived that."

"I can be very stubborn about such things. I tend to get up when I should stay down. I kept breathing, removed the blade so it'd stop poisoning me, and then eventually Bernard found me." She extended her hand to her familiar, and Bernard nudged her fingers affectionately with his muzzle.

"Clearly you and I have a lot in common. I can be very stubborn about staying alive too," Night said. "In fact, I insist upon it daily."

They exchanged a warm grin. And for a moment it was easy to share a space with him and not feel too hot, too stirred up, or overwhelmed. She thought of the quiet moments in the woods when they'd walked together and when he'd read to her, his melodic voice enveloping her in a soothing caress while she lounged in her favorite tree.

If the duke wasn't truly kind, he was certainly skilled at pretending to be.

Ack. All this smiling and flirting is going to make me see my cheese again. Bernard leapt down from the table and scampered up the stairs, granting them privacy.

Night pulled out a chair for her. Rain perched on the edge of the wooden seat, uncertain where to look as he lowered himself gracefully opposite her. His skin was less luminous without the moon's glow, but meeting his tired eyes still made her cheeks burn. She decided to stare at her nails instead. They tapped out an anxious rhythm over a dark swirl in the grain of the wood.

"I wanted to thank you," she said, remembering her manners, "for all that you did last night for the girls here. They are important to me. The constable would have taken their hard-earned coins or left one of us sitting in cold irons for days." She rubbed at her wrists. Pure iron against her skin would have been a torture physically. Allowing Margot to take the punishment for her would have been a different sort of torment.

He laid a hand on the table, not far from hers, his thumb rubbing aimlessly down the edges of his fingers, up, then down again. She watched the movement, her vision going slightly out of focus, hypnotized.

"I helped them for a reason," he confessed.

A flush moved up her neck and into her cheeks. "I assumed as much, though that reason remains very unclear to me."

"I am in want of a bride."

Chapter 5

Rain's eyes flew up to his. They were a dull gray in the daylight and red-rimmed, the pupils nearly nonexistent. She blinked at him. "I wouldn't know how to find a lord a bride."

His breathy laugh surprised her. "I've already found the woman I need. I've spent a great deal of time with her, but I still don't even know her name." He stared back at her pointedly.

It took several rapid blinks and two deep inhales to process his words. Surely, she'd misheard him. He couldn't possibly mean . . . *She is dear to me.* "You sound awfully sure of yourself, My Lord. Aren't you at all worried that this woman might say no to your abrupt proposal?"

His brow remained relaxed and unlined, his face serene. "Oh, I'm quite certain she'll try to say no. Which is why I've come to lay the world at her feet. Should she change her mind, she would never want for anything ever again."

Rain studied his face for signs of dishonesty. As a cultural norm, fae did not tell lies, but they'd become so enmeshed with the mortals in the last century and humans told stories so easily, she couldn't be sure. "But . . . this woman is very, very different from you. She doesn't belong in your world, and she has no real use for wealth."

"Everyone has use for wealth."

"Not me."

"Even you." He was running his thumb back down his fingers again in that captivating way. His hand had shifted closer to hers. "You could use it to keep the women you care for here safe and fed, for instance."

"That is . . ." An excellent point, but she wasn't ready to agree with him. Especially not when he was being so smug about it. "There are rumors of another war brewing between the Seelie and the Unseelie," she said instead.

"There are always rumors of war between them." Irritation edged his words.

Rain suspected he wasn't accustomed to being challenged, and his words were true enough. The Seelie and the Unseelie fae had bickered since the first great war between them.

"Why do I have the feeling any woman who weds you puts themselves right in the thick of that mess?" A mess she'd been in once before already and had no desire to fall back into whether she remembered the details of it or not. She didn't want to end lives. If she was being fae-honest, all she truly wanted from life was the devotion of a family. The *love* of family.

And at the head of that, the love of a husband.

"The fact that you already sense what you'd be getting yourself into is one of many reasons why I'm certain I'm making the right choice." He leaned in closer. "And it blessedly saves time."

Rain shook her head. "I have no desire to be a means to an end, My Lord. Nor do I have a death wish."

He grimaced. "You would not be in danger of death. No one would dare harm my bride. Both the dragon king and the Seelie queen want the night mages on their side in this conflict. They're too evenly matched otherwise. They wouldn't risk driving me to aid their enemy by harming you." A muscle in his cheek flexed, and then his expression smoothed. "Tell me your name."

"Rain." Her voice cracked. She'd spoken it so softly it wasn't likely he'd heard her. All this talk of marriage had her beyond flustered. She licked her lips and tried again. "I'm called Rain."

His gaze dropped to her mouth. His broken smile made her heart stutter. "Rain, I am in need of a wife most urgently." His head cocked to the side, taking her in. She felt his gaze like a caress. "I am in need of you."

She cleared her throat. "Why me?"

"Though you would prefer otherwise, you are a necessary means to an end. I find you very attractive, an additional attribute in your favor given the necessity of the marital bed. For your contribution to our partnership, I would see you cared for and rewarded beyond measure."

"A marriage of convenience?" Her voice had gone quiet again. Disappointment pulled down the corners of her mouth, and that was silly. Had she actually hoped he was courting her and putting up with their differences and her shyness all this time for something other than ambition or politics? How foolish, considering who he was and who she wasn't.

"Precisely."

Rain rubbed a timid hand down her arm. She couldn't look at him. "And what of the love between a husband and wife?"

"*Love*," he exaggerated the word, "is a thing that belongs in fairy stories. What I'd give you is real and true. I'd give you security, dependability, and a beautiful roof over your head."

He didn't believe in love? The notion put a knot in her stomach.

Night shifted in his seat, calling her back to him. "Say yes to me, and desperation will never touch you. You could have whatever you wanted. Freedom from this brothel and its pawing patrons. A home. Clothes, shoes, jewels, an education . . ."

She frowned at him. "You think I'm desperate, uneducated, and a prostitute?"

One of his dark brows lifted. His foot began to tap a steady rhythm under the table. "You're *not* those things, I take it?"

His smile went crooked, creasing the scars at the corner of his mouth. "I hope you won't blame me too harshly for not knowing. You're not exactly a loquacious woman, and we're sitting in a brothel right now."

"I'm not those things." She narrowed her eyes at him. "Shocking as it may be to you, your proposal is not going very well, My Lord."

"I'd like for you to address me by my name, Night."

"If this proposal were less dreadful, I might . . ."

His head tipped back. Laughter rumbled out of him. "Does it help my cause or hurt it if I say that I'm relieved you're not a prostitute?"

Rain folded her arms over her chest, leaning back in her chair. The wood groaned. "My dearest friends are prostitutes. You won't find three nobler souls in all the Row. They don't deserve disrespect or disdain for using their skills to make a life for themselves."

Another charming chuckle. Rain had to admit his smiles and laughs were alluring and disarming, even when she didn't want them to be. She needed to hold on to her irritation. It gave her courage with him.

"I'm disrespectful to everyone, not just them. And I wasn't picking on you or your friends. It's the oldest profession in the world," he drawled. "If anything, I hold some deference toward prostitutes. I was willing to marry one, remember? But I am relieved."

"Why?" Hope edged her voice, and she chided herself for it. He'd made it very clear what he was after here. Wanting more was foolish.

His eyes captured hers and darkened. "Because I've decided I want you for myself, and now I can't stand the thought of any other man touching you."

Though her pulse surged, she scoffed at his fae bluntness. "I'm bound to bump into another man eventually."

"The villain," he teased. "I'm afraid I'd have to rip his heart out."

The duke surprised a chuckle out of her. "You can't mean that."

"Wish I didn't. They'd have to arrest me to keep the peace, and I have no desire to be shackled." His mouth quirked. "I'd look ridiculous in irons."

He'd drawn another laugh from her. She was certain he couldn't look ridiculous in anything he wore. It was unfair in a way. No one should be so pretty. "Never mind that iron burns our skin like hellfire and is poisonous to us."

"Never mind that." Briefly he held his bottom lip between his teeth. A darkness crossed over his expression, an intensity that made her heart thump against her ribs. "It wouldn't matter. I'm already in hell. Have been since I laid eyes on you." His voice roughened to gravel. "I dream of you, Rain. Then I wake up and I don't have you, and it's a nightmare."

She couldn't meet his gaze. He wanted a marriage of convenience. Why was he talking to her this way? *Because he's a trickster,* she reminded herself. She didn't want to become a disposable piece in whatever political game he was playing. Her hands shook slightly. She watched them, willing the tremor to stop. He laid his palm out flat, spreading his fingers so close to hers they nearly touched. He'd stolen her courage again.

"It wasn't my intention to put you in hell," she whispered.

"Then I'll need you to marry me. Now."

"You . . . Now?" She rose to her feet on legs that felt boneless and nearly toppled. It'd taken her a month just to talk to him, and now she was expected to marry him immediately. He was mad. She wanted to shake the confounding male until he made sense.

He stood and reached out to steady her, but she stumbled away from him. Why was it that his presence always seemed to steal her balance as well as her courage? Her agility usually rivaled Bernard's in his cat form.

"Surely you jest," she managed. It wasn't a very nice joke.

"I wouldn't dare tease you." He paced after her with the sleek, dark grace of a panther. "I watched you throw a man twice your size out of a window into the muddy street just last night. Provoking you is not worth ruining my shirt. It's silk."

"I don't want to throw you out the window," she admitted, embarrassed by how her voice had gone low and husky. There were many things she wanted to do to the Duke of Night. Hurting him wasn't one of them.

He corralled her into the corner of the room where the bar met oak paneling, boxing her in with proud shoulders she wanted to touch and a towering presence she could easily lose herself in. He rested an arm above her head, leaning his weight against the wall. "Then what is it you do want from me?"

"I don't know." Her brow furrowed. That wasn't entirely accurate. She knew what she wanted but had no idea how to put any of it into words fit for a lord, especially a roguish one.

"Breathe, Rain," he said with the strength of a man accustomed to giving orders.

She obeyed, sucking in air raggedly. He'd used her name like he'd said it a thousand times before. It rolled off his tongue with enchanting familiarity. "I . . ." She dug for her courage and came up empty. He was too close. Too pretty.

Too overwhelming.

"My eyes are kind when they're looking at you," he reminded her, and his gaze softened. "You never have anything to fear from me. You can tell me what you want, as I have done. There need not be secrets between us."

"I don't . . ." she stammered, his continued nearness making eloquence impossible.

"You left me precious presents. You made lovely things for me with your sweet little hands. You wait for me at dusk." He stooped, bringing his lips closer. "I think you know exactly what you want from me. Only it scares you." His breath warmed the shell of her ear and the side of her scalp.

She swallowed hard. "Women used to leave gifts in woven baskets for the fae males they favored. It wasn't so unusual back then when the world was younger and River Row was new . . ."

His head cocked to the side, considering her. His voice filled with a honey sugariness she could almost feel on her skin. "I remember. Women would leave gifts to draw in a fae so that they could bargain something away. Something that troubled them." He reached out to stroke the velvet collar of her coat, stopping where it buttoned just below her throat.

Her lashes lifted. He was so near, the molten heat of him warmed the front of her body. A crackle of connection sizzled between them, so hot, so compelling, she wanted to open the fastenings and let the wool coat fall to cool her overheated skin, but her hands remained inert at her sides.

"What is it you wished to bargain away, Rain?" He cupped her cheek then, and a new jolt of connection shot through her, his touch featherlight and so pleasant she gasped.

"Loneliness," she confessed quietly. She hadn't felt such

consuming loneliness until she'd seen him for the first time. Rain had lived many mortal lifetimes with her trees and her Bernard. Then she'd added the girls and it had all felt quite manageable until he'd taken that stroll through her woods. He'd broken her into pieces in that moment and made her incomplete. "I would bargain my loneliness away to you."

"Ah." His thumb stroked her jaw, and Rain felt weightless and lightheaded all at once. "But I'd take that from you for free."

Dark spots popped in her vision, and her head tipped. She righted it with effort. She felt intoxicated, drunk on him. Her eyes slid shut. She reached back, flattening her clammy palms against the paneled oak, needing something solid and sure to ground herself. Her lashes were heavy, her muscles melted butter.

"Mate," she whispered, a new connection curling and churning inside of her, a new awareness blooming in her soul. An awareness of him and only him.

And then she felt herself sliding, down and down. Sweet darkness opened up beneath her feet and engulfed her.

Chapter 6

(Night)

Night caught her in his arms before she could fall to the floor.

"Rain?" he said, as her entire weight went slack against his chest. He shook her a little, and her head lolled. She was out cold.

He scooped her up, lifting her in his arms, surprised she was much more solid than she appeared to be under the thick coat. Her eyes were closed, white lashes feathering across her cheeks. She'd pinned her hair up, accenting her slender neck and her sharp jaw.

She was lovely. And not at all in the way of a lady with practiced elegance and charisma. She had a wild beauty. An untamed natural prettiness and a raw charm that reminded him of the forest she was fond of.

Mate, she'd called him. Confirmation that she too felt what he did. Night's blood sang in his veins, pumping so hard his ears rang. With her draped in his arms, he moved them to the door and grabbed his coat off the rack. Bernard yowled at him from the stairwell, and he started. He'd forgotten the familiar was there.

"She swooned," he explained. With a pinch of guilt tightening his stomach, he turned to face the demon. He'd known he was overwhelming her and pushed on anyway. He saw her swaying, knew the bond was stressing her, knew if he gave her space she'd run from him again, and so he'd kept close and let her faint. It didn't usually make him feel guilty when he played people like a hand of cards, bluffing toward the resolution he wanted. This time it unsettled him. When he used people in such a fashion, he preferred they were crass prigs like Sigurd. Not noble and good like Rain.

The cat paced on the top step, his bottlebrush tail twitching side to side.

"She's my mate, and I'm taking her home," Night said sternly. And by the divines, no demon trickster was stopping him.

Another yowl and a hiss.

"Come with us if you insist," Night said, "but your mistress is staying with me now."

Shifting her weight up higher on his chest so her head rested on his shoulder, he turned the knob, then nudged the door open with his boot, balancing Rain and his coat in his hands. Bernard scampered out ahead of them into a busy walkway. Night squinted into the brightness of the morning.

Men removed their hats to honor the duke, women curtsied, all of them staring perplexed at the unconscious woman in his arms. He ignored them. One man offered to summon a physician, but he brushed by the human, attempting to draw as little attention to his mate as possible. Their insistent eyes on her were unnerving. He tossed his coat over her, needing to shield her from their gazes.

Rain stirred in his arms. A line deepened between her light brows.

"You're all right, sweetheart," he said, tucking her in tighter against him.

A little whimper fell from her lips. Her lashes fluttered. This journey would be easier if his mate wasn't trying to escape him while they traveled. Night made a crescent shape with his fingers, the symbol for the moon, cupping his right hand where he held her under her thighs. His connection to the Divine Night was weakened by the sun overhead, but the day was overcast and he was no novice mage.

"Sleep," he whispered. The scent of incense wafted in around him as cool, crisp moon magic swathed her, and her body stilled. Her lips parted, and her breathing deepened.

Bernard hissed before he sunk his tiny teeth into Night's ankle.

"Damn it all," Night grumped, shaking his leg free of the blasted demon. He glowered down at the creature, his face hot with irritation. Bernard licked his muzzle, his yellow cat eyes narrowed to threatening slits. "She's my fucking mate," he growled. "Clearly I mean her no harm."

Bernard hissed, a stripe of hair standing up along his spine, and his claws flexed.

"There's an ice box full of food in it for you if you behave yourself like a gentle-demon," Night said. He had no idea if Bernard's responding meow was acquiescence or not, but he marched onward toward the hackney up the street regardless. The blasted cat could behave himself, or he'd leave the creature behind.

They crossed an alleyway full of factory workers lining up to gather their payment for the week. A dragae stood out in the crowd with his recognizable piercings down his tall ears. He leaned against a doorway at the top of a stoop where the line of workers ended. The bulky brute hid his horns beneath a bowler hat. Their eyes met, and the duke slowed his pace. The dragae dropped his gaze, then strolled off down the alley like he suddenly had something better to do.

Bernard growled low in his throat.

"I see the bastard," Night grumbled. Was the dragae there for him, sent by Sigurd perhaps? Sigurd had a death wish if he thought to have him followed in such a fashion. He'd left the tavern unlocked and unsupervised, he remembered. He'd need to attend to that in case the brute had other nefarious purposes.

His brother exited the hackney and met him on the walkway, his rounded face lined with anxiety. "What's happened? Does she need a doctor?"

The human driver remained at his post, unmoved by the sight before him: the duke carrying a random miss, trailed by a demon cat. Night made a mental note to offer him a job later. The man was discreet and unshakable. He hadn't made a fuss at all when he'd tossed Sigurd out of his coach, and he'd done his bidding the whole night through without demanding a break.

"No doctor is necessary," Night muttered. "Get the door."

Erikson hurried to open the cabin. Bernard leapt inside and turned in circles on the cushions, making himself comfortable.

"Take us around the block," Night called to the driver, "then drop my brother back at the tavern."

"As you like, Your Grace," the driver said, readying the reins.

Chapter 6

"The sloppy little brothel?" Erikson's eyes bulged. He jerked his top hat down like the impropriety of it all might make it pop off.

"Get in. I'll explain." Gently, Night hefted his witch into the cabin, laying her across the bench seat, resting her head in his lap.

Erickson hurried in after him like his boots were on fire. He shut the door and threw the curtains closed over the windows, then he sat down hard enough to rock the coach. "What the deuce is going on here?" he hissed. "Is that an unconscious tavern whore in your arms?"

"She's no whore," Night snapped. He disliked his brother's tone and his staring. "She's my mate, and she's going to marry me and become my duchess."

"Mate? Marry you?" Erikson's face turned three different shades of red before paling completely. He rubbed a hand down his forehead. "Night, if you're thinking of trying to get out of the conflict by enacting some archaic old law, then—"

"That's exactly what I'm going to do." *That and more.* The coach set off slowly. The streets were busy in the daytime, and the hackney crawled forward, waiting for foot traffic to pass.

"But," Erikson spluttered, "that's like trying to hold back a river with a single stone. It's not nearly enough. And . . ." His gray eyes were lingering on Night's mate again. The duke wanted to pluck them out of his brother's head.

Night's nostrils flared. "I need you to stop looking at her."

Erickson's gaze flickered up to meet his. "Stars, the bond instincts are making you cranky already." His lashes lowered once more fleetingly. He glanced between her and the cat curled into a ball beside him. "It's only . . ." He reached for her, lifting one of her lids to examine her eye.

Night slapped his hand away, then maneuvered his coat under her head as a pillow. "Do you want me to rip your arm off?"

Erickson rubbed the back of his wrist like it smarted. "By the divines, you've got it bad. Alright, alright, I won't touch her . . . or look at her." His lips pressed together in thought for a moment. "You realize she's not a young fae female?"

Night shrugged. "I'm not a young fae male."

"I know that, of course, but this one is probably too old to produce an heir, *and* she's a tavern wench and a witch . . . and unconscious for some reason . . ."

Night clutched her to him, scooting her farther onto his lap so that her head and shoulders rested over his thighs. "I told you I don't want a brood, and I already have an heir."

Erikson blinked at him. "Who?"

"You, you idiot. Who else?"

His brother's eyes had gone owl-like. "I had no idea . . . I mean, I understand how succession works, I just always assumed you'd want your own child to inherit . . ."

Night waved his words away. "You and whoever you sire. You're my heir. You always have been."

"But I'm not a mage." Erikson's voice had gone quiet. "I'm half-mortal."

"Most of the province is mortal or half-mortal. That makes you the perfect lord in my opinion, and as my opinion is the only one that matters in this case, you're my fucking heir." Night glowered at his brother. "Don't make me tell you again."

"I don't know what to say," Erikson whispered, emotion clotting his voice.

"Don't say anything, for the divines' sakes. When the hackney reaches the tavern, you're to get out and watch over the place until I send a carriage for you."

"Whatever for?" Erikson's blue brows drew together. "You might not have any taste, but I certainly do."

"My mate is fond of the women who work there." Night gazed down at her. The coach rumbled melodiously over cobblestones. Rain nuzzled into his lap, eyes squeezed shut. "There are scoundrels about. I saw one of Sigurd's ruffians watching the place. I don't like the look of him. See to it that he doesn't try anything."

As the coach rocked side to side, the hem of Rain's coat shifted up, revealing the sheath of a dagger. Night removed the weapon. It was a nasty little blade, sharp and curved. He handed it to his brother and spotted the hilt of another poking out of her boot.

"Stars above," Erikson whimpered, "what's she got so many knives for?"

Night handed him yet another blade from her other boot, and two more from the satchel that hung from her belt. "She was a warrior once . . ."

"She's a warrior still, by the look of it. She's carrying about her own personal arsenal."

"Stars, would you look at this one?" Night found a long thin dagger in a sheath at her belt, tucked behind her satchel. It shone green in the sunlight. The hilt was engraved in an intricate elven style to look like the gnarled roots of a tree. He didn't know much about weaponry—a mage armed themselves with books and knowledge—but he knew this piece was exquisite.

His brother cleared his throat. "You realize, I hope, that you need not complete the bond with this miss to make your plan work? We could find another more suitable mate for you to wed. Someone who understands your peers, someone who won't get eaten alive by the gentry. Someone with skills like sewing and playing the harp. A female who doesn't know how to flay a man alive, perhaps?"

Night ran his thumb tenderly down her cheek. "I want this one." Then his glower sharpened on his brother.

Erikson lifted his hands in capitulation. "I'm saying this as much for her benefit as I am yours. You're a full blue-blooded fae. You don't know what it's like to be an outsider. I do. You'd both benefit from pursuing a different match before it's too late."

Rain's lashes fluttered. Another whimper parted her lips.

Night steadied her with a hand in her hair. "She heard you," he said, a smile in his voice. Rain kicked out at the wall of the coach. "She's trying to wake up. Her subconscious didn't like your suggestion, brother." Grinning like a fool, Night made the crescent with his hand again, calling moon magic to him. "Sleep," he urged her.

Her back bowed, and she moaned. Bernard hissed at him, tail bristling.

"She's fighting it," he said through gritted teeth, struggling to call more magic to him, the morning sun and Rain's stubborn resistance forcing him to double his efforts. She fought him with her will. He couldn't remember the last time he'd come in contact with a force so impressive, and she wasn't even awake. Divine energy filled the cabin, but still she thrashed. In the end, it was his voice that lulled her back into a peaceful slumber.

"Sweetheart, don't listen to a damn thing my stupid brother says. You're coming home with me. You're all mine now," he purred over her, and her breathing slowed.

Chapter 6

"Are you at all worried what this warrior woman with all her knives is going to do to you when she wakes up?" Erickson noted.

"It's good that you have such fight in you," Night whispered to Rain, ignoring his brother. "There's a war coming. You're going to need it, darling."

Chapter 7

(Rain)

Rain felt like she was sleeping on a cloud. The cloud was much too soft and unsupportive, now she'd become accustomed to sleeping on the hard ground. Silk brushed her cheek. She rolled into something long and hard and hot at her back.

Her lashes quivered, realization dawning that the hot thing was a person.

And the person was her mate.

Her stomach did a backflip. She tried to sit up and her head spun. Air caught in her throat.

Long, tender fingers stroked down her arm, leaving a path of pebbled skin in its wake. "You're all right. You're safe," Night whispered, his breath heating her scalp.

Her hair had been pulled out of the knotted braid. Her coat and boots were gone. In her trousers and oversized blouse she felt naked. Exposed. She blinked the room into focus. It was vast and opulent, a splendid space with elegant carvings and images of the divines. A painting of the Night Mother covered the far wall in dark purples and blues, a beautiful woman with midnight skin and the face of the moon. The bed beneath Rain's cheek was large, and as she wiggled, trying to get her bearings, she sunk farther into it.

She tried to sit up again, panic rising in her chest. Her pulse pounded at her throat and in her head. Sitting up failed. She rolled onto her stomach, struggling to put her arms under her so she could push herself upright.

The duke followed her, linking his fingers with hers, and something clicked in her head. She'd never been so aware of a person before, so aware of the height and breadth of them. She felt the expansion of his lungs along her spine, smelled the starch on his clothing, heard the rasp of his stubble against her blouse when he nuzzled closer.

His long fingers laced through hers. Her hand in his pulled her from the murky waves of confusion and panic. For a moment, fingers linked, all was right in the world. The bond purred in her chest, contented, happy.

And then the panic returned like a rapid of icy water crashing into her chest. In a blink she was drowning again. An invisible weight crushed her lungs. She clawed at the blankets, struggling for air. She was hot everywhere, the heat starting at the back of her neck and spreading like wildfire.

"Breathe," Night commanded. He brushed her hair to the side and blew cool breath onto the nape of her neck where she needed it most. "Just breathe." He blew again.

Rain sucked needed oxygen into her desperate lungs.

"Where am I?" she whimpered.

"My home . . . your home." His exhale as he spoke continued

to soothe her, fanning against her skin.

His words sunk in slowly. Her home was the trees. But instead of telling him so, she licked dry lips and leaned back into the comfort he offered. "What happened?"

"You swooned."

Rain groaned, a flush rising in her cheeks. She was a warrior, for the stars' sakes. Warriors didn't swoon.

Night's chuckle shook the pillowy mattress beneath them. "You couldn't help it. Our blooming bond overwhelmed you. Bonding is especially difficult for witches, I'm learning. Something about your broken soul feeling the pull of me and causing you distress . . ."

"Ugh." She rubbed a hand down her face. Her mouth tasted sour. She wanted water and to have her wits back about her. She felt like she'd slept for a decade. The faded light of nearing dusk cast an orange glow through the only window. The room was lit by candles and a small fire in a marble fireplace. "Did anything happen to you?"

Night's laughter vibrated against her back. "Would it make you feel better if I'd swooned too?"

"Actually, I'd prefer it if you'd swooned worse."

He sat up and hovered over her. "No such luck, I'm afraid. But if it's any consolation, thanks to the bond instincts, I gave two of my staff the sack. My valet of many years and a footman."

She craned her neck to peer at him. "Whatever for?"

Night winced. "For looking at you too long."

Rain's burst of laughter helped clear the fog from her mind. She stretched her legs and then her arms over her head, wriggling her fingers and toes, and finally she was able to sit up. Turning in the blankets, she scooched up against the pillows. Her feet were bare. She tucked her toes under the bedding. Her familiar was . . . ?

"Bernard?" She looked around.

"He's helping himself to the ice box."

"Of course he is . . ." She looked her mate over. His eyes had returned to their usual dark gray in the fading light of nearing night. His shirt was rumpled and loose at the neck. What she could see of his chest was smooth and silvery. His boots and stockings were gone. There was something intimate about being able to see the duke's naked feet, and a wave of pleasant heat curled in her belly. "Are you going to give your staff back their positions?"

Night crossed his legs beneath him in a light and unexpectedly boyish fashion, a sight she'd not seen before. She enjoyed it. He seemed so approachable this way, and she sensed that in that moment, there was no trickster mask on his face. No politicking, no games. It was just him.

"I've already sent the butler after my valet." He spoke quietly, adding to the intimacy of the shared moment.

"Not the footman?" She matched his tone, whispering to him like a lover.

He frowned, his dark brows forming a deep V. "He enjoyed himself too much."

Another trill of laughter snuck out of her. She laughed so deeply the scarring in her abdomen smarted, but she ignored it, accustomed to contending with such things. "How will we ever manage these instincts?"

"They aren't all bad." The boyish playfulness left his expression. Taking her in with an unfathomable look, his intensity returned, sharpening his features. Then his lip curled in a broken smile that made her lungs hitch. "You called for me while you slept. You wanted me close. I liked that very much, Rain."

Another flutter tickled through her stomach like she'd swallowed lunar butterflies. "When did you realize I was your mate?"

"The first moment I laid eyes on you. I would have told you so, but you have a bad habit of running away from me when I try to talk to you. An effect of your fractured soul."

Muscles low in her abdomen flexed. "Our potential mate bond is why you've chosen me," she said, putting the pieces together. "You need a mate to achieve your goals? Politically, I assume?"

"I intend to marry you and complete our bond as soon as possible. Our instincts will calm down then for both of us."

Her sigh was sad and slow. She liked that he was her mate, that they were compatible. It explained so much, but she still had absolutely no desire to be a means to an end. Mate or no, he didn't believe in love, the one thing she wanted most of all.

"Can I have my coat back?" She glanced around for it. There was a lounge chair, a basin of water on a stand, an archway that probably led to a dressing room, and a gilded mirror that stood taller than her.

"Is the room not warm enough?"

"It is," she reassured him.

"Then why do you need your coat?"

Rain's eyes lifted to the scarring at his mouth, then trailed up to his temple. She wanted to touch his old wounds, wanted to learn them with her fingers. For a moment she hesitated, thinking it impolite. But then he'd slept in the bed beside her with no such worries, so her restraint seemed unnecessary. Tentatively she reached for him, giving him a chance to pull away.

He didn't stop her, even as her thumb glided across his bottom lip and then lingered over the torn skin in the corner of his mouth. "You wear your scars well and boldly. I've always admired that about you." Her lashes lowered. She laid a hand over her navel. "I prefer to keep mine covered in armor, only my armor went out of fashion ages ago."

"Do you have many scars?" he asked, his voice gentle, his eyes kind.

"Yes, but please don't think I'm complaining. My body has served me well, and I appreciate it. I've just put it through a lot over the years, so I try to treat it better now and then, when I can. It likes the layers."

His face fell. "Your scars hurt you."

Rain shrugged. "A twinge here and there. An uncomfortable numbness is more common. Nothing that is worth your worry."

"Your every discomfort has my worry and is well worth my concern." He laid a gentle hand on hers over her belly. She felt a corresponding tug behind her navel. Then his thumb stroked along her knuckles. "One day you'll have to tell me about how you got each of them."

"So many of my memories are lost to time, but I'd like it if you told me about yours . . ."

He scratched at the old wound at his temple, and his eyes fell. She'd forgotten all about her worries, all about her panic, all about their differences. There in that room, seated on the bed, they were protected from outside woes. Nothing else mattered but them, like the space between encapsulated an intimate magic.

And then the salty, metallic smell of iron wafted to her. Her nose wrinkled, and the spell was broken.

She shifted her weight so she could see the window better. "Iron bars?" His returning smile was devilish. Her stomach flipped, and a spark of heated panic flared at the back of her neck. "*New* bars by the look of them," she added, stressing the word, filling it with her mounting displeasure. New to the window, she'd meant. They were makeshift at best and welded together haphazardly, but they'd confine an immortal well enough. Wood scrapings she hadn't noticed before scattered the floor, and the carpentry around the window didn't match the walls.

He studied the backs of his fingers. "I may have had a quick renovation or two added since you arrived."

She blinked at him, taken aback. "How long have I been here?"

A wrinkle in the bedding stole his attention. He straightened it, avoiding her eyes. "Several hours. It only took one to install the set of bars, though."

"I was unconscious through the whole thing?"

His grin widened into something wicked. Something that shouldn't have sent a pleasant tremor down her back but did anyway. "I helped."

She frowned at him. "You used moon magic on me . . ." Rain clambered out of the bed, casting around for her things. She spotted her boots and coat folded on the bureau by the door. She marched for them, then stopped. Her fingers balled into fists. "If this door is fucking locked—"

"It's not," he said soothingly. He remained seated on the bed. Slowly he lowered his feet to the floor, crossing his arms casually over his front.

Rain touched her side where her sheaths lay empty; her

satchel was gone. "You took my things."

"You mean your weapons? I removed them," he said dryly. "The bond sometimes makes us impractical. I dismissed my staff, for instance. I wouldn't want you to do anything you regretted later. Especially not to me, and especially not if it involved your daggers. I may wear my scars well, but I don't want new ones either."

She glared over her shoulder and regretted it. It was positively unfair how attractive he looked when he was acting like a rogue. A lock of blue-black hair spilled into his eyes. "If the door isn't locked . . . what will happen when I open it?"

"You'll get to see the courtyard. I thought you'd like a room that opened onto the outside the best." Casually, he thrummed his fingers against his folded arms.

She took a calming breath, tension loosening in her chest. "Then I haven't been kidnapped?"

"Oh no, you've definitely been kidnapped." His grin went lopsided, and her heart lurched. "But . . . gently."

Her laugh lacked humor. "You can't keep me here."

"I beg to disagree." The dark intensity in his expression softened, melting into a comely playfulness that was as aggravating as it was beguiling. "Your shock surprises me. I assumed a mature fae woman such as yourself would appreciate some good old-fashioned imprisonment for the sake of marriage. It's all the rage in the best fairy stories. You love fairy stories."

Now she wanted to throw something at him, but her boots wouldn't do. She needed those for her feet. Then again, he'd lost his senses completely, she was sure, and perhaps a boot to the head would knock them back into place. The ladies in legends who'd been captured by a mate driven mad by his instincts were taken from castles. They were princesses of enemy lands in warring courts, a mate worth dying in battle for because they brought wealth and title and power. They didn't live in muddy trees, and they weren't old and covered in scars.

"You're not as charming as you think you are," she grumped.

"Yes I am." His smirk all by itself nearly made her swoon again.

Drat. Yes, he was. She cursed their compelling bond which was clearly as senseless as he was. Rather than admit what he already knew, she stuffed her feet into her boots, pulled on her borrowed coat, fastening it over her tender abdomen, and hurried outside. She liked the strength she found in her aggravation more than she liked the other overstimulating emotions he brought out in her, the ones that left her head swimming and made the bond pulse through her desperately, threatening to pull her under again.

Rain came to a slow stop on a narrow walkway paved with flat stones. The wide courtyard was expansive and fortified on all sides by the slate walls of Night's manor, decorated in columns, low burning oil lanterns, and spitting fountains all wrapped in lichen and greenery. Straight ahead, a balcony loomed, the dimly lit room above hidden behind heavy velvet curtains. Centered in the courtyard, one massive oak tree stretched leafless limbs toward a darkening sky, its trunk so fat it would take five of her standing hand in hand to encircle it.

Taken aback by all the beauty before her, she came to a slow stop and swallowed hard, realizing for the first time just how massive the duke's home was. And it probably wasn't even his only home . . . Their lives were so very different.

She couldn't even begin to fathom such wealth. Just like he probably couldn't wrap his head around what it'd be like to live contentedly outdoors with nothing. It would baffle him to learn she'd rather sleep on the ground at the base of that old tree than in the pillowy bed he'd provided.

He saw her poverty as a thing she needed saving from. She saw it as a satisfying state of her choosing, an expression of her love of nature and freedom. Night believed she was the only prisoner in these walls, but she could imagine the ruthless expectations that came from such an estate as this. Trouble brewed on the other side of the Eventide, and all of it fell on him. He was as much a prisoner here as she was.

The duke was the one who needed saving, and he didn't even know it. It actually made her feel sorry for him, cooling some of her irritation.

The door opened at her back. Night joined her, clothed and shoed. Ignoring him, she moved to examine a bird perch, an ornate one with clever woodworking—not elven, but well-crafted.

"Falconry?" she guessed of the perch. It appeared to be built for a large creature and held a bowl full of treats a hunting bird would like.

In answer, he cupped a hand around his mouth and hooted, mimicking the call of an owl. Moving shadows caught in her periphery. She looked up, watching as a large gray barn owl flew from the roof to alight on the perch, large wings rustling. Night removed a dead minnow from the bowl attached to the ornate stand and tossed it to the bird. "This is Katy."

As the owl gulped down the little fish whole, she twisted her neck in a most absurd manner to gaze upon Rain.

"Hello Katy." Rain waved to her coyly.

"She taught me to fly," Night said.

"Oh? When you use—" She'd nearly called it trickster magic, but at one time "trickster" was considered a derogatory term. She didn't want to offend her mate, even if it might no longer be the case. She enjoyed his smile too much. "When you use your connection to the divine to transform, is an owl the beast you become?"

Night shook his head. "Just the wings. Birds are too fragile, even large ones like Katy here. I'd never risk becoming one fully."

Rain stared at him, imagining a great expanse of silver wings at his back, similar to the set on Katy, only grander, large enough to lift a man as tall and solid as the duke. She had to admit the image in her head wasn't unattractive—quite the opposite in fact.

Her belly fluttered. "Do you go flying often?"

He chuckled humorlessly. "Hardly ever. I don't enjoy flying," he admitted.

Rain took a minnow and tossed it to Katy. She ignored the offering, letting it fall. Apparently, she was only interested in treats from her master. "Such a shame . . . Do you have an affinity with other nocturnal creatures?"

Night's eyes smiled at her. "All of them."

"You're bragging," she accused, turning away from him to hide the telling spread of her lips that would have stolen the bite out of her reproach. She continued along the path of flat stones.

"I am." He followed her at a distance, trailing one of his hands along the wall, stopping when she stooped to examine various flora. Purple flowers bloomed untamed up a short trellis beside a makeshift archery range. After pistols had been banned in the fae provinces, recreational and competitive archery surged.

They reached the gates next, which were barred, chained, and secured with three padlocks as big as her fists. The locks and chains were iron, capable of dispelling magic and poisonous to the immortal races.

She couldn't decide if it was exasperating or amusing that he thought he could keep a witch here so uncreatively. She chewed her cheek, thinking it was probably both. Night saw her studying the exit and moved in closer, hands fidgeting at his sides. The bond swelled pleasantly in her chest, pleased by his nearness.

But he couldn't stand there staring at her all night long, as much as their instincts would like that. His duties would pull him away eventually. And then she'd find her freedom again. Her stomach dropped at the thought of parting from him, even under the circumstances.

They wanted different things, she consoled herself. She'd have to say goodbye to him eventually. It'd be easier to do so now than later.

Why do you look so pensive? Bernard's thoughts caught her off guard. She searched for him and finally spotted him in the form of a large crow perched on the balcony overhead.

I was kidnapped, she thought grumpily, *while you stuffed your gut.*

Bernard's head cocked. He shuffled side to side across the stone rim on clawed feet. *I won't pretend I understand fae romantic gestures, but isn't this the pinnacle of that sort of nonsense for your kind?*

Rain scowled up at him. *He can't just do as he pleases with me because he's my mate.*

I thought that was exactly how that worked . . .

Males are all obtuse. Rain scoffed aloud and drew Night's eyes. She translated for him, "I told Bernard you're obtuse."

His lips twitched. "Are you hungry?"

She could eat, but she wouldn't give him the satisfaction. "I won't break bread with you."

"Your form of protest?"

"You'd enjoy it too much." Nourishing one's mate was a well-known bonding ritual fueled by instinct. One that seemed incredibly appealing now that the idea was in her head. She wrung her hands together, suddenly wishing to busy them. She found a patch of fading flowers to stare at, digging her boot at a small rock she found in the lawn.

She was *not* thinking about what it'd be like to sit in his lap and place food in her mate's mouth . . . *Was . . . not.*

"I would enjoy feeding you, but that can wait until you're feeling less stubborn." His voice drew her eyes compulsively. He pursed his lips at her, and Rain had to suck in her cheeks to prevent an involuntary noise. He was pouting.

He was *adorable*. It made her furious how adorable he was.

Standing so close to him in his finery, she was reminded how much she didn't belong here, how little they had in common, and how they wanted different things. He needed a marriage of convenience. She needed one with heart. It disappointed her so, and she sighed. It could have been the joy of her life falling in love with the charming, complicated duke. She wanted to remove all his masks and peer at all his layers.

She turned away from him in search of another distraction and found one on the rack along the far wall. "Is that an elven bow?" she asked.

"It is." His voice was low and cautious. "If you promise not to shoot me with it, I could let you see it up close."

She squinted at him. "Are you trying to distract me from the fact that I'm a prisoner here with rare elven weaponry?"

"I saw your dagger and may have moved it in here just for you . . . I thought you'd appreciate it." The curl of his lip pulled at his scars. "Is it working?"

"Unfortunately yes." There was so little elven beauty left in the world. It had once been elves and Seelie fae in the northern provinces. Over time, the fae populations grew and dominated as they so often did amongst the immortal races, and the two groups intermingled until only the Seelie Tree Court remained.

"You could delay your attempts to run away from me again," he said, "and shoot with me instead."

"I could . . ." she said cautiously.

"Shoot *with* me," he stressed, "not *at* me."

She rolled her eyes at him.

Night retrieved the bow and gave it to Rain, watching her closely. It was lighter than it looked and intricately decorated, made of living wood that had a green tinge veining through it. All trees had life, but only rare living trees never died, even once they were separated from their roots—immortal trees, they were sometimes called. The bow's limbs told a story in carved detail of Rae, a goddess of nature, and her lover, a Vanir demigod of night, day, and dawn. She took her time inspecting it with her fingers, weighing it between her hands, reliving a story she knew well.

Night stared at her with the same scrutiny she gave to the bow. Finally, she could stand the pressure of his attention no longer. She looked up at him and her breath caught. There was passion and longing in his moonlight gaze. She'd never been looked at in such a way before, never felt so picked apart and *seen*, never felt so wanted.

The duke broke away first, collecting a quiver of arrows with white fletching. Then he joined her a few yards from the makeshift target of straw and wood.

He handed her an arrow, and when she accepted it, his grip lingered on the shaft. A bolt of connection shot up through the wood into her hand. Her fingers tingled, and they were staring at one another again, wordlessly allowing time to pass around them, trapped in that intimate magic born of their blooming bond. Nothing else mattered. She could stare at him like that for ages . . .

Rain interrupted the moment this time, aiming and firing the arrow, nearly striking the center of the target. She stretched out a hand for another bolt, and Night obliged her. She pulled the string back to her cheek, more comfortable with the weight now, and fired a second shot, striking center. It wasn't a difficult shot—they were standing rather close to the target—but he seemed impressed. His approving nod made her blush. She returned the bow to the duke.

Night took two shots seamlessly, and then they agreed to extend the distance, adding several more yards between them and their target. Rain struck center with her third shot.

"Excellent," Night said.

Bernard cawed above them and flapped his ebony wings, cheering her on.

She shrugged. "It's not impressive when there's nothing about to distract you like bad weather or an enemy hoisting an ax or blinding hunger."

"Spoken like a true warrior," he said, awe in his voice.

They exchanged stories as they shared the bow. Once he'd

gotten her talking, it felt surprisingly easy to continue. She was at times too distracted by aiming to feel nervous. He wanted to know how she'd made her living in the woods all this time. She shared about the archery competitions she'd entered to earn coin early on, the furs she'd trapped and sold, and the skills she perfected until trade became her method of bartering. She'd had no use for coins for ages now. She made her own clothing or traded for it, hunted and foraged for her own food, slept at the brothel when it was too cold . . .

"That bow belongs to my brother, Erikson," Night confided. "A Divines Day gift for a fledgling fae, now a man for many centuries."

"It's an extraordinary gift," she said warmly. "I'm sure he loved it."

"Actually, he's never had much use for it, but I didn't know Erikson well when I took over raising him after our father died. He accepted the bow with grace, however. Erikson was never truly a fledgling. He was too mature for his age and prone to worry. Sadly, that bow has gone largely neglected over the years. It's good it's getting attention now." Night raised one midnight brow in irresistible challenge. "How about a friendly wager?"

She hesitated to ask, but he was hard to withstand when he was being roguish. "What'd you have in mind?"

"Next best shot wins. If I'm the victor, I want a kiss." He smiled the way a cat might at a mouse it was toying with.

The suggestion put images in her head she'd have some trouble dislodging later: the hard heat of him pressed against her, his mouth claiming hers. In the back of her mind, an unfriendly voice reminded her that she couldn't stay, couldn't give him what he wanted, because he couldn't give her what she needed. "If I win, I want my freedom."

He rubbed at his pointed chin, considering her. "How about if you win, you get to keep the bow?"

"Oh, I couldn't . . ."

"It needs a good home."

She studied it between her hands. She wanted it, wanted something from him, wanted to put it to good use. And he insisted . . . She kept her expression flat and free of mischief. "If you're certain your brother wouldn't miss it, you shoot first."

They were several yards out now, and she'd lost count of how many times they'd fired, but her arms were beginning to burn. Night took her place down the line and accepted the elven bow. He readied his shot.

"Grow," Rain shouted. The living tree in the bow responded to her voice and to her affinity with nature. The limbs extended, stretching the string taut. Startled, Night's shot went high. Laughter bubbled out of her at his vexed expression.

He spun to face her. At the sound of her utter delight, his look of consternation melted into bemused humor.

"Is something wrong?" she said, her smile so wide her cheeks hurt. "I told you a good archer can fire even if there's a distraction. Don't you want to be a good archer?"

"You cheated." Night moved out of her way but loomed close. "You're no mage, but you're quite the little trickster."

You did cheat, Bernard said.

Whose side are you on anyway? Rain refused to be intimidated by the duke's proximity, keeping her expression placid.

"You can't pressure me. I've been threatened by far worse than you, My Lord. Loose," she said, and the limbs of the bow returned to their original size. She aimed with confidence, pulling the string back to her cheek and holding her next exhale to steady her shot.

Night leaned in nearer still until his lips were by her ear, his breath tickling the tender skin of her neck. "Do you dream of me?"

She released the shot, and it went wide, striking the outer edge of the target. Her face flamed. She'd dreamed of him every night, another symptom of their blooming bond. Vivid dreams of her legs wrapped around his waist, him moving between her thighs with sleek grace, dreams she awoke from hot and slicked with sweat, her core throbbing . . .

"I'll take that to mean yes," he said smugly.

On the way to fetch their bolts, they argued about who'd won. Both arrows were lodged in the outer edges of the target. The disagreement grew increasingly spirited. Rain handed back the bow and attempted to measure the distance between the center and the arrows with her arms. Night accused her of bias.

"Prejudice can't change the size of my arms!" she shouted, surprised to find that she quite enjoyed yelling at her mate. In fact, she'd never found shouting so pleasant in all her life. She felt free in that moment to say whatever she wanted to. A feeling that was completely foreign to her.

Better still, he shouted back with a secret grin that creased the corners of his eyes. "Then your arms aren't the same size."

Rain pressed her limbs together in demonstration. "My arms are *perfectly* even!"

"They may be perfect, but they're certainly not even. Clearly my arrow is closer to center than yours."

"Bernard can decide who won," Rain suggested.

"Not a chance." Night shook his head. "He'll pick his

mistress."

How dare! Bernard cawed and flapped his wings, drawing the duke's attention. *And it's clearly a draw. You both shot horribly.*

"He didn't appreciate your accusation, and he says it's a draw," Rain explained. "Demons feel the same way about lies as the fae do." Then she peered up at her familiar. "Although, he's developed an irritating fondness for human jesting that I hope he tires of eventually."

I won't, Bernard vowed. *Humans are weak fools, but they know what's funny.*

"No matter," Night said evenly. "As this is your home now, there will be plenty of time for a rematch."

"*You* don't get to decide where my home is," she said through her teeth.

The battle picked up again then. They shouted at each other. She jabbed a finger at him. He shook the bow at her, carrying on about his need for a bride. She repeated her desire for immediate freedom.

"You have an entire court full of proper ladies with proper manners at your disposal," Rain barked. They'd ended up by the oak tree somehow. "You wouldn't even have to abduct them. They'd come and stay in your absurdly large house all on their own!"

"I don't *want* a proper lady who dresses well and has all the silly social graces. I want *you*!" He made a sweeping gesture with the tip of the bow that encompassed her from her ashen hair to her worn boots.

Rain frowned. "You want me because I dress poorly and have no grace?"

"No, no . . ." Night groaned. "I mean I don't want a soft woman that's never experienced adversity in her sheltered life.

That's not what I need." He met her perplexed expression and pinched the bridge of his nose. "By the divines, I swear I'm usually much better at complimenting women than this."

"Are you sure?" She raised a brow.

That got a laugh out of him. His shoulders shook. Then Night's gaze fixed on her face, a tenderness in his features that didn't match his argumentative tone. It made her knees threaten to buckle. In her fleeting recollections of her past, she was certain she'd never been wanted like this before. Not by anyone. It was *delicious* to be wanted so intensely. It made her feel pleasantly warm all over and a little needy herself.

It was very hard to say no to the duke. But once complete, the bonding instincts would settle and fade over time, and what would she be left with when her true mate still didn't believe in love? Just a vast wealth she didn't care for and the duty to re-involve herself in a fae war she didn't want to be a part of ever again.

He would have to find . . . someone else. The idea made bile rise in her throat, and suddenly she had no appetite at all.

"Rain?" All humor left his expression. He shuffled in nearer, concern etched in the lines of his forehead and bracketing his mouth.

She waved him off. "I'm all right. Just a stomachache."

Brows drawn together, he looked like he wanted to say something else, but there was movement behind the gate, and the plodding of a mortal's heavy footsteps sounded alongside the light graceful strides of two fae. The first immortal wore a uniform tunic and heavy gloves and worked a large key through the padlocks. He was flanked by two others, one a half-fae male responsible for the heavy steps, with long sideburns and full cheeks. He greeted Night with a tip of his top hat.

Night returned the elven bow to the rack, looking irritable. Then he joined the new arrivals at the gate.

She noted familial similarities between Night and the half-fae in height, the blue in their hair, and the shape and color of their dark gray eyes. Beside him stood a younger fae female decked in a midnight blue tunic with fringe at the shoulders and a crescent moon emblem at her breast. Thin, ribbed ram horns curled off her crown. Her hair was cut short at her chin and shone a vibrant magenta in the lamplights.

It was a mage uniform, Rain guessed. The female probably hadn't reached her first century yet. Her eyes were bright and light. She was likely a guard of some sort, as was the other with the gloves. Night hissed words at them Rain could barely hear. The female appeared bored.

"I told you to make sure I wasn't disturbed." Night's hands formed fists at his side.

"I wouldn't have bothered you, but it's urgent . . ." The half fae glanced around the duke to peer at Rain.

She shrunk back from the unfriendliness in his scrutiny. *I don't think that man likes me,* she told her familiar.

Bernard flapped his ebony wings overhead. *Do you want me to shit on his hat?*

Rain repressed a snort. *You probably shouldn't.*

Are you sure? I've cleaned out most of an ice box. I've plenty of ammunition.

I'm quite certain.

Is the duke going to leave us? Bernard sounded almost as sad about it as she felt. The knot in her stomach hardened.

Night and the half-fae continued to whisper urgently at each other. The half-fae was called Erikson, and he was Night's half-brother. Picking up on bits of conversation, Rain discerned that he was an advisor of some sort.

Rain sighed. *The duke is a very important man. This is how it would always be, Bernard. Duty will always pull him away from us.* She swallowed hard, grounding herself. *And when the bond instincts have settled, it'll be even worse. We'd never see him. We are a means to an end.*

But I love . . . his ice box.

Rain shot him a look that had him crowing loudly, something that to Rain sounded like chittering.

"Half an hour," Night groused at Erikson. "That's all you get." He turned to Rain, an apology in his gaze.

"Go on," Rain said. "It's not as though I'm a guest here whom you're being rude to. Not exactly."

His flash of teeth was full of mischief. He crossed to her and took her hand in his. Her whole being came to attention at his touch, muscles warming and loosening, and her mouth went dry.

He pressed a cool kiss to her knuckles, his thumb skimming across hers. The contact made her head swim. "I won't be gone long."

"Goodbye, Night." She hadn't meant to say the words so solemnly, but they were out of her mouth and she couldn't put them back in now.

He hovered over her, dropping his forehead to hers. She felt the velvet curve of his antlers brushing the top of her scalp. "I like my name on your lips," he whispered, pressing their linked hands to his heart. His pulse thumped with unfettered power, the expanse of his chest hard and unyielding.

Her eyes slid shut, absorbing the satisfied thrum of their bond along the surge of her pulse in her neck and thighs. "We have an audience," she reminded him.

He frowned at that. "*You* have an audience."

She couldn't resist the grin that curved her mouth. "Do you want to sack all of them now for looking at me?"

"A little." His smile was slow and satisfying, crinkling the lines near his eyes. "A lot," he confessed.

They shared a long breath, and then he straightened, separating himself from her with what looked like great restraint. He turned, posture rigid as a soldier in formation, hands balled at his sides.

The young female guard and the advisor Erikson led their lord out through the metal gates. The fae mage wearing thick leather gloves entered the courtyard, shut the bars with a clatter of metal on metal, and re-secured the fat padlocks. A long leathery tail tipped in black fur curled behind him.

Rain glared at the mage's back, sizing him up. He was broad and muscled and had several inches on her in height. The dagger at his hip was as large as Rain's forearm. He would try to knock her down, but Rain would just get back up again . . . She could take him. "Are you my new nursemaid?"

"While our lord is away, yes," he said drolly. "Won't be long now, though. He seemed eager to be back with you."

Rain's attention returned to the oak tree. She crossed to it and introduced herself, pressing her palm to the trunk, exchanging heat and energy with it. The oak was old and lonely. She ran friendly fingers along the ridges of its bark, sympathizing with the ancient tree.

Bernard came to rest on her shoulder, his claws catching gently at her woolen coat. She hoisted him back toward the room, the only other door in the courtyard.

"Where are you going?" the mage demanded.

"Back to my quarters," Rain said without turning around.

"Just . . . behave yourself. I'll have to put you both to sleep if you try anything."

Bernard cawed at that. *Ack. Moon magic makes me positively itchy. Let me shit on* his *head, at least.*

Leave him be for now. It took a moment to cross the expansive courtyard. She pushed open the door. It still smelled like Night inside, like old books and peppery cologne, and her stomach flipped. *Are my daggers in here?*

I smell elven metal and living tree in the bureau over there.

Rain crossed to it and opened a drawer. She smiled down at her satchel and the familiar weapons which glinted in the candlelight and the dim glow cast by the low fire. She returned them one at a time to their sheaths, reflecting again on the loss of elven beauty in the world. Her coloring reflected her elven-fae ancestry and something else . . . something lost to her memories. Something Bernard didn't even recognize.

She had sensed Night wouldn't keep her things from her entirely. She appreciated that. He didn't like her to want for anything, an instinct she could relate to. She felt the pull to give him whatever he desired just as strongly.

But he couldn't have her. The thought turned her more and more morose by the second. Not even the comforting weight of her blades or the nearness of her familiar cheered her.

We're leaving then, Bernard guessed.

The guard threatened to put us to sleep. Why don't you put him down first? Choose something small so you don't have to take my blood.

Bernard spread his wings and burst into a cloud of shadows. He shrunk down and down, forming a small scorpion on the carpet, stinking pungently of sulfur. Little legs wiggling, he scuttled to the door, tiny enough now to slip below the crack and sneak up on the unsuspecting mage.

Rain caught him by his segmented tail, careful of the sharp barb on the end. "Put him to sleep *temporarily*," she urged, lifting him so he met her eyes. "Not forever. Try again. And don't you dare eat any of his fingers."

His pincers clicked at her irritably, then he was a black cloud once more, writhing and spinning before shrinking farther into the form of a furry spider.

"That's better," Rain said warmly.

The little spider pitter-pattered across the floor, sliding easily under the door. Rain sat on the corner of the bed and tried not to think about the way Night had held her hand, the feel of his urgent lips against her knuckles, or the sweet way he'd blown on her neck to soothe her when she'd awoken in such a panic . . .

Flashes of the dreams she'd had since their courtship began popped into her mind. Intimate muscles between her legs tightened and heated. Memories of bare skin and the glide of their lean bodies fitting together so perfectly, the sheen of sweat on their flesh . . . He would be tender, patient with her shyness, a generous lover. An experienced man like the duke would teach her all the things she didn't know, lessons that made her hot and curious—all dangerous thoughts. She squeezed her thighs together and bit down on her lip so hard it hurt.

The sharp pain helped a little to ground her.

Leaving would help more. She needed to be far away from him to dampen the ache.

There was a bit of parchment on the bureau and an inkwell that was almost dry. She went to it. She'd said goodbye already, but she felt compelled to say more. It was good manners amongst the fae to leave best wishes in a note for those you cared for. Rain found a fountain pen and filled it with the ink. Her handwriting was rough, but not leaving a note would be the height of poor manners. She hadn't used those skills in a great while—another reason she'd make a dreadful duchess.

I'm sorry. Please let me go. It's for the best.

-Rain

Her eyes welled with tears that threatened to spill over. She chided herself. This was not the behavior of a warrior, a woman who had held life in her hands and taken it, had survived battle, who lived on the land, and who frightened the predators of the night. She sniffled against the sting in her nose and rubbed her wet lashes, the deep pit of her loneliness opening wider within her.

After a time, she peeked out the door and found the mage lying face-down in the grass, his legs spread behind him. Bernard was a crow again, perched on the balcony, waiting for her. She took her time crossing to him, letting crisp fall air cool her clammy skin. Her breath misted around her. Stars glinted overhead.

Bernard joined her as she climbed the old oak tree. He didn't comment on her watery eyes or the hitch in her breathing, and she was grateful for it. Cradled in the tree's branches, she laid both hands on its trunk. "If I promise to see to your loneliness, my friend, will you help me?"

The tree rattled its limbs. They knocked together like chattering teeth.

Rain kissed the bark. "Thank you."

The tree stretched, the wood groaning. Branches grew and elongated and reached until Bernard and Rain had a clear path to the manor roof. She patted the limb beneath her with gratitude. As she scaled the limbs, Bernard cawed on her shoulder unexpectedly.

Surprised, Rain hunkered down. "What in the name of all the divines was that?"

Sorry. Apparently, the part of your soul you gave me was hoping you'd get caught by your mate so you couldn't leave.

Rain's eyes formed murderous slits. *Do that again and I'll pop you in your beak. This is hard enough for me as it is.* She studied the mage below, checking for signs of movement, then the gates and the gaps between. All was well. They made it to the roof without another issue. Rain stepped carefully, testing the rounded clay tiles beneath her boots.

Ear-splitting howls rent the air. Startled, she jumped, nearly falling.

Bernard took flight. *By the moon mother's knickers. That sounded like wolves.*

Rain clutched her chest, willing her heart to slow to its usual rhythm. "It is wolves. The duke must keep them as pets . . . Let's hurry."

Chapter 8

(Night)

Parting from her, even temporarily, was hell.

Night hated it. Every instinct, every taut muscle, every beleaguered breath, and every thought wanted to curse Erikson off and return to Rain.

But mating was a matter of state, not the heart. He had a duty to his people, and that must always come first, even before the bond, compelling though it was. He followed his brother and Elayna, a mage captain, out of the courtyard.

Elayna was too young to hold such a position, according to most. She hadn't yet reached her first century, but Night had never met a more capable fighter or a more talented trickster. Clearly the Divine Night favored her, and so he'd promoted her quickly and trusted her council because she spoke plainly and never bothered with flattery. She was not a valueless card to be used and discarded for the greater good. She was an ace in his sleeve. A rather deft and deadly one.

Erikson led them down the walkway and into the main house, removing his top hat. He guided them to the parlor, set aside his hat, and retrieved a wire from the bar. Night didn't bother sitting down, ignoring the overstuffed chairs, and so Elayna remained standing as well, her hand on the hilt of the dagger in her belt.

"Summarize it," Night said, not bothering to conceal his irritation, "and be quick."

"I'll start with the bad news before I get to the worse news," Erikson said, hoisting the telegram closer to his eyes. "The Seelie queen wishes to inform you that because you have not responded positively to her suggestion that you pick a spouse within her line, and soon, the Tree Court will no longer be making use of the river Eventide's ferry system for travel or the transportation of their goods. She urges you to contact her should you suddenly come to your senses." He let the telegram go, and it fluttered slowly toward the floor.

Night crossed his arms over his chest. "We knew she might try something like that."

"And we were dreading it," Erikson reminded him, "because it'll bankrupt a large portion of the province. Not just the ferry workers, but the factories waiting for their supplies of redwood and coal."

"We have plans in the works with the railyard—"

"The railyard is actively being purchased by your friend, Sigurd."

"Damn it all." Night rubbed a hand down the back of his head, smoothing his hair.

"Outbid him," Elayna said, her voice toneless. "Outbid him significantly and do it now."

Night considered her proposal. She wasn't a financial advisor, but she made a good point. "Outbid him anonymously," he said. "Change the name of the railroad to sound mortal and foreign. My estate will control transportation once more under a secret trust. The new production will replace jobs lost at the ferries. Trains will take over deliveries. Now, tell me the worse news."

Erikson tossed the wire aside and picked up another. This one had singe marks at the edges. "King Yaga wishes you well—and that concludes the only pleasant thing about his thinly veiled threats of violence and destruction. He regrets to inform you that, due to a lack of action on your part regarding securing an alliance with his family, he has decided to no longer stop giants and trolls from traveling through the mountains and heading north at their leisure. But do contact him should you decide to make an advantageous match with his kin. He will award such a decision with title and land in the Unseelie provinces."

"Divine's blood," Night grunted. Even Elayna, a soldier, flinched at his blasphemy. Giants were not something the duke had foreseen. He'd expected more threats. More demands. More unwanted gifts and bribes. This was *nearly* an act of war.

"My thoughts exactly." Erikson crumpled the wire and tossed it. Then he laid his hands on the bar and sagged over the countertop.

"Patrolmen are no match for giants and trolls," Elayna said.

Night nodded sadly, eyes downcast in thought. "I need more mages . . . Send my house guard."

"My Lord," she said, disapproval sharpening her tone.

"Take my house guard, the novice mages too," he repeated. "See to it that other Lunar nobles do the same. Giants and trolls will be told to target the factories and the bigger buildings along the Eventide, the better to make us desperate and cause the most damage. Station the mages there. Run them in shifts. No one gets leave except to sleep and eat. Make sure they understand how serious the threat is."

"I will, My Lord." She hesitated then, her lip catching on her teeth.

"What is it, Elayna?"

"Permission to stay with you, My Lord. You need someone watching your back. You and your mate's."

Night's smile lacked humor. "I am very capable of guarding myself and Rain."

"Normally, My Lord," she said in that unfiltered way he usually appreciated. Now it set his teeth on edge. "The blooming bond has its grip on you. It'll heighten some of your senses and impair others. You're not yourself."

"She's not wrong," said Erikson. "You sacked your valet and an innocent footman earlier today."

Night shot him a glare. "Fine." He hadn't the time nor the temperament to argue the matter further. "You stay here with me, Elayna. But see to the others first. Attending to my mate just got twice as crucial. It's more imperative than ever that I get her to accept my proposal. The moment the wedding announcements are sent, the sooner we can all breathe a little. See that I'm not disturbed."

Erikson gaped. "You want to set a wedding date even if the bond isn't complete?"

Night started for the door and stopped. "We don't have the luxury of time, so that's exactly what we'll do."

"But they'll know," Erikson protested. "Only a true mate meets the law's requirement. If they visit the two of you or send spies—"

"She'll be my true mate before long. I'll see to that." He aimed a threatening finger at him. "*You* see to my estates and make sure I'm not disturbed. I need *time,* Erikson. As much as you can give me."

"I'll . . . do my best."

Night straightened his shirt and hurried for the doorway. Elayna and Erikson followed at his heels, firing the odd question at him about logistics and planning.

His pet wolves howled, not a strange occurrence given the position of the new moon in the sky. But then, just as they reached the gate, Night sensed something was wrong. There was an unnatural stillness in the air, a quiet that was loud.

"Arne?" he called through the bars, careful not to get too close. "Rain?" There was no response. "Give me your coat," he snapped at his brother.

Elayna produced a spare set of keys from her belt. Erikson stripped off his coat and passed it over. Night wrapped his hands in the thick fabric. He took the keys from Elayna, hurrying to unlock the door, handling the iron padlocks with trembling fingers through the wool.

His throat tightened. "Rain?" he called again.

The silence was deafening. His pounding pulse made his ears ring.

Night shoved the gate open. It bounced against the slate wall as he raced inside, Elayna beside him.

The guard captain pointed at the oak and gasped. "What magic is that?"

The old tree's limbs stretched to impossible lengths, winding and twisting, forming a bridge to his roof. Night howled a curse at the sky. He ran to the base of the tree and looked up at the limbs, studying the rooftop for signs of his mate.

"She's a wily thing," Erikson mused.

Night started to climb the tree, to pursue her. The branches dipped and groaned under his weight. They couldn't hold him. He wasn't as slight as Rain. Then Elayna called his attention to the guard, Arne. He was sprawled in the lawn, face pressed to the grass, his leathery tail in a limp pool at his side.

"She's long gone by now, My Lord," she said softly. Elayna was never soft.

"Is he dead? Did that wild thing kill him?" There was horror in Erikson's voice.

Night wanted to throttle him. "He's not dead, you idiot." He dropped down and joined Elayna. She'd turned Arne on his back, slapping his cheeks, searching him for injuries. Night picked up his hand. It was swollen and red around the pad of his thumb. "He's been bitten."

"By your mate?" Erikson asked.

"By a demon," Night growled. "Stop talking about my duchess as though she's some sort of animal, or I'll speak death into your ears."

Elayna stared at him with wide eyes. Night's lips pressed together. He'd regretted the words the moment he'd spoken them. Very, very few Lunar mages were powerful enough to speak death into another.

Night was one of those few. It was yet another reason why the Seelie and Unseelie fought for him with such reckless abandon. With the fae Duke of Night and his potent mages at their disposal, their enemies would fall dead at their feet in droves. If only he had enough power to strike them both down on his own. If only his court weren't so small compared to the others.

Chapter 8

Erikson cleared his throat, allowing the uncomfortable moment to pass without comment.

Night made a circle with his fingers to mimic the shape of the dark new moon overhead. He called the Divine Night to him, and the air thickened and became coated with scents of autumn and incense. A crisp breeze picked up around him, jostling his hair. He lowered onto his knee and moved his circling fingers over Arne's injured hand.

"Divine healing," he whispered, and the fine hairs on his arms rose. The swelling receded, and the guard's damaged skin paled.

Arne stirred awake.

"Look alive," Elayna said.

Night stood and kicked Arne's boot, jostling him. "Up with you."

The guard blinked at the sky, appearing lost. He glanced at Elayna, then around at the courtyard.

"What happened to you?" the duke demanded. "You were warned she was a witch. You knew her demon was a trickster."

"Yes, My Lord. I'm . . . I'm so sorry, My Lord," he said thickly. "I've failed you."

Night stared gloomily at the branches stretched over his head. His nostrils flared. He couldn't leave it standing now, knowing what she could do with trees. "Cut it down."

"The tree? Er . . . of course, My Lord." The guard lumbered to his feet. "Right away, My Lord." He turned, taking in the project before him, scratching at his hair.

Anger simmered under Night's skin. He sucked autumn air into his lungs and fought for clarity. Then he grabbed Arne by his bulky shoulder. "Wait."

"Yes, My Lord." Arne met his gaze reluctantly.

Night groaned, chin dropping. He rubbed at his eyes. He hadn't gotten enough sleep that day. His mate in his arms had been too distracting. In her slumber she whimpered his name over and over. He pinched the bridge of his nose, thinking of the weight of her, the places where she was firm like a hardened soldier and the curves of her that were feminine and petal soft. He thought of the way she'd melted around him when he gave her what she wanted and came closer . . .

The sweet sound of her voice would turn shrill in his ear should he hurt her by bringing down her tree. She would harden in his arms . . .

"Don't cut it down. Just . . . move it."

"That big tree, My Lord? Move it?"

"You heard correctly," the duke said, resigned.

"I'll do my best, My Lord."

"Are you a mage of the Lunar Court or aren't you? You'll do it," he said firmly. "Or you'll find yourself a new posting."

The guard rubbed the back of his neck. "I'll need to consult with mages in the Tree Court, My Lord."

Night winced but waved him off. "Do what you must."

The duke hesitated before leaving. The urge to pursue Rain was growing stronger, but curiosity brought him instead to the room he'd prepared for her. For older fae like himself, it was considered the highest disrespect to leave the home of a dear one without a word or a note. She technically was not a guest, but . . . The door was unlocked. The candles had burned down, but a small fire continued to crackle. He caught the scent of her, the little white flowers that bloomed in early fall and smelled of vanilla.

He checked the bureau where he'd stored her knives and satchel. They were gone.

Then he spotted the note she'd scribbled on a loose piece of parchment, and a knot grew in his throat.

I'm sorry. Please let me go. It's for the best.

-Rain

He traced the lopsided letters with the pad of his fingers, ice water thickening in his veins. "I can't let you go, sweetheart," he whispered to the dark. "You've infected me so . . ."

He returned to the courtyard, new purpose in his gait, his long strides eating up the lawn. Erikson and Elayna trailed him out. His steps were loud on the pavers, with none of his usual immortal grace. Worry and anger churned inside him beside the bond that wrenched at his insides. "Elayna, ready my wolves."

"Yes, My Lord," Elayna sped off in the direction of the back lawn.

"You're going after her?" Erikson said. "I hesitate to say this, brother, but I think she's made her choice rather plain . . ."

"She's a witch. The bonding process is uniquely complicated for her," Night muttered.

"I don't know why I bother. I know you're not going to listen to me when I say going after her is—"

The duke spun on him. Erikson's mouth snapped shut. "Then don't say it, *brother*."

Erikson's throat bobbed. "In that case, may I suggest an alternative? One to give us time?" He raised his hands in surrender when his brother shot him another scathing look.

Night clenched his jaw. "If you can keep up, you can suggest what you wish, but I can't wait on you." He entered the main house through a side corridor. Their steps echoed on the marble floors.

Erikson elongated his strides to keep pace. "We know you'll

never select a bride from the Tree Court or the Mountain Court, but—"

"Of course I won't."

"—but they need not know that."

"What are you saying?"

"I send word that you've changed your mind and would like time to interview their favored candidates."

"No." They passed the parlor and the drawing room, entering a wide foyer with white stone walls and domed ceilings. "You suggest we lie like we're mortals."

Erikson huffed at him. "You never even need to meet them. *You* don't need to lie at all."

At that, Night paused before a mural of starlight. "Who would interview these potential brides?"

"I would, of course." He grinned. "I'm excellent at asking inane questions. I'll take up absurd amounts of their time, one after the next. I'll *stall* for you, brother. I'll bring a short reprieve to their incessant demands and threats."

"All right. But have them visit you in one of the country manors. I don't want them here."

Erikson shook his head. "We need it to look like you're taking the offer seriously. Until we have an official engagement announcement sent out to the papers, it should be here."

"Fine . . . Stand back."

Erickson did so.

As a trickster mage, the duke could take the form of any night animal he'd familiarized himself with, or simply borrow attributes from them. He'd considered calling forth the wings of an owl so he could hunt for his mate from the skies, but the forests were dense. He needed sharp senses.

Night linked his fingers and crossed his thumbs so the tips

of them jutted out past his hands, resembling ears. "Wolf," he whispered. Some spells were stronger cast in the quiet.

The scent of incense filled his nose, and a crackle of lavender light illuminated his vision as his body began to change.

Chapter 9

(Rain)

Rain returned to The Red Boot. She'd left so abruptly before, she didn't want her girls worrying about her, and she longed to see them. Her soul hurt with an ache that made her limbs weary. She wanted their good humor to lift her souring spirits. On the off chance the duke didn't come to his senses and he decided to continue to pursue her, a public place would make abduction rather difficult.

The Duke of Night was undoubtedly above the law, especially in River Row. She couldn't imagine a constable ever daring to arrest him for taking her, but there had been a time when fae behaved how they pleased in the Lunar Province. It was through fear of the Lord of the Lunar Court that they'd learned to carry themselves in a more civilized fashion, especially when interacting with mortals. Rain sensed he wouldn't undermine that.

Bernard kept at her ankles in his cat form, nimbly dodging

plodding feet.

The tavern was overly full, the effect of the popular lord's recent visit, no doubt. The rumble of voices was a dull roar inside. Susan worked the bar. She flashed a customer her breasts for a copper crescent between filling a short glass with gin. Margot sat in the lap of a wealthy business tyrant Rain had never liked, a fae named Sigurd. A ruddy fox tail draped the back of his chair. She frowned as he ordered Margot to fetch him another ale, shoving her off his lap. Then Sigurd clapped her on her generous ass with enough force to make her stumble.

Rain corrected an earlier thought: *most* fae had learned to behave in a more civilized manor out of fear of the duke. Sigurd was a lost cause.

Margot took it all in stride. Her mischievous grin never faltered.

Rain sidestepped patrons to catch up with her. "He hit you," she grumbled when she reached her.

Margot waved the notion off. "Pfft. That was an appreciative pat and nothing more. Besides, he's fae. They don't always realize how strong they are."

Rain frowned. "Yes, we do. Who fed you that line? Show him to me, and I'll hit him for you."

"Oh . . . ?" She chuckled. "Don't worry your head. It'll put creases on your face, my mother always said. Sigurd is a prig, but he tips well and he doesn't smell horrible. But can I get a hand with the ales? He puts them back faster than I can keep up." Margot tapped the bar four times. Susan laid out four mugs and began pouring. Margot eyed them, then seemed to think better of it and tapped for another four.

"He enjoys humiliating you," Rain grumbled. "I'd like to

pluck off his tail and throw him out on his ass."

We could bring him down, Bernard said encouragingly. *He's a mage, but his connection to the Divine Night is weak. If you let me have his fingers, he wouldn't be able to cast at all, and then you could have fun with your daggers . . .*

The thought was a tempting one. Planning it out cheered her.

"Let me tell you a little secret," Margot said, moving in close so only Rain could hear. "A man can only humiliate you if you let him. And I let *no one* humiliate me."

Rain wasn't convinced, but she let the matter drop. She filled her arms with ales and hefted them back to Sigurd's table with Margot in tow.

Sigurd's ruddy face split with a smile. "Rain," he purred. "When do I finally get to spend time with a raspberry like you? Have a seat, darling." He shifted in his chair and patted his lap.

Rain plopped the drinks down on the tabletop, nose wrinkling. "I'd sooner spend time with giants. They'd try to eat me, but that would be a vast improvement on an evening with you."

Sigurd's bark of laughter drew unwanted eyes from around the room. Rain spotted Penny at a corner table by herself, a haphazard stack of books scattered before her. Rain moved to join her, but Sigurd caught her elbow.

Bernard hissed at her feet. *He can either let you go, or I'll bite his hand off . . .*

"Let go, or my familiar is going to bite your face off." He didn't deserve a warning, but it had the desired effect. His hand dropped.

Face! Bernard chittered. *Even better. The vain bastard will hate that. Wish I'd thought of it.*

Chapter 9

Sigurd paled. Then he peered down at the furry feline, looking unconvinced. "I just wanted to have a conversation with you, Rain. Why do you always have to be so frigid toward me?"

Rain put her back to him, ignoring the surly mage.

"Is it 'cause you're bedding the Lunar lord now . . . ? Don't look so surprised—the entire Row is talking about it," he taunted, and conversation at the nearest tables ceased. Sigurd's thick chortle made her neck hot. "Is my blood not blue enough for a tart like you? What's he paying you?"

Margot intervened. "Oh Sigurd, you terrible tease. You know Rain doesn't turn a trick for anyone, whatever the color of their blood. That's what I'm here for, sweetie. For you and every other great lonely heart . . ."

Rain hoped Margot took him for every last coin.

The witch moved on, crossing to Penny with more urgency. The girl's narrow face lifted, and her eyes brightened. She pulled Rain into a tight hug, squealing in her ear, and as quick as that, Rain's frustration was forgotten. Sigurd wasn't worth her time.

Besides, as soon as he left, she was going to suggest that Bernard return to his crow form and shit in his hair, and all would be right in the world then.

"Tell me everything," Penny crooned, her feet tapping out an excited beat beneath the table. "The duke's brother was here when we returned from our shopping. He said you and his grace got on well and that we shouldn't expect to hear from you for a while. It made us sad, but we were happy for you."

Mention of the duke put an ache in her chest. Rain immediately changed the subject to the variety of books on Penny's table, gesturing to them. "These look interesting."

Rain could read, but language and the shapes of certain letters had changed quite a bit over the years, causing her to stumble. She preferred to be read to as a result, and Penny was always eager to oblige her. The thought made her think of the duke again and his warm, resinous voice washing over her all those weeks ago, and she flushed.

"I'm taking a brief break from turning tricks while I've still got your beau's coin in my purse," she said, hoisting a book with the image of a hand on the cover. "In the meantime, I thought if I learned more about astrology and palm reading, I might be able sell my knowledge for a half piece or maybe a copper crescent, something fresh to bring in more coin. Margot thinks the boys'll go for it as long as I'm topless . . . What do you think?"

Rain had an urge, not for the first time, to scoop the young girl up and tuck her away some place safe and cozy, some place full of books and warm blankets. She was too soft for this life. Too sweet. And one day, brutes like Sigurd were going to ruin her and . . . Well, she hoped she was there to chuck them all out the window before they could manage it.

Rain pushed those thoughts away because they never got her anywhere. Penny hadn't chosen this life for anything less than necessity. Making her feel bad about that would do no one good. They were grown adults by human standards, and there were mortals on this very street who lived worse, with less, and were even younger.

But those poor souls weren't *her* girls . . .

Rain forced a smile and extended her hand. "I'd love a reading from you—even with all of your clothes on."

Beaming, Penny took her hands. She hovered over her palms in turns, running her touch so lightly over the creases it tickled. "These are undoubtedly the hands of a fighter. What I've learned so far is that one palm reveals your actions and personality and then the lines of the other, when interpreted correctly, reveal what might be." She flourished her fingers with a playful air of mystery.

"Sounds fascinating. What do my lines say?" Rain knew very little about mortal religious and cultural practices, save for the bits of information she'd gathered spending time at the tavern.

"This is your heart line, and here's your life line . . . Oh, you're an immortal, so it's strange how it's broken here in the middle and then it just keeps going. Ha. It's like you died in the middle of your life . . . . And this shape here either indicates you're going to have an adventure or . . ." She flipped open one of her books, turning the pages rapidly. Squinting, her eyes bounced from the illustration to Rain's palm. "Or it means your 'habits indicate you'll soon expire full of tumors.'" Releasing her hands, Penny smiled brightly. "Well, let's hope it's the adventure, yes?"

"I'll tolerate an adventure over the tumors," Rain said. Bernard's laughter echoed in her head.

"Would you pay a half piece for that?" Penny's brows lifted, and her brown eyes filled with hope.

"Oh, definitely."

You lie like a mortal, Bernard scolded.

I do not. She gave him a nudge with her boot. *I'd give Penny all my coin if I had any.*

Ack. Stop being sentimental. It's making me ill. Bernard brushed against her leg like a cat with an itch, curling around her.

Good. If you vomit, do it on Sigurd's boots, please.

Happy to.

* * *

Rain wasn't ever going to get Bernard to let go of human humor now.

For most of an hour, Penny whispered common mortal jokes into his ears. When the cat laughed, he fell on his side and appeared to be hyperventilating, which startled Penny. Rain was quick to reassure her that Bernard was quite all right and very amused.

Penny stroked his back from neck to tail, and Bernard was too tickled to complain. "How did he become your familiar?"

Rain leaned back in the chair across from her, pondering the question. It was a loaded one. She didn't know how much a mortal would be able to understand. "I gave Bernard a piece of my soul through bargain magic. Are you familiar with immortal bargains?"

Her brow furrowed. "I read about them in a book once. If you break the bargain, you die, yes?"

"That's right." Absently, Rain opened one of the books on the table, flipping to a random page, a chapter on the implications of warts and scars. "I bargained a piece of my soul in exchange for his service as a familiar."

"Then is he your slave?"

Bernard's ears went back at that. He snarled.

Rain laughed. "He's not my slave. I made it part of the bargain that he'd have free will. I didn't want a slave. Just . . ." She hesitated, unable to explain exactly what it was she'd wanted from him. "Just a companion." She peered at the illustrations in the book and couldn't make sense of any of the graphs. The language was modern, and the spellings were strange to her.

Penny lowered her voice like she was about to tell a salacious secret. "And he's a *demon*?" Her eyes were round and bright, full of coltish inquiry.

"That's right." Rain chuckled. "In order to become a familiar, one has to be able to wield blood magic. Demons, dragons, and fairies can do that—though I've never heard of a fairy becoming a familiar. They're so very rare to begin with, though, so it's possible, just not probable. When demons reach the end of their life after an era or so, they can choose to be reborn in hellfire."

Penny winced. She scratched behind Bernard's ears sympathetically.

"Yes, exactly," Rain said. "I'd want to avoid that too. When Bernard reached the end of his life, he went in search of someone to preserve him and found me."

I only regret my choice half the time, Bernard said.

Rain grinned down at him and continued. "Bargain magic is fed by blood and by the soul. Bernard wields blood magic. The fae access their souls through will, which they use to connect to the divine." She'd lost Penny there—the girl's eyes went blank. "Suffice it to say, he's my familiar because he chose to be," Rain finished with a shrug.

A half hour later, Sigurd left with a trio of dragae henchmen, and Rain was glad to see the back of him. She suggested Bernard follow them home and decorate their hats from the sky. Bernard pursued them gleefully, transforming into a crow after he slunk outside. Her head echoed with his snickering until all went suddenly silent. She'd learned over time that they could only hear each other through their link from about a block away. She knew he was well and alive, could sense his life force which was strengthened by its connection to her own, but his soothingly familiar voice was gone for now.

Rain put out a patron who arrived already half rats on liquor and looking for more. He had coin to spend, but he reeked of sewage and was upsetting the other customers. Susan asked the witch to assist with a weary look Rain recognized. She was relatively gentle with the older human since he hadn't hurt anyone, escorting him to the side door when he refused to depart, instead of shoving him out a window. Older humans were more fragile than younger ones, she'd learned. The fae were the opposite. Age hardened a fae's body. They tended not to move as quickly or have as much energy, but they were stronger and more solid.

As she shut the door behind the old man, a chorus of howling wolves shattered the evening quiet and the trees swayed as though caught in a gale. Rain gasped. There hadn't been wolves in her woods for nearly a century. Another howl—deeper and louder than the others—followed, and her knees went weak. She recognized those wolves. The foul-smelling drunk tore off toward the street, lumbering and shouting about beasts in the woods. Rain had to brace herself against the door.

She'd chased the wild wolves out because they were scaring her food away: deer and rabbit. Then the coyotes came, and she chased those off when they tried to take her place, and the bears after that . . . Only the occasional lone passerby came through her trees now. Never a group or pack.

She touched her chest; the blooming bond reverberated through her with such intensity she trembled. The great wolf's next cry was solemn and low. Grief-stricken. And in that moment, so was she. She wanted Night to appear before her so she could make him all better. She would give him a gift and nourish him with food she made, and he would quip at her and smile his striking broken smile, and he'd no longer be so devastatingly sad . . .

And all at once she wanted him to stay the hell away from her.

She felt like she was drowning in the confusing whirl of emotions and sensations. It was enough to make a person completely mad. The sound of padding paws and snapping jaws brought her to her senses. She couldn't see the creatures yet, but she sensed them looming closer, heard the snap of limbs and the rustle of disturbed leaves. She leapt back, slammed the door shut, and threw the lock.

Rain dashed for the front entrance, but the sight of her trickster mate in the window made her boots catch on the floorboards. A small crowd from inside the pub began to press their faces against the glass, pointing.

"By the divines," she gasped. Night made a beautiful wolf. Silver fur glinted in the starlight. He was the size of a small horse and well-proportioned, all sleek muscles and heavy paws. He had a mane of darker gray around his neck, and unmistakable piercing silver eyes.

In a burst of lavender moon magic, the wolf was gone. Night stretched to his full height, rolling his neck and shoulders like he needed a reminder of how they worked, dressed in his silk shirt and tall boots. His eyes captured hers through the window, the same captivating silver. Amongst the growing crowd, he'd picked her out easily.

The duke crooked a finger at her, his jaw firm. A heat pooled in her belly, growing and expanding down into her core. She stood her ground on legs that felt like soup and shook her head defiantly. She knew she wasn't going to make it to the front door before he got there. She was fast, but he was younger.

She backed into a tight corridor that led to the scullery and hid in a shelved closet full of linens and old cutlery, feeling like the worst sort of coward, but she needed a minute to think, and she needed away from the bustle of the tavern to do it. Her breath sawed out of her so loudly she couldn't hear the dull roar of the crowd.

The door cracked open, and Rain's hand went to the hilt at her hip under her coat, an instinctive response. She didn't have it in her to harm her mate, no matter how firmly she was against the idea of being kidnapped again.

Margot pushed inside. "I saw you slip in here after your beau turned up. Thought you might need a talk— Oh dear, you're sweating."

Rain dabbed at her face with the sleeve of her coat. The bond pulsed through her so demandingly her ears were ringing. "Will you let me know when he leaves?"

Margot turned about in the tight space and peeked out. "He's just planted himself at a table in the back. I don't think he's going anywhere, sweetie," she said with her eye pressed to the crack she'd made. "He's staring over here with that fae-intensity of his that makes me want to climb up his lean body and latch on like a randy monkey . . . Does he not have that effect on you?"

Rain's long, tortured exhale said more about that than her words ever could.

The door opened fully, and her stomach plummeted, but it was only Penny. "Why are we all hiding in here?" the girl asked, squeezing her willowy frame in between them.

Chapter 9

Before either could reply, Susan filled the threshold, a hand hooked on her hip. "I'm all alone out here. Could I have some help, please?"

"Rain's beau is back," Margot said in a stage whisper, jerking Susan inside and shutting the door. "We mustn't be seen. We're waiting for the duke to get bored and go away. Though, I think the stars will fall from the sky before that happens." She and Penny giggled.

"What's he done?" Susan's concerned gaze fell on Rain in the dark closet. "Didn't he treat you well at his estate?"

"He treated me very well," Rain said in a tiny voice—not the voice of a warrior. "But then he ruined it by kidnapping me."

Penny gasped, covering her painted mouth with her hand.

Margot's dark brows shot up in surprise. "He kidnapped you? But then why are you smiling?"

Rain touched her mouth, shocked to find it curving upward at the corners. "Damn." She *was* smiling. Biting her misbehaving lip, she cursed the bond that thrummed excitedly in her chest.

Susan snorted. "The fae have *strange* ideas about romance. That's why she's smiling. Do you want me to try to get rid of him?"

"I don't think you can. Just distract him a bit," Rain said, "while I slip out the side door."

"Is sneaking away without speaking to him another strange fae romantic gesture that I don't understand?" Margot asked.

"Yes," Susan said before Rain could explain herself. Then she decided not to bother. It was too complicated anyway, and there wasn't time to discuss mate bonds and marriages of convenience and the brewing war.

"I can help," Penny said, her voice like a merry tinkling of bells. "I'll go read his palm. I need the practice anyway." In the dark, she stepped on Susan's foot on her way out. Susan grunted in pain, then followed her, limping.

Margot hung by the threshold. "I'll give the door a tap when it's safe." She closed Rain in.

Bernard? she called out along the link of their souls. There was no response. They didn't like to be separated long. He'd panic if he didn't know where she'd gone. But she couldn't stay. Night's nearness was a beautiful torment.

Why didn't he just let her go already? When she'd awoken in his home, he'd mentioned bonding was hard with witches because of the piece of their soul they'd shared with a familiar. Why in the name of the sacred stars didn't he make life easier for himself, then? He could hold a ball like a practical lord and nab the next lady he spotted who was mate compatible and *not* a witch.

The idea of her replacement made every muscle in her body go tense, and her fingers formed claws at her sides. She'd like to think she was too old for petty jealousy, but apparently the bond beating in her chest was not.

A knock at the door stole her attention, and she braced herself. Inhaling sharply, she shuffled out, back into the heat of the busy tavern, keeping low. Her sneaking was made easier by how much shorter she was than everyone else. She caught a glimpse of Night at the table nearest the entrance, legs crossed, body turned toward Penny. Penny stooped over his palm. He was being kind to her. She could see it in his eyes and his smile, which made young Penny light up from the inside out.

He was wrong when he said he was only kind to her. He was responsible for great kindness in River Row. This was the man who'd scared the fae into treating mortals like citizens.

Chapter 9

The man who kept a war out of the Lunar Province. A busy man who had walked her silently through the trees for nearly a month because she liked the quiet and the woods. He was kind. Much to Rain's frustration, she liked that about him very, very much.

She made it to the side door, unlocked it, and shouldered it open. The cry of wolves had her snapping it shut again. "Drat," she hissed. She wouldn't make it far with them at her heels carrying on and giving her away. He'd just snatch her up again and haul her off.

Like the old fae used to. *Do not smile,* she scolded herself.

There was only one path left to her. She'd have to go over there, use her words and talk to him like a proper lady. Her eyes went heavenward with a wish to the divines. She so hated words. Her words, not his. His were always annoyingly lovely. The words of a practiced trickster.

"Your heart line is complicated," Penny was saying as Rain drew near, dragging her feet the way mortals walked. "Oh, hello, Rain. I didn't see you there." Her smile was warm and bright. A line formed between her brows, advertising her brief confusion, as this was not the plan.

Rain forced her expression to smooth, and then she slid into the chair across from the duke.

"Would you like a refreshment, Your Grace?" Penny offered.

"I'll have whatever Rain would like," he said quickly, "and for me, do you have milk?"

Penny giggled. "Yes. But does Your Grace not want something stronger?"

"I don't drink spirits," he explained. Then he gave her one of his disarming smiles. "And I love milk."

"Me too. Rain prefers water—"

"Wine please," Rain said. It had been a long while since she'd had wine. She remembered not liking it much, but it tasted better to her than other drinks and she was counting on the alcohol to help with her courage.

"I'll see to both." Penny winked at her before trotting off in the direction of the kitchen.

Night had a way of saying so many things with his eyes. They turned on Rain, covering her in their moonlit glow, and in a moment she felt terribly guilty and uncomfortably hot all at once. She saw his frustration, his worry, and felt his loss. But she swallowed and held her ground. He'd kidnapped her, after all. He'd been the one in the wrong.

Her jaw firmed. "Do I need to remind you that you'd look ridiculous in irons?"

"I hoped I'd catch up to you in the woods." His lips twitched. "Coming to a public place was clever. I can't abduct you in front of all these sods, now, can I?"

"No, you can't."

"I could, though, you know. No one would stop me." He tapped his fingers against the tabletop like he was pondering it.

"You could. But you won't."

He raised a dark brow. "I might."

"You won't, because you're kind," she said accusingly. His eyes went wide, and his lips parted in surprise. For a moment, Rain worried she'd overstepped. But he was her mate, and he'd certainly done worse, so she pressed on. "You wear your masks well, but I see you through them. You are a kind man, Night. And you aren't going to take me in front of all these people. You've worked hard to make River Row and the Lunar Province a more civilized place."

Chapter 9

He folded his arms in front of him and leaned his weight across the table. "If there was time, I'd do things so very differently with you. I'd visit you and read to you and walk with you, exploring every deep and dark place of the woods you love." His voice dropped to a liquid purr. "I'd sleep beside you under the stars. I'd take you in the grass like the old gods used to, not caring who saw us there. I'd earn your trust and then get you to speak to me freely." He sighed. "But there just isn't time for all of that, I'm afraid."

"This isn't an issue of time," she groaned, picturing everything he'd described in her mind's eye in deliciously vivid detail. "I already speak with you better than I do anyone else, believe it or not. I'm just terrible at it in general."

He pressed on. "I'd learn you if it were up to me. Your every thought. Your every scar. Your every wish and every desire. I want that time." He dropped his chin, and his voice went husky. "Do you dream about me, Rain? You never answered before."

Her lashes fluttered shut. She felt pulled toward the crooning of his voice. She could feel it on her skin, and it was as compelling as it was frightening. "You know I do," she whispered, and there was that intimate magic between them again. Nothing else mattered. The tavern might as well have been completely empty.

"Trust the bond. Follow your instincts. Your fear of me, of us, is just your broken soul in panic. I'd sooner rip my own heart out of my chest than see you harmed."

"We want different things." Chin lowering, she shook her head. "The bond is overwhelming, yes, but I could endure it if—"

"Could endure it if what?" He straightened in his chair.

Rain clammed up as Penny returned. The girl laid a cup of milk and a glass of wine before them. "Would you like something from the kitchen before we cool the oven for the night?" She studied Rain as she spoke, checking in.

Rain forced a reassuring smile.

"We're all sorted. Thank you." The smallest crack broke through his charming façade, his hurried tone revealing a hint of his irritation at being interrupted.

Penny jogged off unawares.

"You were saying," he prompted.

"I don't want a marriage of convenience."

Night lifted out of his chair, the movement so fast it caught her off guard. He snagged the back of her seat and dragged her in closer so that their thighs touched. "I need you near," he said in her ear, his arm fitting around her shoulders with sure and steady pressure, fingers grazing the nape of her neck.

Hot, wet warmth pooled between her legs. She squeezed her thighs together. *Hang it all*, if that's all it took, what else could he do with his hands? "The more sensible thing for you to do is—"

"I don't want to be told what's best for me. If you don't want a marriage of convenience, then what do you want? Speak plainly."

Rain met his eyes head-on. His body warmed her side. She stretched her hand out and planted her palm over the hard plane of his chest. "I want your heart, you fool." The thing she desired most thumped against the flat of her hand like it had heard her.

Understanding turned his expression pensive. "You don't just want the trappings of a marriage. You want the fairy story."

Chapter 9

"Don't call it that." Feeling twice as heavy as before, her hand dropped from his silk shirt. With difficulty, she lifted her wine to her lips and took in a mouthful. It tasted sour on her tongue. She spat it back into the glass, coughing. "Apparently I still don't like wine . . ."

Night's full-bodied laugh brought water to his eyes. He had a laugh like coffee: rich, warm, and dark, but with none of the bitter undertones. Another drink she didn't usually like, but the sound pulled her mouth up into a resistant smile.

Sobering, he touched the scar at his temple. "You wanted to know how I got this, yes?" At her nod, he continued at a neutral clip, not unlike a man commenting on the weather. "When I was a boy of sixteen, my father bashed me in the head with a fire poker. An iron one. He had been drinking—he was always drinking. He had the idiotic idea that evening that he needed to go spear hunting while deep in his cups. I stopped him. He'd have killed himself or someone else if I hadn't intervened, and he scarred me for my trouble, nearly robbed me of my life. The mage who rescued me said I almost lost my eye. My father burned himself to the bone picking up that poker and was too pickled to feel it."

Rain sucked in a breath. "Your father, he's dead?"

"Died in the first war." His slow smile had her blood simmering pleasantly in her veins. His fingers stroked her neck, sending seductive tremors down her spine. "Why? Would you like to kill him yourself now?"

Her chin dipped in assent. "I'd like to put him in the ground again for you."

He chuckled. "Thank you. That was not my mother's response. She sent me away to be raised by my uncle, the last King of Night, back when we were more than a neutral province. The war stripped us of our kingdom at my uncle's passing and made me its lord. Now the mortals call me duke." Night grimaced. "We must pay taxes to both Seelie and Unseelie alike, but thanks to the many advantages of the Eventide and our mages, River Row prospers still. Our overlords have hoped for centuries that we'd crack under their tariffs and choose a side, pledge allegiance. But we won't. We are the descendants of the gods, the Vanir, the children of the divines and the Moon Mother herself. We don't belong to the Seelie or the Unseelie, and we won't be dragged into their conflict."

Rain's head was spinning. "I have a hard time imagining a mother sending her child away from her like that." Her stomach hardened with the awareness of her own loneliness. She couldn't remember her parents at all. She often wished she could recall something about them, but then it was more likely that her mind had let them go, the memories too painful perhaps.

Night sipped from his cup, then licked the shadow of milk off his lip. He missed a spot and Rain helped him, swiping at the corner of his scarred mouth. He had that disarming boyish look again, another endearing peek behind the trickster mask. She brought her hands under her thighs and sat on them, smothering the urge to touch him more.

"I'm not angry with my mother," he explained. "I understand now what I didn't when I was so much younger. Her first responsibility was as a lady of this court and a wife to my father. She did her duty, kept me safe, and eventually died with honor as a mage in the war."

"But what of her duty to you? Her son?"

Night swirled the milk in his glass, smoothing out the lumps of cream in it. "She fulfilled that as well, if not in the way I wanted. She saw to it that I was cared for and kept from the brute who sired me. My uncle, the Night King, was a very busy man, but I was always seen to. I was fed and clothed and educated. And when I did get to spend time with him, he was kind to me. All in all, I made it out better than most. I have a great deal to be thankful for. So you see, when we wed, you will be my duty. In that way, I can give you what you seek. I can show you the kind of devotion they write about in fairy stories."

Rain's heart sunk to the floorboards. "Except when a higher duty calls you away." There would be many, many higher duties. "And there wouldn't be a chance for love. Just responsibility."

"Of course." He set his cup down.

This was more than a lack of belief for her mate. He'd been so terribly betrayed by love—his mother's and father's—he wouldn't know how to open his heart to her if he tried. What she insisted was a necessity, he shoved away, seeing only responsibility and purpose. Her soul ached for him and for the boy he'd been, for the lonely existence he offered her should she complete the mate bond with him. If his father were standing before her, she'd kill him with her bare hands and bury him in a shallow grave for the scavengers to dig up later. There was no greater fae dishonor then feeding a body to animal foragers.

She cupped Night's face, fingers light on his cheek. The tips of them tingled with connection. "You would try to please me, and for that I'll always be grateful."

His nostrils flared. "But it changes nothing between us?"

"I'm afraid not." Her lip trembled. For he was incapable

of making himself vulnerable to the love that had hurt him so. It had scarred him more deeply than any war wound she carried, more deeply than the markings on his face, and he didn't even realize it. She could see how, if she were him, it might be less agonizing to simply not believe in love at all. "Please find another, Night. Though it pains me deeply, we are not suited, you and I."

This big proud man whom she'd once believed unbreakable splintered before her. Night's face fell, his shoulders rolled forward, and he deflated in his chair. She'd remember that wretched look twisting his features until she took her last breath.

His lips pressed together and thinned. Color bled from his cheeks, turning his face from moonlight silver to a sickly gray. He didn't speak, and that was worse still. He was the one who was good with words. Night stood slowly. He bent in half and pressed a cool kiss to her brow, a kiss that prickled across her skin long after it was gone, and then he left.

The desperate chorus of crying wolves filled the woods beside the tavern. Her mate joined them in his wolf form, howling at the sky for the remainder of the night.

Chapter 10

(Night)

When the sun rose over the trees the next morning, Night didn't return to his estate with his wolves. Instead, he found himself inside the home of the witch Sora Yaga. He laid his forehead down on her wax wood table. Shifting his weight, the curve of his antlers struck the surface with a gentle clatter. The wood was cool along his brow and soothing against his burning eyes. Beyond the narrow windows, the landscape whirled by, but from the inside, Night couldn't feel the hut's movement as it lumbered across the province on long chicken legs.

Sora filled a short egg-shaped glass with a coffee liqueur. The color burned amber, reflecting early morning sunlight. It reminded him of the shade of Rain's eyes, and he groaned, covering his face with his hand. The noise hurt his throat, which he'd made raw carrying on in his wolf form the way he had. He chided himself for behaving like some schoolboy who hadn't yet seen fifty winters, let alone more than five hundred.

"You say you don't believe in love," Sora chuckled, "and yet you look positively lovesick."

"I'm not lovesick," he said sourly, then added with sarcasm, "but it pleases me dearly that my philosophy on life amuses you so."

"It's either funny or it's sad, and I'd rather laugh." She poured another egg-like glass and pushed it toward Masha.

Her familiar had taken the form of a small dragon with black scales. No bigger than a cat, Masha perched on the tabletop beside her mistress's elbow, her leathery wings and tail tucked in around her.

"Endless witness accounts of being in love are told with regularity," Sora said to her familiar in a chiding tone as though Night were no longer in the room. "Poets wax on and on about it. Astronomers, scientists, academics, songwriters, playwrights too . . . Some of the greatest minds of the last age speak of love. Apparently, the Lord of the Lunar Court believes all these minds suffer from the same powerful delusion."

"Shared delusions *can* be powerful," he grumbled. He accepted the glass that she pushed at him. He wasn't in the mood to explain that he didn't drink alcohol, so he held it between his fingers, turning the glass without consuming it, watching the liqueur throw the light, enjoying the scent of roasted coffee, orange rinds, and vanilla.

Masha dipped her diamond-shaped head into her cup and drank with a long forked-tongue.

"Have you explained to your mate," Sora said somberly, "the seriousness of the situation? Does she know what's at stake? Does she understand the mind-bending power a true mate bond could protect you from?"

"She's clever. She knows war looms close, but no. I didn't explain about the Seelie queen." Night stopped turning the glass to meet her large blue eyes. "I know why you think I should have, but . . ."

The look she gave him was surprisingly gentle. "You didn't want her to say yes to saving the province. You wanted her to say yes to *you*."

Night didn't confirm her words were true.

He didn't have to.

* * *

Night's brother was waiting for him in the foyer when he finally made it home. It was nearing noon, and he'd never felt so bone tired in all his years. As he entered, he stopped at the sun altar beside the double doors and lit a stick of incense with a long match, letting the perfumed smoke climb up the metal engraving of the Divine Day: a bright red sun.

"Has Elayna seen to my wolves?" Night asked. Eager to reunite with his bed, he headed toward the stairs, not waiting for an answer.

Erikson followed dutifully behind him. "Yes. They arrived hours before you did—made me nervous when they made it back and you hadn't. Arne asked me to inform you that he managed his task. The oak in your courtyard has been relocated . . . Your mate is not with you. I assume your efforts to fetch her were unsuccessful?"

Night paused on the steps to glare at his brother, annoyed both by the judgment in his tone and the poorly veiled eagerness. Clearly, he'd wanted him to fail. "I was unsuccessful," he said somberly, then plodded on up to the second floor and down the elaborate corridor.

Erikson followed for a time, then said cautiously, "In that case, I'll make plans for Baron Dagrun and his daughters to join us for the midnight meal."

Night stopped in his tracks, frowning at his bedroom door. "Why?" he said acidly.

Erikson shuffled his feet. "Because his daughters are eligible and attractive. And your idea of marrying a mate and bonding her is the only one we've got. You need a mate . . . one that won't run off. The province is likely full of potentials."

Night pounced. In a blink, his brother was pinned to the wall, his fingers tightening around his neck. A growl rumbled deep in the duke's chest. Erikson's eyes widened, the whites stark in his paling face.

Then Night's grip loosened, the heat and fire melting from him to quickly be replaced by shame. He moved his hand from his brother's throat to his cravat, and he straightened it. The duke bent forward and touched the curves of his antlers gently to the crown of Erikson's head, a fae display of humility and deference.

"Brother," Night said sadly, "you always get the worst of me. I spent too much time in a wolf's body last night. Please forgive me."

Erikson pulled at his own cravat and worked his throat. "There's nothing to forgive. Perhaps it was a bad time—"

"No. Don't make excuses for me." He lifted his head and stepped away. "You're right, and your judgment is sound. There's no reason not to identify who's out there, see who else has mate potential, in case . . ."

"I'll see to it," Erikson said, and Night was grateful for the interruption. He hadn't wanted to finish his thought.

Chapter 10

Shoulders sagging, Night resumed his path to his chambers.

His brother stopped him. "You're nothing like Erik, you know?" His eyes were on his boots. He straightened his cravat again, though it didn't need straightening. "In case you were worried about that. Father was a nasty and hateful man constantly in his cups. He was not even a quarter of the fae you are. You . . . aren't like him."

Night couldn't place the emotion that welled inside him. It prickled sharply like thorns in his chest, and yet it was also warm and comforting too. It occurred to him that if he didn't love his sweet brother after he said something like that, then either love truly wasn't real, or he simply wasn't a man capable of the emotion.

He nodded at Erikson, uncertain what else to do. Then he entered his chambers and closed the door carefully behind him, shutting out the world: the duty, the impeding war, the looming threats. All of it. The heavy curtains were already drawn to block out the sunlight pouring in from the balcony. He didn't bother undressing before sliding into his bed.

He was almost too tired to sleep. His mind whirled mercilessly. Then he stirred awake, not realizing he'd slipped under at some point.

Rain.

He longed for her so fiercely he thought for a moment he'd seen her standing at the foot of his bed, but then he stirred awake again and the vision of her was gone.

Night rose at dusk and readied for his day in a fog. His valet assisted him with none of his usual good humor. Apparently, he was still sour about being let go unexpectedly before when Night had been seized by mating instincts. The valet was a mortal and unfamiliar with the impact of the blooming bond.

A refreshment cart was wheeled in by a maid as the valet fastened the duke's cufflinks, the mage Arne following her in. The duke straightened, made immediately alert by the sweat on the guard's brow. He waved his valet off and turned to face him.

"My Lord," Arne began, rubbing the back of his head with his large palm. His leathery tail dragged the carpets in defeat. "About the oak tree . . ."

"My brother informed me that your efforts to have it moved were successful."

"They were, My Lord . . . but . . ."

Night stared back at the guard with growing impatience.

"Perhaps you should see for yourself." Arne gestured at the balcony.

Curious, Night crossed to the heavy velvet curtains and pulled them back. His valet tended to the curtains on the opposing side, and the duke squinted out into fading sunlight. The oak had returned to the center of the courtyard.

And it flourished.

It was surrounded by a handful of bright green saplings freshly planted. The ancient tree had seemed near death before. Now it stretched tall.

"I'm so sorry, My Lord," came Arne's quavering voice from behind him. "Your witch must have . . . snuck back in here while I slept the sun away and . . . she left a note."

"Of course she did." Her antiquated manners wouldn't allow her to visit a place without leaving a note. Excitement pumped up his pulse.

Arne removed the folded parchment from his pocket, and Night took it from him with so much exuberance he nearly tore the page. He read hungrily.

Leave my trees alone or suffer my wrath.

Hope you are well.

-Rain

Laughter bubbled out of Night, so much so he felt a little lightheaded afterward.

"My Lord?" Arne sounded alarmed.

Night swiped an amused tear out of his eye. "Leave it, Arne. If she wants it there that badly, we'll keep it there."

"As you wish, My Lord."

Chapter 11

(Rain)

Rain spent the next week walking amongst her trees and foraging for her food. At night she slept on the floor of the tavern in front of the stove for warmth, then she left again at sunrise. The quiet of the woods usually cheered her, but at the moment nothing had the power to soothe the ache the bond put in her chest. She would climb up her favorite trees and lounge in their branches, soaking up the sunlight that bled through the canopy, longing to be held by a very different set of limbs. The sad thrum of the bond reverberated inside her, a constant reminder of what she'd given up. Her appetite was gone. She avoided sleep, dreading the vivid dreams fashioned by instinct.

When she did fall asleep, she'd awake hot all over, a dull throb between her thighs, craving the man she'd ordered away. It was the worst sort of torment.

The duke hadn't returned. The chase was over. He'd finally

chosen reason and let her go. Bernard did his best to console her, but he understood so little about what it was she'd lost. He pulled away from her, keeping his distance, and she couldn't blame him. She wouldn't want to be linked to her miserable head either.

She tried reminding herself that hurting, feeling the bite of loneliness now when she had a way out of it, was better than being alone as a lady with a husband who didn't believe in love and didn't want it in their relationship, in a massive house full of political backstabbing and looming war, true-mated to a man she could never leave.

It was late in the afternoon at the end of the week when she decided to visit the tavern before it opened to patrons. She hoped the girls' sweet voices would drown out the gloomy one inside her head. Bernard joined her in his cat form. When she opened the side door, he snuck in ahead of her, slinking between her legs, only to be scooped up into Penny's willowy arms. Bernard gave a frustrated yowl that was immediately smothered by affectionate rubs and pats.

I hate everything, Bernard said, tail curling and uncurling.

"Pretty kitty," Penny cooed, disappearing with him down the corridor toward the scullery.

Rain made her way to the bar where Susan busied herself organizing shelves. The moment the woman spotted Rain, she abandoned her work, coming around to her side of the island to pull her into her arms.

"We're so sorry, love." She hugged her close, pressing her face to her slender shoulder.

Rain was taken aback. She hadn't said anything to the girls about what had transpired between her and Night, and they hadn't pried. An old newspaper lay open on the corner of the bar. The duke's name in a headline caught her eye, and a fresh pang of grief shot through her. She drew in closer, picking out the letters she recognized, piecing together the meaning of the modern ones using context clues.

A fae feast was scheduled late next month, to celebrate something. "Susan." Rain pointed to a word written in the modern common tongue she didn't recognize. "What's that say?"

Susan peered over her shoulder, then gave her a pitying look. "Engagement," she read quietly. "You didn't know about the duke . . . ? We assumed that was why you'd been so quiet lately . . . I'm sorry, love."

"Oh." Rain sat down hard on the nearest stool, her limbs suddenly too heavy to keep her upright.

Susan's hand was a warm, friendly weight on her back, but it wasn't enough to stop the sting of tears that clotted her throat and burned her eyes.

"I told him to pick another mate to bond," she choked. "I have no right to feel so dreadful and yet . . ."

Penny reappeared, shuffling quietly into the room. She dropped Bernard on the bar and took Rain's hand in hers. "But of course you have every right. Wounds of the heart go the deepest and hurt the very most, everyone knows that."

Susan patted her back. "You haven't truly lived until you've felt the sting of love lost. It's what all the poets go on about. It's one of those spices of life that, though bitter, remind you you're still breathing. So have a cry, love."

Rain's breath caught on a sob, as though she'd needed the permission to let her eyes well over. She told them through her tears about the things she'd discussed with Night, about his political needs conflicting with her desire for a love match.

Chapter 11

Susan's palm moved in a comforting circle on the center of her back, over the woolen coat she'd given her. "Get it all out. Then wash your face and put it behind you. You know what you want now, and there is no nobler thing to pursue than love."

"Then you don't think I'm a fool?" Rain rubbed her eyes clean with the backs of her hands.

"Not at all," Penny crooned.

"Maybe a little," Susan said, and a laugh choked out of Rain. Susan had always been the most fae-honest of the lot.

"It's romantic of you," Penny insisted. "Courageous, I say. Good on you, Rain."

Bernard nudged Rain's chin with his muzzle. She scratched behind his ears with gratitude. She realized then she couldn't hear movement up in the loft. "Where's Margot?"

Susan's face, already fair, paled further. The blue vein in her forehead stood out. "She's . . . decided to work elsewhere."

"What do you mean?" A knot grew in her stomach, her instincts roiling within her.

"Sigurd," Susan said like the name tasted sour. "He made her an offer she couldn't refuse."

Rain shook her head. "He's scum and a brute. He's—"

Susan waved her off. She rounded the counter, returning to her shelves. "Margot's done this before. Hoped the grass was greener, then realized it's not. She'll be back."

Penny remained quiet, playing with the end of Bernard's tail, not meeting anyone's eyes.

"I don't like it," Rain said, leaning against the edge of the bar. "How long has she been gone?"

"I don't either," Penny confessed in a quiet voice.

"She's been gone three days," Susan said over her shoulder,

stacking upturned mugs in neat rows. "One of those dragae brutes covered in ink came to gather her things. He had a note from her written in her hand. She's always hated goodbyes, and she said so in her letter."

Rain fiddled with the end of the newspaper, wrinkling the story about the duke's engagement. "You haven't seen her, then?" The knot in her stomach grew spikes and twisted.

"Margot's a grown woman." Susan straightened a bottle of gin so the label was facing outward. "I know you don't see us that way, but she is. And like I said, she's done this sort of thing before. She's always complaining about how little the men around here can pay. It was only a matter of time before she tried something new again . . ."

"But it didn't go well for her last time," Penny said meekly.

Rain had heard enough.

* * *

Walking through the city was an assault on Rain's senses. Bernard knew where Sigurd's offices were, having followed him home the other day, dropping wet presents on his hat and coat from the sky in his crow form. One of the most delightful days of his life, he told Rain, as he led the way.

It was a long hike through busy side streets. The walkways were crowded. A crisp fall wind whipped between the tall buildings more bitingly than what she was accustomed to amongst her trees. The air was dank with human smells, river, and smog. When they finally arrived at the stone and steel building full of windows, it was near dusk.

The front and side entrances were crawling with unfriendly dragae, their skin steaming in the cooler air. Bernard fell over her in his shadow form. At his touch, he took some of her blood to conceal her from sight as she moved in closer to peek inside. She peered through each window in turn, looking for signs of Margot.

Finally she spotted her and gasped. Margot served drinks in the lobby topless, balancing a tray full of clear liquor in iced glasses. No corset or stays, her bodice draping down her front. Her warm skin was two shades paler than normal and covered in bruises. Her right eye was swollen shut.

Rain's fingers made unconscious fists at her side. The sight of her confirmed her suspicions. Margot hadn't volunteered to work for Sigurd. She wasn't here of her own volition.

I could handle three of them if I took the first by surprise, Rain told Bernard. *If I gave you as much blood as I could spare, how many could you handle?*

These dragae are marked, Rain. Do you see the ink on their arms? An immortal would need to be at least as old as you to recognize it.

Rain strained to see the marks and cursed. *These men are warriors. The dragon king's favored. What are they doing here, pretending to be mercenaries . . . ? Diplomacy it is, then. Transform into something intimidating, please.*

A cat?

No.

A large cat with lots of unnerving fur and big bulgy eyes?

A wolf, please.

Bernard dropped his shadows, and the air warmed around her, stinking of sulfur. He appeared beside her in the form of a black wolf with midnight eyes. He'd taken some of her blood in his shadow form to manage it. Not very much. Just a sip and he was so big his wolf's head came to her chest.

The arches and columns of the building hinted at Lunar

craftsmanship, but as she led them inside through the front door, the influences changed. The lobby was too warm with so many dragae in one space. The furniture was spartan, the walls papered in drake art made to look like dragon scales. The urn in the corner bore the image of the Divine Terra, a dragon with an island on its back. Smells of mountain cuisine dominated the space: beets, sautéed mushrooms, creamy gravy, cooked rice, and lentils. Several sets of unfriendly eyes turned toward her. None of them seemed surprised to see her.

Margot paused and released a breath. She didn't acknowledge Rain, however. She kept moving, kept passing out drinks and food to the soldiers spread out in the lobby. They spooned food into their mouths out of clay bowls and ignored the witch and her familiar. Against the far wall was a dragae with tall ears and several piercings. Rain recognized him.

That's the bastard I bargained out of The Red Boot, she reminded Bernard. *The one that held the girls hostage for two nights. I should have just killed him.*

You can't now, Bernard said glumly. *You agreed to let him live. And you didn't put a time limit on it. You have to be careful with your words when you make bargains.*

She made it to the center of the room undisturbed, Bernard beside her looking properly menacing. "Sigurd?" she demanded, calling out to the brute she recognized.

"He's expecting you," the dragae with the piercings grunted. Then a smug smile flittered across his thin lips. She hadn't noticed it before, but on the back of his wrist was an inked image of crossed dragon wings. "Try anything, witch, and we'll pluck your pointed ears off your tiny head and hang you by your thumbs from the rafters. Now go inside." He indicated the door on his left with a jut of his chin.

Chapter 11

"Dusan," came the taunting call from the nearest dragae, who paused in spooning more food into his face. The rest of his words were in the language of the mountains, a crisp, bold tongue with heavy "r" sounds—a language Rain had forgotten long ago.

Dusan, the dragae she recognized, smirked at her, eyes unfriendly. The other laughed uproariously at whatever cruel joke he'd made at her expense.

Rain wanted to put a fist through their faces. Her fingers itched for one of her blades, but thinking of Margot and how she didn't want to make things worse for her, she kept moving, expression placid.

Rain made a circle with her fingers and displayed the crude gesture for the dragae.

"Cunt," Dusan said under his breath, and he spat on the floor by her feet as she passed.

On the other hand, Bernard said, baring his large teeth, *I didn't make a bargain. I could bite his insolent face off.*

Margot first. Bite faces off later. Rain crossed to the office door and pulled it open. Bernard reluctantly followed her through, growling low.

The office was lit by dull gaslights. Leaning against the walls were stacks upon stacks of political signs: *Vote Sigurd for Councilman.* An empty secretary's desk sat cattycorner to Sigurd's. The mage didn't look up from his work, even as Rain closed the door loudly behind her. His fox tail flicked against his seat, and his beady eyes narrowed on the correspondence he was writing.

Rain stepped farther into the room. "Sigurd?"

He raised a finger at her, silencing her. The scratch of his fountain pen filled the quiet.

Rain rolled her eyes. "I'm not going to stand here all—"

His finger rose higher. Bernard growled and snapped his jaws, but Sigurd was unmoved.

Finally, the fae finished writing, adding a signature to the bottom with a flourish. He lifted his beady eyes. "Rain," he greeted warmly like he would an old friend. "I've been expecting you. Forgive the delay. Between managing my businesses and campaigning, I've been burning my candle at both ends."

"Going to become a politician instead of just bribing them?" Rain guessed.

Nice one, Bernard said.

Sigurd's chuckle lacked humor. "There's no reason to be unpleasant."

"I'm very, very tempted to make you look like Margot does now with matching bruises and a fat eye," she said through her teeth. Her hand went under her coat to the sheath strapped beneath her satchel, where her elven blade made from steel and living tree rested. "That would just be the start, though."

Sigurd's laughter burst out of him. "You're so droll." He gestured at the armchair across from his desk. "Have a seat."

"I'll stand."

"Suit yourself." Sigurd leaned back in his chair, his red fox tail pillowed behind him.

We can take him, Bernard said confidently. *I'll go for his beady eyes. You stab him in the balls. Then we'll grab Margot and run . . .*

He's a Lunar mage, a trickster, right? If I take off his fingers, he should have a hard time casting.

He's a weak one. You won't even need to bother. Bernard snarled deep in his throat. Jet fur stood up along his back.

Chapter 11

Sigurd snorted at her familiar's show of aggression. "I didn't like ruining Margot's pretty face, but it was effective. It certainly got your attention."

Rain's nostrils flared. "You didn't need to hurt her to get an audience with me."

He scoffed. "It's not as though you keep a post box in those woods of yours, Rain. And hurting her was necessary to ensure your cooperation. You see now what's at stake, and you can threaten me all you like, but we both know you don't stand a chance against the force waiting for you in my lobby."

Sigurd dug in a desk drawer, removing a clear flask full of a glowing liquid that caught the gaslights and threw stars about the room. He fetched a tall glass out next, then he opened the cap and poured the entirety of the liquid into the cup. The liquid glittered with gilded flakes that swirled about as though caught in a whirlwind.

Fairy wine. It smelled like overly ripe fruit and dead leaves.

Bernard's ears went back. *If he drinks that, it'll strengthen his connection to the Divine Night tenfold for days . . . It'll still hurt if you stab him in the balls, though.*

We have to get Margot out of here before we do any stabbing. Rain hadn't forgotten that just outside was a lobby full of King Yaga's soldiers she'd have to contend with if she went the route of violence.

"Where'd you find that?" Rain kept her tone level. All things fairy, including the beings themselves, were extremely rare and very powerful.

Sigurd's smug chortle needled its way under her skin and made the small hairs on her arm and the back of her neck prickle. "I planned to expand my wealth into railyards, but I was outbid by some foreign company made up of mortals and lousy with coin. Purchasing this"—he hoisted the glass—"was a small consolation. I always wanted to try fairy wine, and now I have good reason." He saluted her with the glass and tipped it back, swallowing hard. His eyes squinted shut. "Ack. It tastes like farts . . ." His ruddy face went redder still. Then Sigurd flexed and unflexed his fingers, studying them as a small smile spread his lips. "But I can feel it working."

Moon magic filled the room, cooling the air. Papers rippled, then lifted off his desk. Office supplies and political signs began to shudder and shake. Sigurd chuckled.

"Margot," Rain said evenly. Her temper had fled her, replaced by a serene bloodlust that had always served her best in times of conflict. Bernard pressed his side against her thigh, a show of camaraderie. He'd go with her into hell and worse, she knew. She patted the top of his head, filling her fingers with his coarse fur, taking strength from him.

Sigurd's face returned to its usual ruddy shade, but the cloying scent of moon magic lingered. He flapped the collar of his dress shirt, cooling himself as papers and objects returned to their places. "What do you know about dragon hoards?"

Rain's brow knitted. What connection could she or Margot possibly have with that? "Dragons favor items of worth. The more valuable a thing is to someone, the stronger their desire to possess it. They keep them in secret places up in their mountains."

"Hiding their hoards in their mountains is a bunch of fairy story flimflam." He tapped the side of his nose as though he intended to bring her into his confidence. "They keep them on their person, magically. And there's one such hoard here in the Lunar Province. A hoard I know to be full of ancient wyvern coins, enough for a man to buy their own country."

Greed glittered in his small eyes.

"Did your marked mercenaries tell you that, the dragae with the crossed wings inked on their flesh?" Under her coat, Rain found the decorative hilt of her elven dagger, and she fingered the metal grooves. It eased her.

Sigurd raised a brow. "What's it to you?"

"Those men don't serve you," she said evenly. "They're the dragon king's favored soldiers. They are loyal only to him. All this talk of hoards and wealth—I see it now. You're being played like a fiddle."

Sigurd swatted a hand at her. "Those men are loyal only to coin. Coin that I have in abundance."

"Whatever you know, you know it because King Yaga wants you to know it. If you were a smart man and wished to stay safe, you'd run the other way fast and far."

"Being safe isn't always good for business," he said, leaning back in his chair. "If you want to see an end to Margot's suffering, you'll make a bargain with me and help me claim my hoard."

"Finally, he gets to the point," Rain grumbled to Bernard. "You already know what I want. Margot's freedom and you far, far away from her and the other women of The Red Boot."

"Yes, so predictable," Sigurd drawled. "It is said that witches hold no allegiance to anyone save each other. Is that true?"

Rain shrugged. "True enough."

"There is another witch living in the woods outside of River Row."

"Sora Yaga."

"You know her?" He grinned.

Rain was tired of seeing him smile. She hoped to see him looking scared and hurt soon. "Yes, I know of the witch who lives in a hut that moves about on great chicken legs. She's impossible to miss. Witches are not pack animals, but we do hold a certain deference toward others like ourselves. That said, I won't hurt Sora Yaga. She's never wronged me, and her falling out with her wicked father amuses me."

Sigurd smacked his lips together like his mouth tasted tart. He pulled out another flask from an inside jacket pocket, a silver one, and he drank from it greedily. "Ack. I can't get the taste of farts out of my mouth." Then he waved at her like he was shooing away flies. "You won't hurt the witch. I'm going to do that until she gives me what I'm after. I just need you to get me *to* her."

Rain thought his words over. Bernard whined at her, uneasily. "I would not have to harm her?" she clarified. "I need only bring you there?"

His smile was full of sharp pearly teeth. "You couldn't in any way warn her of my presence, but yes. Bring me inside her hut. I can't get close to it without the great blasted bird legs trying to claw me to bits."

"And what if Sora Yaga kills you?"

Sigurd's chortle was full of malice. "Do you know nothing of fairy wine? At this moment, there is no greater mage. Not even the duke himself could outmatch me. With my connection to the Divine Night, I can take a man's sight, make him deaf, paralyze him. I could turn myself into any nocturnal beast I choose or just gift myself their attributes. I could sprout the wings of a bat and the head of a wolf and the ass of a beaver right now if I wanted. I'm unstoppable, Rain. I need only be in a room with her. Sora doesn't stand a chance against the power coursing through me, don't you worry."

"Oh, I wasn't worried for you. I'm hoping she rips you

apart. Assuming she does, what happens to our bargain? What happens to Margot?"

"It's like I said. I didn't enjoy hurting the girl. You get me inside that dratted hut and our deal will be done. Come what may."

Rain lifted her chin defiantly. "I want Margot free and sent home *now*. I want to see her to the door of the tavern. I want your guarantee that you and all of your dragae bastards will never darken her door again. You and your men won't *ever* hurt any of them at The Red Boot. And—"

"And then you will agree to the bargain and bring me to Sora or death take you?"

Rain nodded. "I'll agree."

Speak the words so very carefully, Rain, Bernard urged her.

I know what I'm doing.

"On my life, I will set Margot free this night," Sigurd said, "and allow you to see her to her door. Myself and my mercenaries will never step foot in that putrid little establishment known as The Red Boot ever again. We will bring no harm to the women at the tavern, in exchange for your cooperation. You will get me inside the hut of Sora Yaga, and while there, you will not interfere. You will do nothing to warn her. You will accomplish all of this before sunrise."

"On my life," Rain said, and her pulse thumped, "after escorting Margot safely home, I will bring you inside the hut of Sora Yaga for you to do as you will. I will not help you hurt the witch. I will not warn her of your presence. I will only gain you admittance."

"Do we have a bargain?" Sigurd extended his hand across his desk.

Rain stepped to him and took his hand reluctantly. His palm

was dry and cool. "Yes," she said, and the weight of the bargain magic cinched around her ribs.

"Yes," Sigurd echoed, squeezing her hand in his.

* * *

Rain held Margot in the back of Sigurd's coach as she sobbed. Bernard lay across their feet in his wolf form, whining miserably. Twice Margot tried to tell Rain something, but she couldn't get the words out. Her eye was swollen shut and leaking tears. Rain planned to see to her injuries as soon as she was certain she wouldn't need the spare blood.

"Everything is going to be all right now," Rain said as the coach rounded on Dimmet Street and the brick face of the tavern loomed closer.

Margot clung to her, dribbling snot and tears onto the shoulder of her coat. Rain wanted to stab Sigurd in the balls for that. Margot never lost her spirit, come what may. Now here she was, a mess of nerves and trembling uncontrollably.

I'm going to bite that bastard's head off, Bernard hissed.

We'll get the job done and then come back and heal her.

Bernard rose to his feet with a snarl. *Let me heal her now. Explain to her that I'll need to borrow some of her blood. I'll have to take more because she's mortal, but it won't be much, and all I'll have to do is touch her. She won't feel it, and she won't miss it. I won't even complain about how bland human blood tastes.*

Rain explained what was needed. Margot nodded her head, and Bernard set to work, evaporating into a shadowy mist that fell over her, darkening her skin, tinting it the color of smog. Slowly the flesh around her eye began to tighten, the swelling receding. Her bruises lightened to a yellow color and then vanished completely. Her skin regained some of its warm glow.

Then Bernard was a wolf once more, sitting back on his haunches, looking pleased with himself.

Margot wiped her nose as the coach came to a halt in front of the tavern. She patted Bernard's head in gratitude, then turned to face Rain. "Thank you."

"Of course."

"No, I mean it, Rain. Thank the divines and the ancestors and the gods and whoever else is out there wanting it. I thank them for you. I've been treated poorly by men before, but . . . the last three days . . . the horrible things they said to me . . ." She swallowed hard.

Rain took her hand in hers and pumped it. "One day I'm going to make all of them hurt for you." She choked on the words. "I'm so sorry I wasn't there sooner. I didn't know. I've been a bit stuck in my own head here of late." Her reason for being stuck in her own head tugged at her. She pushed it down, not allowing herself to think her mate's name.

"It's not your fault. Sigurd had me write a letter. He expected me to tip Susan off, I think, and then they'd go and fetch you, but I ain't no traitor. And Penny gets a little wild sometimes when she thinks someone she loves is hurt. She might not have waited for you. I didn't want any of you lot wrapped up in this. I don't know what trouble he's got planned for you now, Rain, but I'm worried sick—"

"Don't worry." Rain's fingers tightened around hers. "Sigurd is a dark-hearted louse. And he'll get what's coming to him soon." Thinking about the arrogant fae made her painfully aware of the bargain magic that clung to her, and she swallowed down her own anxieties.

Margot's throat bobbed. Then the door to the tavern was thrown open, and Penny and Susan ran out into the street to greet them. The bar was full of customers, but they went ignored in favor of rushing the side of the coach, asking questions so rapidly Rain couldn't parse their words.

Rain handed Margot off to Penny's wide embrace. She'd leave the explanations to her. Then she shut the coach door and tapped on the roof, and Sigurd's driver set off again down the cobblestones.

She'll be all right now, won't she? Bernard asked.

She'll be all right. We'll see to it.

Chapter 12

(Rain)

The coach dropped Rain and Bernard off at a secluded hunting cabin deep in the woods outside of River Row. She was familiar with the area and friendly with the trees. Sigurd was waiting for her outside. He ordered the driver to stay his horses until he returned, and then they set off on a hike through dark woods, headed in the direction of the meadow Sora Yaga seemed to favor. It was nearing midnight.

Before the next tree line, Rain stopped and unhooked her satchel. "I'll need to conceal you in this now."

Sigurd frowned. His scruffy tail drooped at his back. "That old, smelly thing?"

"Do you have a better idea for how I'm to get you inside Sora's hut without her noticing you're there to commit murder?"

"You could hide me in your shirt." He leered at her.

"The stars will plummet from the sky before I ever let you anywhere near the inside of my clothing. Now, are you a trickster or aren't you? Transform already, and make it something small." She held up the satchel for sizing.

Sigurd formed a tight fist with his fingers, then stuck out his thumb and held it up toward the moon. "Rat," he said, and the cloying scent of moon magic radiated from him. His body shrunk down and down, letting off a fragrant red mist until he was no bigger than her boot—a rat with a long twining tail and ruddy fur.

Rain bent low and picked Sigurd up by the scruff of his neck. The beady eyes were a bright magenta. "A rat. How fitting . . . Are you hungry, Bernard?"

She flung the rat into the air toward her familiar. Sigurd squeaked and squealed. The red mist returned, puffing out of him, but Bernard was quick. The demon's wolfish jaws clamped down around him with a crunch and snap of bones, and Sigurd went stiff and then still in his maw. The familiar shook the fat rodent once, then twice.

Don't swallow him! Rain warned. *I still have to bring his body to Sora's hut . . . he just never specified that he had to be alive while I did so.*

Clever. He didn't specify that he had to have all of his blood either, Bernard pointed out. *Ack! He tastes like fairy farts, though.*

Bernard dropped a beheaded, shriveled mass of bloodless rat on the forest floor by Rain's feet. He coughed up the head next, and she grimaced down at the mess.

Bernard smiled a wolfish smile up at her, tongue lolling out of his mouth. His teeth were stained pink. *Ha. I bit his head off after all.*

Nose scrunched, Rain gathered up Sigurd's remains, tucking

them into her satchel, and then reattached the bag to her belt under her fawn coat. Beside her, Bernard grew in size and in energy. He began to shuffle his paws in place, battering up a cloud of dust, breathing heavily. Soon he was bounding about the forest.

Weeeeeeee! His cackles echoed in Rain's head. When he finally came to heel, he'd grown his wolf to be the size of a horse. *I could make myself as big as a tree if you wanted.*

"I don't want that," she chided. "Stop playing about and take me to Sora." Rain climbed onto his back, clutching handfuls of the black scruff at his neck for balance.

You're no fun at all. The fairy wine in his blood won't last forever, you know. It's use it now or it's gone. Can't I at least make myself as big as—

"No."

How about a dragon or one of those dirigible contraptions? We could travel in lavish comfort or—

"No," Rain groaned. She could still feel the weight of the bargain magic pressing in around her. "Come on. We have a time limit to keep. Dawn will sneak up on us before we know it, and then I'll be as dead as that rat. I'm not in the clear yet, and need I remind you that if I die, so do you?"

Oh fine. Sourpuss, he said but with all the malice of a raspberry tart. He bounded off between the rows of trees, giggling like a schoolgirl.

Wind whipped through Rain's hair, and soon she was grinning. She hadn't smiled like that since Night . . . An image of him sipping milk came to mind. She shoved it away. Bernard's whoops and cheers lifted her spirits. She felt lighter.

Then they came to a creek bed which looked like a sleek expanse of damp rot in the dark, and it smelled no better.

Bernard wasn't slowing.

"No . . . No you don't! *Bernard!*" Rain gripped his fur so hard her knuckles went white. She squeezed her legs together along his back.

Cackling and squealing through their linked souls, Bernard leapt the creek in one sleek jump. Rain screamed with her face buried in his neck. They glided through the air at a speed that sent icy autumn wind raking across her cheek. He landed with a thud, casting up a great wall of mud.

Splattered in wet filth, Rain sighed with relief, grateful to have survived the ordeal. "You wicked thing . . ."

I AM A WICKED AND MAJESTIC DEMON! All the immortal provinces shall fear me and tremble!

"You're full of farts is what you are," she said mildly, her smile restored.

Large tongue hanging out of his mouth and tossing spittle, he galloped through the trees and into the meadow. Lunar butterflies shot into the air, ousted from the massive flora that grew only in the fall, like the star lilies and the turnip roses and grape daffodils. Bernard bounded after the bird-sized insects, bouncing from one to the next, spooking them into flight, like a kitten playing with a ball of string.

"Will you control yourself, please," Rain said, unable to hide the laughter in her voice. "Sora's hut usually rests beside the arm of the river Eventide. It's not far now."

Bernard charged forward, stirring up a great kaleidoscope of butterflies, blue wings luminous in the moon's soft glow. Sora's hut leaned crookedly beside a copse of pine trees. Rain's stomach flipped. It would be a gross exaggeration for her to claim she knew the witch well. Over the last several hundred years, they'd spoken only once.

Chapter 12

The dragon princess had made a borscht, the smell of which had called Rain and a hungry Bernard out of the forest after an unsuccessful day of hunting. Bernard had recognized the out-of-favor dragon princess immediately. Rain offered a trade of furs for a bowl of the beetroot soup, but the witch accepted chores instead. They'd spoken briefly about the migration of the wolves in the area, while Rain and Bernard worked dutifully, and then neither had attempted to repeat the endeavor again.

What if Sora wouldn't open her door for her?

The hut shuddered, shaking the lunar butterflies off its thatch roof, and then the house rose up on its great chicken feet. It stood there stiffly, leering at Rain with its slanted windows.

"Sora Yaga? I need to visit with you. Because . . ." Rain hesitated. The bargain magic cinched around her ribs. It was difficult to draw a full breath. She'd vowed not to warn her of Sigurd's presence. She needed to be wise with her words. *What should I say?*

Ask her . . . for some coffee?

I hate coffee.

You hate everything.

Not everything . . . Rain cleared her throat and decided to be as fae-honest as she could be. "My life depends on whether or not you open your door to me."

The hut lowered itself to the ground with a thump that shook the earth. Moments later, the door swung open, the frame sprouting razor sharp teeth, and a hot blast of air hit her, smelling of brimstone and ash. Rain unhooked her satchel and chucked the bag inside its dark maw. The moment it crossed the threshold, she felt the bargain magic fade from her, and her lungs expanded.

The razor sharp teeth shrunk, fading into the wood, and Sora's familiar showed herself in the form of a little dragon with black scales. The familiar slipped out through the shadowed opening, into starlight.

Oh? What have we here, Bernard said, charmed. He shook Rain off his back and evaporated into a puff of dark mist, reforming into a matching little dragon with glistening black scales. Sora's familiar became a sleek panther next, followed by an owl, and Bernard mimicked her one shape after the next. Only familiars could become objects as well as living things. Before long, the two of them had run out of animal forms and began to shift into various weapons: an obsidian great sword, an ax made of dragon scales . . .

I need more blood, Bernard said eagerly.

Rain rolled her eyes. *I'm not giving you my blood so you can win some asinine trickster contest.*

Lamplight illuminated the doorway, and Sora stepped outside, holding Rain's old satchel ahead of her with the tips of her fingers, her nose wrinkled. Her flaxen hair was down around her shoulders. She wore a velvet gown and a gilded belt that wrapped at the waist, its ends tasseled and dangling over her bare feet, a formal dress of a time long ago, a time familiar and dear to Rain.

The witch shook the satchel out, and the rat carcass tumbled into the tall grass beside a spool of string, a metal and flint striker, a jar of various needles and buttons, and two sheathed daggers.

"You brought me a dead Lunar mage?" Sora narrowed large indigo eyes at Rain.

"His name was Sigurd," Rain said. "He made a bargain with me, but the bargain didn't suit him. A rat, even one full of fairy wine, is no match for a hungry wolf, you see."

"I see." Sora crossed her arms elegantly, considering her. "Sigurd was a pain in my side, always showing up uninvited."

"Dragae soldiers filled his head with tales about dragon hoards. He wanted yours."

Sora nodded. "I owe you a boon, then."

"You don't." Rain dug her boot at the earth, feeling uncomfortable. "Sigurd hurt someone dear to me. I'd have—"

Movement in the doorway drew Rain's eyes, and air left her lungs in a rush. Night ducked so his curved antlers didn't scrape the lintel. He was dressed in traveling clothes and his long cloak, the same one he used to wear when he'd visit her in the forest. Even in plain clothing, he seemed too majestic for such dull surroundings, too proud and blue-blooded for the simplicity of tall grass and dilapidated wood.

That was probably how the two of them appeared together standing side by side. Majesty and old wood.

Sora's slow smile curled her lips. "It's my understanding the two of you are acquainted."

"We are," Night said in a silky purr that made Rain shiver.

She stumbled back a step, heart thundering in her chest. *Time to go, Bernard.*

Bernard had returned to his cat form and was pouncing about, batting at butterflies with the dragon familiar. He groaned in protest through their link but joined Rain's side promptly.

"It's good to see you again . . ." The words felt like sandpaper leaving her throat. Good was the wrong word for it. The sight of the duke was a reminder of her loss and a knife in her chest. She backed away, eager to part from the handsome vision that made her recall long walks through the woods, his melodic voice like warmed honey reading her fairy stories, an archery competition, awaking in bed beside him with his cool breath on her neck—all visions that caused her great pain.

She made it another step before Night prowled after her.

What in the name of all the divines was he doing? Rain scowled, retreating faster. Her boots caught in tangled weeds. She stumbled and caught herself.

He answered her thoughts with a roguish grin that crinkled the scar in the corner of his mouth.

"Stop this," she scolded. *Bernard!*

I'll get him. Bernard jetted toward the duke.

Night cupped his hand, forming a crescent shape with his thumb and fingers. "Sleep," he said, and Bernard tipped onto his side, disappearing below the tall grass, snoring loudly.

Rain spun on her heels and sprinted for the tree line. "What are you doing?" she shouted over her shoulder.

"Stop running, and I'll tell you!" Hints of wicked amusement colored his words.

Absolutely nothing about this was funny. How dare he toy with her in this way? Under her breath, she cursed him and the tug of excitement low in her belly.

"Hang it all," she grumbled.

Rain lowered her head and sprinted as fast as her legs would carry her. The steady thump of the duke's boots followed her, drawing nearer. She was quick, but he was younger. He caught her before she made it to the trees, wrapping her up from behind. She stepped on his foot and shoved his hands away. Undeterred, he snaked an arm around her waist and held her firmly against his chest. When she fought his hold, he lifted her off her feet, grunting from the effort of confining her thrashing body.

Chapter 12

She gave up the fight quickly after that. It wasn't usually in her to do so, but he was a Lunar mage. She didn't want to be put to sleep, and the scent of moon magic mingling with his peppery cologne was rich in her nose, alluring, distracting, and threatening.

His touch warmed her against the chill, and what if this was the very last time she got to be like this with him again? In his arms. Touching her mate.

Not alone.

She was so painfully lonely the ache in her chest opened like a gaping wound. Beside the wound, the bond thrummed in her heart—and between her legs—so hard she thought she might swoon again.

"What could you possibly gain from chasing me?" Rain asked, her voice unsteady.

"A bride." Night's breath warmed her ear. He set her back down on her feet, holding her firmly. Head lowered, his chin nudged her neck.

Rain's brow knitted. "But you . . . you have a betrothed now."

"Do you still dream of me?" The naked passion in his voice sent a liquid heat coursing through her. "I dream of you every day. Then every night I awake in hell."

"But the papers," she said, breathless. "You've a fae feast scheduled to celebrate . . . ?"

"Do you think of me as often as I think of you?" He brought his lips so close they skimmed the shell of her ear.

Rain turned in his arms. He let her, gazing down at her with two silver pools she could drown in. His hands rested on her hips, a heavy welcomed weight. In that moment, Night was the living embodiment of a fairy story. He had stars in his smile, obsidian in his hair, and the moonlight of his eyes was so piercing, so extraordinary, Rain couldn't get enough oxygen into her lungs. Being near him made her weightless. If he let her go, she might just float right out of the meadow.

Pulled by a force greater than herself, she came up on the tips of her toes and pressed her lips to his.

It took only an instant for her to realize she was about as good at kissing as she was at words. She missed part of his mouth, catching only his bottom lip in a hard pucker. She pulled away, frowning. If he'd noticed she didn't know how to kiss a man, he hid it well behind a look of absolute astonishment.

"There," she grumped. "You win. I admit it. I'm an absolute mess. I don't eat. I barely sleep, and when I do, I dream of you—now get your fucking hands off me. You've an engagement to go and prepare for, and we still want very different things."

Instead of letting her go, he pulled her in tighter until she was pressed to his hard body, her hands caught between them. "We have differences?" he teased. "What differences?"

"You don't believe in lov—"

Night nuzzled her ear with his nose, and she forgot how to make words.

Rain turned her head away from him. "And I don't want any part of your war. I'm sure you have more important things to do between all of your political maneuverings and your new engagement."

He towered over her, his chin nestling in her hair. "Our engagement," he said, the words muffled against her scalp.

Rain blinked into the wool of his cloak, certain she'd heard him incorrectly. A weight she hadn't realized was there lifted off her shoulders. "What did you just say?"

Chapter 12

"I told you before I don't have a lot of time, so I'm cutting quite a few corners. For the benefit of the Seelie and Unseelie monarchs, I've already sent out the announcements for *our* engagement."

She was so dazed and confused, a steady gust of wind could have blown her over. She wanted to hug him and hit him at the same time. Of course, she didn't want her mate off marrying someone else, but that didn't change anything between them. "But I didn't accept your proposal!"

He pressed a light kiss to the side of her head, one she leaned into despite her better judgement. There was nothing hurried or hard about his kissing, she noted glumly. "I knew if being apart made you even half as miserable as it made me, you'd come back soon enough, and here you have."

She squinted up at him. "But I didn't come back to you. I came to Sora. I didn't know you were here."

"You came back to me," he insisted. "You planted saplings in my courtyard, and I'm certain you visited my room that day too. Now here you are, whatever the reason. . . close enough," Night said, and then he scooped her off her feet, ignoring her squawk of protest, lifting her onto his shoulder.

"I only visited your room for a moment to . . ." She couldn't complete that thought. Anything she said would have to be a lie.

Or the truth. The truth was even worse, though.

She'd visited his room because she *had* to see him again. She'd told herself it was because she wanted to plant the saplings and needed to be sure he wasn't awake to catch her, but that wasn't all of it. She needed to be near him again.

"I'm taking you home," he said merrily.

Rain made a fist and struck him near his kidney. He dropped

to a knee with a groan. "You're not kidnapping me again, you damned—"

"Sleep," he coughed.

Her fingers went numb first. Then her arms and legs were suddenly too heavy to lift. "What did you do to me?"

A pained chortle choked out of him. He rose slowly, adjusting her on his shoulder. "I'm not going to harm you, Rain. You know that, yes?"

Her exhale shot a burst of vapor into the cool night air. "I know, but you don't just get to do whatever the bond wants you to. You're forgetting to use words like 'please' and 'may I' around me. It's making me feel . . ."

"Feel like what?"

"Like I'd like to stab you with something," she confessed, trying to wriggle her fingers and toes. It was unnerving that she couldn't.

"Wonderful. You make me just as violent. The audacity of forcing me to come and kidnap you again." His tone was aggravatingly playful, flustering her in a fashion that was equal measures torment and pleasure. "I can't think of a single fae legend where the bride had to be stolen *twice*. You deserve a thorough spanking for that."

The act he described played out vividly in her mind, right there in the woods, bent over his knee . . . Her pulse went thudding out of control. "Threatening to spank a witch is a great way to get yourself turned into a rotting pea. I ought to ruin all of your pretty shirts with dagger holes," Rain carried on under her breath, certain she didn't know how to turn anyone into anything, including a pea, rotting or otherwise. Then she grunted from the effort of trying to move her numb arms and legs. "What'd you do to me?"

Chapter 12

"Your body is at the command of the Divine Night. If I can see you and my will is greater, I can steal your voice, make you blind with darkness, or deafen you for however long I wish it. I can paralyze your limbs with sleep. I can put all of you under if I like, but I enjoy listening to the sound of your voice, even when you're being contrary. I can heal, and I can send one to an eternal night by speaking death into their ears."

"Such a formidable mage," she goaded, "carrying off a little witch half his size . . ."

"An equally formidable witch covered in knives," he quipped, pretending to be affronted. He carried her back in the direction of Sora's hut, tall boots cutting through grass that came to his hip. "When they turn our romance into a legend, I'll make sure the poets know exactly how many daggers you had on your person."

"Twice as many as I actually have?"

"Three times that at least." His grin was clear in his voice, and then he continued, his gait long and sure, jostling her gently on his shoulder. "A Night Mage can take away pain or give it. Likewise, I can take pleasure or grant it . . ."

She worked her throat. "Is that what you're going to do to me when we get back to your home? Play games with your magic?"

"*Our* home," he corrected briskly, then he stooped to pick up Bernard's sleeping form. "And no. First, I'm going to feed you. And then I'm going to bathe you."

His words sunk in, rooting to the marrow. Liquid desire caressed her spine, raising the fine hairs of her arms, and her skin broke out in gooseflesh. Her mouth opened and her tongue tied. She made an incoherent noise, a keening whimper. Then with great effort she managed something more coherent.

"Why does everyone want to bathe me?"

"Hmm?" He patted her thigh reassuringly, his hand threateningly close to where she was growing wet and needy. "You smell like mud, sweat, and vanilla. I like all of your smells but prefer the vanilla."

Bathing was a bonding ritual. It wasn't one commonly discussed, but she recognized it the second he spoke the words. She wanted to be bathed. She ached for it.

He was going to strengthen their bond . . .

Would she let him? Her mind went blank like it had given up on helping her entirely. Her heart and soul continued to whirl and battle. The last week without him had been dreadful, but what was a week to an immortal? Even if it had been the longest of her life.

Rain glanced about for her things that had been dropped in the grass. None of it was there. Not Sigurd's rat body or her spare set of daggers. Sora must have collected them. Rain would probably have to trade her for them later. She sagged against his shoulder, too tired at the moment for further battle.

Night hefted her across the meadow, nearing the forest. "When I reach the trees, are they going to behave themselves? If they don't, I'll have to put you and them to sleep."

Rain sighed. "Trees are not gentle things. I'd hesitate to call on them. They might accidentally crush you."

At that he picked up his pace. "Five hundred years is a long time to live amongst the trees. It makes me curious. The Seelie fae I'm acquainted with usually prefer warmer climates—they're more sensitive to the cold. So why these trees, Rain?"

The answer put a lump in her throat. "Everyone comes from someone," she said quietly. "Surely even me."

"Naturally," he said, and his voice had gentled.

"I don't remember much of what happened before Bernard and I used bargain magic to make him my familiar. Or maybe it was the injury, the dagger in my stomach, or the pains of a war that refused to end. I'm not sure. Either way, I can't remember my family. But I miss them all the same, you see."

"You don't remember them but hope that perhaps they remember you," he offered.

"Exactly. If I leave, they might finally come looking for me. I'd like to be here if they do."

The arm over her legs softened. "I see . . ." They walked on in somber silence for a time. When he spoke again, his tone had found its usual irreverent humor. "Hmm. How much of you is relieved I'm here with you now, and how much of you is still thinking about stabbing me?"

"I don't recognize my own feelings," she confessed. "I haven't since I saw you for the first time. You make everything feel like a desperate whirlwind. Hot and icy. Passion and the brink of insanity trapped together in a hurricane. That's what you do to me." She worked her throat. "So I suppose my answer is both equally."

"Hmm. That's close enough to a declaration of your affections for me as I'm likely to get, I think." They walked on in silence for a time, Bernard snoring loudly in Night's arm. The gentle sway of his body reminded Rain of how tired she was, what little sleep she'd gotten, and it was well past midnight now.

"You can't carry me like this the entire way," she said, fighting back a yawn.

"I'll be just fine. You're light as a sparrow." Then he rested his hand high on the back of her thigh, just under the curve of her bottom. "And the view from here is highly motivational."

She snorted at him. Reflexively her eyes were drawn to his backside, lean supple curves flanked by narrow hips that flexed with his steps. Her view was definitely better. "It's not *you* I'm worried about. I don't want others to see me this way."

"No member of my house would shame you or speak a word of it."

"No, they won't, because they won't see it," she said firmly. "When we're in sight of your estate, you'll let me walk in at your side, not over your shoulder like a captured criminal."

"Would you walk alongside me now? Your hand in mine?"

The image that played out in her head at his words, strolling hand in hand through her trees, was frustratingly lovely. Then a surge of panic shot through her at the very thought, and she was flying into the whirlwind again.

"I . . ." She hesitated. Her fingers tingled. She was starting to get feeling back in her hands. Rain had a very strong will. She'd be able to move again soon, and he wouldn't know, if she was careful not to give herself away. The moon magic was still there, still filling her lungs with its cloying scent, still raising the hairs on her arms, but her strength had weakened it.

"Hmm. That answers that," Night said, adjusting her along his shoulder, jostling her out of her anxiety.

She sagged over him, letting her chin rest on his back. "I wish I could explain my feelings better. I simply don't have the right words."

"Bonding with me makes you feel like you're drowning in deep murky waters full of monsters," he said placidly.

Rain crooked her neck to stare at the back of his head. "That's an apt description, actually."

"I've recruited a witch to consult on the matter."

Chapter 12

"The dragon princess?"

"I was consulting with her when you arrived unexpectedly. She owes you a boon now. You should hold her to that. It took me seven months of laborious errands and chores to earn a boon from her." He stepped over a protruding collection of roots and into a glistening pile of leaves.

Rain grinned against his back. "I earned her boon in one evening."

"Don't gloat," he said with a chuckle. "It's unbecoming."

"Everything I do is becoming to you," she grumbled. "You've gone mad with bond lust. You're not thinking clearly about what a poor match we are." Not that she was doing any better. The parts of her that enjoyed a good hunt, that fueled her bloodlust in times of battle, all the primal pieces of her makeup, loved that she was being hauled away in the manner of the old fae. That portion of her mind was thrilled that he'd chased her through the meadow, happy to be touching him, whatever the reason.

Unfortunately, the other parts of her were drowning.

He asked about the events leading up to Sigurd's demise. She answered him honestly, sensing that his loyalties would be to his mate over another mage, especially one as repulsive as Sigurd.

"You tricked a trickster," he said, sounding amused. "I'm not surprised. You can be quite resourceful in a pinch."

"He underestimated me," Rain said. She tried to shrug, and slowly her arms let her. Her will was winning against the moon magic. "Sigurd over-valued the strength of his hand and significantly miscalculated mine. It's as simple as that."

He fell quiet then. Rain wondered what thoughts ran through his mind, before deciding she'd rather not know what political machinations she may have just inspired. Bernard continued to sleep soundly—and loudly—in the crook of his arm.

"You miss your family," he said, and his words surprised her. She'd been sure his thoughts were on trickster mischief.

"With everything I am," she admitted solemnly. "I miss having family even if I can't remember what that feels like exactly."

"Rain, we may have different ideas about love, but I understand the importance of family . . ." The honey sweetness of his voice coated her in comfort. "My family wasn't always the most functional, as you know, but I wouldn't trade any of them for another. Not even my father."

She was quite certain she could move now. With a word, she could distract him using her trees, then while he used moon magic to subdue them, she'd grab Bernard and escape.

But his musings about family brought her pause.

Night kept his word as they reached his estate. He released Rain from the magic that put her limbs to sleep, not realizing she'd already broken their hold with her stubborn will. He set her on her feet. "Do I need to remind you that I can cast the magic again in an instant should you try to flee from me?"

Rain rubbed more feeling back into her arms. "Do I need to remind you how many sharp objects I have on my person should you become too presumptuous?"

A grin lit up his handsome face. He extended his hand. "I could be your family, Rain."

His voice was a silky purr full of a promise she could feel on her skin like a caress, and her heart stopped. When she took his hand, the organ started again with a great kick against the cage of her ribs.

Chapter 12

Their connection was ice and embers. A thrill shot up from their linked fingers, into her chest, warming her. A burning flush stole the sting of the cool night from her cheeks and nose. She was weak in the knees, and she couldn't decide if it was the aftereffects of his moon magic or their bond or a debilitating combination of the two.

Night was not unaffected. He kept stealing glances at her as they walked, his thumb following an eager path along her knuckles. Stone steps led to an elaborate set of thick double doors which parted for them, hauled open by two stout footmen.

An underbutler took Night's cloak. The duke waved him off when he tried to accept Rain's coat. She appreciated that, though the human underbutler eyed her mud-splattered appearance with grave concern, like she might dirty some of the many exquisite things about the great house.

Her hand in his, Night walked them to the altar in the foyer on the left which honored the Divine Night, opposite the Divine Day. He allowed her to light the incense with a long match. Perfumed smoke rose up before an engraved metal image of a gilded moon.

Then Night handed the bundle of snoring cat to the underbutler. "I'll allow him to wake in a moment. He'll be very cross when I do," Night said. "Be prepared to feed him heavily until he's been appeased."

"Don't put your fingers anywhere near his mouth, though," Rain warned.

Night walked her straight to the kitchen next, ignoring the curious eyes of staff. His house was a labyrinth of marble halls, sleek stones, and elaborate arches, oil paintings, and fine woodwork. Rain was overly aware of the prints her boots were leaving on the floors and rugs.

Kitchen staff bustled about, preparing several dishes. A large stove heated the room, letting off a heavenly aroma of mutton and ripe fruit.

A half-fae woman balked at the duke's appearance. Her skin was a light shade of pink and her ears were subtly pointed, but her face was round and soft like a mortal's. She led with a polite curtsy. "My Lord . . . supper isn't ready just yet. Is there something I can do for you?"

"I need you and the staff to clear out for a few minutes," he instructed.

Rain squeezed his hand a bit tighter, moving behind him to avoid the many sets of intrigued eyes that had latched on to her with overwhelming interest.

"My Lord . . ." The cook worried her hands in her white tunic.

Night's voice was warm and reassuring. "Nothing will sour in ten minutes, Cook. Then we'll be out of your hair."

She looked uncertain, but she couldn't very well deny the Duke of Night. "Of course, My Lord. As you wish," she said meekly. Then she clapped her hands and shooed her staff out of the kitchen.

Alone, Night towed Rain to the scullery in the back. He turned on the taps and filled the sink basin with warm water. She watched him with interest as he removed his cufflinks, tucking them in his pocket, and rolled up his shirt sleeves, revealing more smooth gray skin and veined forearms. Then he gathered up a cake of tallow soap that smelled like almonds and washed his hands. Rain wondered at the number of boilers a house of this size might possess. It was a relatively new technology. Only wealthy homes had taps, and even fewer had hot water.

Night motioned her over. She shoved up her coat sleeves and obediently came to stand in front of him at the sink. She was painfully aware of how covered in mud she was and how filthy her skin had become. Night caged her in with his long arms, grasped her cold hands in his sudsy ones, and took his time washing her. He moved his fingers languidly over hers, brushing his thumbs down the creases of her palms, working gently at the sensitive spaces between her digits.

His tender touches made the bond thrum in her chest with nearly unbearable exuberance. He laid his chin in her hair, rubbing her small hands between his larger ones until they were pink and hot and clean. There was no part of her wrists and fingers he hadn't caressed. She was so dirty he had to drain the sink and fill it again. He washed her up to her elbows, his touch lingering on the shallow nicks and scars at her knuckles and the callouses on her palms. He ran an inquisitive finger over a long scar turned white on her forearm but didn't ask about it.

Then he found a scrub brush with clean bristles and applied it to her coat. Dried dirt flaked off of her with each careful stroke.

"Thank you," she said softly when he was done. Something prickly had thickened in her throat. No one had ever been so tender with her before.

He nodded his head, his gray eyes bright as though caring for her in this way did something to him, fed something deep in the recesses of his fae being. It certainly did hers. He linked their fingers once more and brought her back to the kitchen. If he held on to her because he was worried she'd bolt, it wasn't necessary, especially once she got a proper look at the food.

She was hungry, and so was her mate.

And she *needed* to nourish him. The bond sent her pulse surging in her neck and thighs. She moved instinctively, following his cursory gaze to the bread on the counter. It was full of nuts and sprinkled with cinnamon. She broke off a piece and turned to him.

Obediently he opened his mouth. She fed the bread to him with great care, watching as his lips closed over the morsel, skimming her fingers. She studied him as he chewed and swallowed, drinking in every sign of his enjoyment.

"Did you like it?" She knew he did but needed to hear him say it out loud.

"Mm-hmm. I liked it," he said, nodding his head, a secret smile in the corner of his mouth. His satisfaction grew hers.

"This one next." She pulled him along to the roasted leg of mutton because he'd glanced at it. She picked off a piece, the meat nearly too hot to touch, and she blew on it. He moved to help, but she batted his hand away, instinct taking over.

The corners of his eyes crinkled with mirth. When it was the right temperature for her mate, she brought the cooled piece to his mouth. He parted his lips. Delight surged inside her at the contented sound he made as he chewed.

This was excellent, but she needed to make him something to eat with her own hands . . . One of the servants had started to mix whipping cream. Stale bread had been added to a collection of overly ripe Seelie berries which were brighter and larger in size than raspberries and grew year-round. Its juices had turned the bread an inviting pink. She fed him a bit of the pudding, and then she mixed the whipped cream. When it had thickened, she offered him some, first on a piece of pinkened bread, then on the end of her finger. He took her offered digit into his mouth and sucked the whipped cream off, and she felt the pull of his lips deep in her core and in a tug behind her navel. Intimate muscles fluttered.

She wanted her lips on his again but didn't dare repeat her disastrous first attempt. Then he was feeding her in turns, pudding and bits of mutton and buttered bread until they were both full to bursting. Seeing that he was sated, she felt the same. Not just full, satisfied in every way possible. There was no room for worries, no conflicts in that intimate space between them. Only contentment.

Rain glanced about at the mess they'd made, and it had certainly been longer than ten minutes. The poor cook was probably chomping at the bit by the doors.

"It was such a pretty meal . . ." she said.

"It served its purpose," Night reassured her. "And the others won't mind . . . Or they will mind, but they won't dare complain."

As they left the kitchen, Night stopped a maid. "Have a bath readied in my room. I want the water hot, and add lots of warmed towels. Lots of them," he stressed.

The human girl nodded her understanding and scampered off to do his bidding.

Rain's stomach dropped and then filled with butterflies.

Chapter 13

(Night)

Her innocence and timidity went straight to Night's heart.

With gentle encouragement, he walked Rain up to his chambers, and once they were there and the door was shut, the blinds drawn, candles lit, he knew with certainty he'd never be able to play her like some hand in cards. No tricks, no traps, no bluffs.

Just kindness. That's what his protective, noble mate deserved, and that's what she'd get.

Rain was not a card. She was a player. A warrior who tricked tricksters. There was no doubt in his mind that she was worth the effort, worth the chase, worth his bond. She was the wife he wanted, the partner he needed, the true mate that could save his court.

Leaning against the far wall near the crackling fire to give her space, he let her explore his bedroom. She visited the various hangings and art on the walls first, poking her head into the dressing room. Her amber eyes constantly flitted over to the copper tub centered on the carpet. As she took in the steam curling off the clear waters, delicate muscles in her throat flexed with her swallow.

A high-backed chair sat beside a bench seat and a stand with a ceramic basin and a pitcher full of more steaming water. Two cakes of vanilla-scented soap—the soaps she'd made for him—were situated on the stand beside a rubber dropper, a vial of almond oil, and a box of soap made from various plant oils the mortals called palm soap.

She crossed to his bed, running her fingers over the stacks of thick towels, testing the plushness of the silk and cotton mix. "What now?" she said so softly he almost couldn't hear her.

"Rain, look at me."

She did eventually, her bottom lip trapped between her teeth.

He pointed at the entrance. "That door isn't locked. I hauled you here to my house, I know, but I'm not going to make you do this. I'll tell you what I want, what my instincts want, but nothing happens unless you want that too. Do you understand?"

Her chest filled with a deep inhale and released slowly. "You think because I'm quiet and I'm small that I can be pushed around. It's a common mistake made regarding me." She met his gaze, and there was fire and steel in her tawny eyes. "You can't make me do things I don't want to do, Night. No one can. I'm only here because I want to be here."

A smile tugged at his scarred mouth. "Good. On the bed beside the towels is a robe for you."

Rain lifted the robe in question, a thin silk piece in a cream color. She held the fabric up under her neck and let it drape her body. It fell above her knees with large hanging sleeves, and her cheeks flushed. "You want me to wear this?"

"I want to undress you slowly, then wrap you in that myself. But we'll do what you're comfortable with."

Her lips twitched. "Turn around. I can undress myself." When Night hesitated, she made a twirling motion with her fingers. "And no peeking, My Lord."

Night groaned playfully in protest, but he obeyed, facing the wall. The sound of shifting wool and rustling fabric was a gentle sort of torment, but he dutifully kept his curious eyes forward. Then silence swept over the room, and Night could feel the uncertainty radiating from his mate. The gentle padding of her footfalls against the carpet disrupted the quiet as she crossed the room.

"Do I have to keep staring at this wall?" he asked eagerly. "I'd much rather stare at you."

"Hmm. I'm not sure . . ."

Night glanced over his shoulder and found her standing in front of the mirror, tightening the corded belt of the robe around her middle, studying her reflection. The cream of the silk highlighted the golden hues of her skin, those not covered in dirt. Her hair was a tumble of loose snow down her back. Her amber eyes darted to his in the reflective glass. The strength of will in the little half-smile she gave him stirred him down to his core.

This was what a force of nature looked like wrapped up in silk, he decided. When it came to keeping his duties in order and his priorities straight, having her in his life would make that very difficult. He'd want to shove everything to the side. Hopefully that desire calmed once their bond was cemented.

Chapter 13

Night gathered her clothes and coat and left them out in the hall for the servants to launder and press. Her satchel and knives he placed on his nightstand, then he retrieved three of the lush towels from his bed. The first he unrolled and laid on the floor on the broad side of the tub. The others he set folded on the chair.

Rain padded over to him. "What are you doing?"

"Preparing." He placed the bench seat, one that likely belonged to a vanity, on top of the towel. Then he positioned the chair across from it alongside the tub. He retrieved the stand with the pitcher, basin, and supplies next, maneuvering it within reach of the chair.

Rain watched him work, worrying the belt of her robe.

Night gestured to the bench seat. "I'd like to wash your feet. Please sit."

Biting her lip, she did as he asked, tucking the short robe beneath her. The silk stopped at her knees, little knobby things that he wanted to kiss, they were so dainty. Night pushed aside the towels and sat in the chair. He added a cake of soap to the basin along with a fold of terrycloth, rubbing them together under the water until the curls of steam came up smelling like vanilla, the little white autumn flowers that would forever remind him of his mate.

When Night reached for her foot, Rain tensed. He gentled his touch, lifting her leg at the ankle and setting it in his lap. Folding the terrycloth in half, he let the warm mixture run down her shin bone, then he followed the trail it left behind with the cloth.

The state of her feet made his stomach drop. "You even have scars on your toes."

A breath of humor escaped her. "Not so many there," she

said, and he caught the warning in her tone. The number was higher elsewhere.

He washed her from her knees to the tips of her feet, one leg after the other. Night retrieved a new cloth and started again, attentively cleaning the slight spaces between her toes, feeding the thrumming bond that warmed his blood.

Rain squirmed, and a little gasp parted her lips.

Night lifted a brow. "Is my fierce warrior mate, who lets no one push her about, *ticklish*?"

She giggled, the sound so sweet and pure and good that his chest went tight.

"Lausat, you precious creature," he whispered, and her skin pebbled before his eyes. His lips curled. "I thought you might like that term."

"It's an old, old word," she purred. Her arms fell to her sides, gripping the edges of the bench seat. "And I'm an antique. Naturally I like it."

"Is a diamond an antique? You are lovely, is what you are." He lifted her foot and kissed her damp flesh. "Even these little toes of yours are charming. In fact, I think they might be my very favorite part of you." They curled in as he spoke of them, and another raspy laugh brightened her face. "There isn't a part of you that isn't beautiful to me, not even the scars, but your toes are most precious. If not your toes, then certainly your knees."

"My knees?"

"They're positively dainty."

Her amber eyes glinted brightly, set afire by the candlelight. "Say it again, would you please? That old word . . ."

"Lausat," he said sweetly, and a shiver went through her, "my bride mate. Thank you for the honor of letting me wash you."

Chapter 13

A new emotion crossed her expression, furrowing her brow as he lowered her now clean feet from his lap one at a time. The toes he adored curled into the towel on the floor.

"You need a bride," she choked out, appearing to want to say more, but her eyes misted. Quickly, she blinked the emotion away.

"There is war all around us, Rain. Securing and marrying my true mate puts out a small fire for the Lunar Province. It stops the Seelie and Unseelie from forcing us into an alliance that will devastate my court. Marrying *you* puts out a larger fire . . ." He returned the terrycloth to the basin, watching it float amongst the bubbles. "I need someone I can depend on in the coming crisis. A survivor. A warrior who tricks tricksters. My every instinct confirms that partner needs to be you."

Rain's chest rose, pressing her small breasts to the thin silk. "I was never more tempted to leave my forest and seek a new home elsewhere than when whispers of war reached me . . ." She lost her voice. Her lip was back between her teeth.

Night gathered one of the towels, lowered onto a knee before her, and began drying her legs. "One war is more than enough for anyone to fight in, but it isn't fighting that I have in mind for you this time. I need help *avoiding* the battle," he said encouragingly, then compulsively he kissed her little knees, each of them in turn. Her skin was welcomingly cool under his lips. "Without you, I foresee the trees that are your home destroyed by Seelie war machines, and the human girls you cherish enslaved by the dragon king."

Her cheeks colored like blooming rosebuds. "Spoken like a true trickster, using my love—a thing you don't believe in—to manipulate me."

"I am," he admitted, and he met the fire in her eyes without flinching, "because the passion and responsibility you feel for those girls in that shabby little tavern is the same passion I feel for my entire court. I won't let the Lunar Province be destroyed by this conflict. I. Won't."

She reached for him and smoothed back his hair, fingers grazing the base of his antlers. "You can wish to stay out of it, Frey Magis, but I think we both know the day is fast approaching where staying out won't be possible for anyone. Even the great Duke of Night."

"I know." On his knees, peering up into her eyes, he breathed the words like a prayer, "Help me, Rain."

"I don't want war. But I don't want to be alone anymore either." Sagging, she hung her head, and her ashen hair curtained her face. His poor mate. Night's heart dropped to the floor. "All I've ever wished for was family, Night. Not war or riches or wealth beyond measure. Not politics and the battle and blood favored by the gentry. Just freedom and trees and love."

"I need you, Rain." Pain infused his words, tightening muscles in his arms and shoulders. He was on his knees begging without shame. He'd stopped carrying about such things as his pride ages ago, the weight on his shoulders had flattened him so. "And in exchange for your help, I vow to you I'll do my very best to give you the things you want, whatever they look like to you, however you want them. Marry me, bond with me, help me." Her mouth opened, but he silenced her with a raised hand. "Don't answer tonight. Think on my request and be sure. I know the cost of what I'm asking. I need you to be certain."

Her throat bobbed. "How long do I have to think about all of this?"

Chapter 13

A breath of amusement broke free of him. "Well, our engagement feast is scheduled for next month, so before then, please."

Her smile was wistful. "I can manage that."

He rose to his feet and offered his palms. "I assume you'd rather not remove your robe."

Without hesitation she took his hands, her slender fingers disappearing inside his, and she stood beside him. The blind trust in her quick actions pleased him and the bond down to his bones. Their connection beat fiercely through his veins.

"I would rather keep it on . . . this time," she said.

Night moved the bench seat so that it was beside his chair, parallel to the tub. He helped her perch on the cushion, facing away from him. Then he rolled the towel he'd been using and combined it with the other. He sat in the chair and placed them in his lap, creating cushions for the back of her shoulders and neck as he pulled her down over his thighs. With some adjustments, her head rested on the rim of the tub, neck supported by the towels. Her ashen hair tumbled over the rim, the ends rippling the water.

He combed her locks with his fingers, loosening snarls. Then he parted the strands and used a dropper from the stand to apply almond oil. He worked the golden oil into the roots, raking his fingers along her scalp. Her eyes fluttered shut, and a murmur of contentment slipped through her lips.

The bond rejoiced. It sung in his chest.

He retrieved the pitcher of water and tested it to make sure it wasn't too hot. Satisfied that it was the right temperature for his mate, he poured it lightly around her scalp. Wetting her hair, he caught the stray rivulets that tried to run down her face or toward her eyes.

She started to cry then, and the sight of her tears turned his throat raw.

His mate was trapped in murky water full of monsters, and here he was holding her under, insisting on bonding. "My poor Lausat," he cooed. "I'm so sorry, sweetheart. But I just can't let you go."

Every fiber of his being clung to her. She was his. His duchess. His salvation. He needed her. He set aside the ceramic pitcher, now empty, and wiped away her tears with his thumbs. She chewed her lip, her mouth trembling.

Night chucked her chin, willing her to cheer up, to defeat the swell of emotion caused by her distressed soul. "None of that now," he said gently. "You're safe in my arms. My little warrior who tricks tricksters. You don't even need my arms, do you . . . ? That's better now . . ."

She swallowed audibly and sniffled. He made a lather with a bar of the palm soap. Then he scrubbed it through her hair while she struggled to stifle a whimper so pitiful it put an ache in his chest.

As he massaged her scalp, her eyes closed and her breathing slowed. He whispered reassurances until her body loosened over him. Her hands had been folded tightly around her middle. They went lax across her abdomen. The lids of her eyes softened, and for a moment, he thought he'd eased his mate to sleep, or perhaps she'd swooned again.

Then her white lashes fluttered open, and there was something new and determined in her gaze.

Night refilled the pitcher from the bath water and rinsed her hair, combing the wet through until the strands were sleek and smooth and glossy clean. She smelled of vanilla and the meadow he'd chased her through.

Chapter 13

He squeezed the excess water from the strands, then helped her sit up. She turned on the bench seat, her legs spilling over the edge, the curve of her knee brushing his. She kept her leg there, the hem of her robe riding up her thigh. Both the touch and the flash of skin brought him pause. There was something significantly intimate about them. He sat there for a moment staring at that expanse of golden flesh, feeling the heat of her knee resting against his.

Rain bundled her dripping hair into a knot at her nape, likely unaware of his runaway thoughts, his growing fascination. Night unfurled one of the towels and tossed it over her shoulders, protecting her robe and skin from the wet droplets. With the other towel he replaced her hands, gripping sections of her hair and squeezing it dry between the cotton fabric.

Her eyes were fixed on his chin, her expression thoughtful and determined. Night ruffled her hair playfully, stirring the strands, and a lightness lifted the tension out of her features.

She kissed him then, her weight falling against his chest. Her lips were gentle and careful and salty from her tears. This was not the passionate and bumbling kiss of before. With her first kiss, he'd been too shocked to absorb any of it. Too surprised to taste her, to respond. She'd kissed him angrily, a flash of hot skin taken away too quickly.

This time her lips parted over his, soft and delicate. The contact only lasted for a moment, but it was an excruciatingly beautiful moment, one he clung to.

"I couldn't help myself," she confessed, eyes down, her shoulder propped on his chest.

"I'm glad you couldn't." Then he pulled her into his arms, and he claimed her mouth with his. She came willingly, lounging over his lap, his arm supporting her weight. He deepened the kiss, tipping her back.

Her mouth warmed. Her lips parted for him. He touched her tongue with his, a gentle encouragement. She mimicked the movement, searching his mouth tentatively. Night teased her lower lip with his teeth, and she did the same, repeating every caress, every playful touch with timid wonder. He kissed her until her lips were bright and swollen, and her breathing turned labored.

Night cupped her face. Her hands went to his hair, fingers grazing the base of his antlers. Heated blood surged through his veins. His cock, already alert, stirred beneath her, straining the wool of his trousers.

He broke the kiss to gaze down at her. "You're a quick study," he teased, "based on your first attempt—"

"Let's never talk about the first attempt," she groaned.

"What if I want to talk about it?" A chuckle reverberated through him. "It was the first time you kissed me. A good mate would wax on eloquently about the shape of your lips and other such nonsense. I should write you lines about its swiftness."

"Stars help me, please don't." Rain covered her face with her hands, her cheeks coloring. When she looked at him next, she stared with tired watery eyes. Her lids were heavy. She yawned and stretched in his arms.

"You must be exhausted." Between the bond battering at her and the events of her evening with Sigurd, she had to be beat.

She was so tired, in fact, that she didn't put up any fight at all when he stood her up and tucked her into his bed, burying her in blankets. He stripped down and dressed in a nightshirt. Lips quirking, he caught Rain watching him.

"And here I thought you had your eyes closed," he said

playfully.

"You didn't tell me not to look," Rain said, no longer appearing nearly as sleepy.

As he blew out all the candles, she muttered to him about the softness of the bedding and mattress.

"I sleep outside," she said groggily. "Beds make me feel like I'm sleeping on mushy bread."

He slid in next to her, took her into his arms, and rolled onto his back. She draped over his chest, her weight an insignificant thing, her hair dampening his shirt.

"Am *I* too soft?" he asked.

She nuzzled her cheek against the smooth expanse just above his heart. "No," she murmured, "you're just right."

Tucked together, they didn't need as many blankets. He pushed them off as one of her legs tangled about his. She fell asleep first, her breathing deep and even. He followed swiftly after her.

Chapter 14

(Rain)

Rain awoke burning and touch-starved. Her core throbbed, her blood boiled, sweat beaded her brow. She was accustomed to awaking from her dreams in this way, her head full of images of her mate, intimate muscles between her thighs clenching with need.

But this time, as she dabbed at her forehead and tried to sit up, everything felt different. Images of her mate didn't fade from her. The dull ache didn't lessen. It strengthened.

The duke was a solid force beneath her, his nightshirt rumpled. Rays of daylight broke through the velvet curtains, casting diamonds in his hair. She sat up, momentarily straddling his waist, uncertain what time it was. He slept with one arm behind his head, antlers curving back into the generous stack of pillows. Her hair had dried in wild waves around her shoulders.

"Night," she said on a ragged exhale. "Night, I need you to . .

." She couldn't finish the thought, didn't have the words. She had no experience with seduction, though this didn't feel like that anyway. This felt like demand. Like desperation.

Like he was hers to order about.

His eyelids fluttered, but he remained motionless, deep in slumber. She rolled off of him, tangling the bedding. He stirred then as though he'd felt the loss of her.

With heavy movements, he turned onto his side, blinking his moonlight eyes, illuminating the shadowed spaces between them. "The sun is still out. Come back and go to sleep."

"I can't," she gasped. "I . . ." She swallowed, and her voice turned husky. "I feel like I'm on fire, and I need you . . . I've never . . . but I need you."

She was not making any sense. How he could possibly understand her was a mystery, but understand her he did. He slid an arm under her shoulders and pulled her in close. Propping his weight up on an elbow, he hovered over her. "In your dreams, where did I touch you?"

"Everywhere," she panted.

He proffered his free hand, his face serene. "Show me."

Rain grasped his wrist and ran his touch across her body, over her breasts, down her stomach. Her nipples pebbled. Her breasts felt full and achy. Guiding his hand lower, she lost her nerve just below her navel.

"Did I really stop there of all places?" he asked archly, his voice warm and thick with sleep. "Surely not even the dream version of me would stop just before the very best part."

Laughter loosened something in her chest that had gone tight. She felt lighter, freer, and grateful for his good humor.

Her hands drifted over to his shirt while his hovered below her scarred belly button, a gentle pressure that was as lovely as it was intimidating. She plucked at the top buttons uneasily, her brows knitting. "When it comes to matters of intimacy, I'm afraid I'm significantly inexperienced."

"You're innocent," he said matter-of-factly.

She rolled her eyes. "I'm old and I've killed people—stole the life from someone just last night, in fact, in case you've forgotten. I'm hardly innocent. But I haven't ever shared my body with another. I didn't used to care about such things, but then you walked into my life and turned everything upside down."

"How rude of me," he said dryly. "Then you have an interest now in such things?" The teasing tone failed to fully disguise an edge of hope.

"A growing interest," she admitted, squirming closer. His body responded to her nearness, muscles tautening, his chest radiating heat. Her mouth opened, and she hesitated. He stared at her, eager for her words, so eager he shook her playfully to make them come faster. "I want you to teach me," she confessed finally.

His brow lifted. "About pleasure?" The gravelly change in his voice was subtle but unmistakable. It sent a thrill through her.

She wetted her lips and worked her throat. "I want to know what you know. It's a dream I keep having. I ask you to teach me, and you promise to show me all, and then I always wake up well before I'm satisfied."

His arm tightened around her. He pressed his body along hers, evidence of his desire hard and hot against her side. "I'll teach you if you want that, and I won't leave you unsatisfied."

"Please." Her voice broke.

He kissed her nose, running a gentle finger from her chin

down to her sternum between her breasts. He stopped once more just below her navel. Pinching the silk robe, he tugged on it. "Do you want to keep this on?"

Another nod. "Please," she repeated, quieter than before.

"Then it stays on." He brushed the back of his hand along her cheek, encouraging her eyes up to his. "Have you ever touched yourself before?"

A line was back between her brows. "Touched myself how . . . Oh! You mean . . . I guess I've never bothered with that either. I frequent a brothel. I understand the mechanics of things. I'm not woefully ignorant."

"Of course you aren't." He pressed a kiss to the crease in her brow she hadn't realized was there until it relaxed. An impatient breath sawed out of her. "I'm going to touch you," he warned.

"Where?" The word was more prayer than whisper.

"Absolutely everywhere."

He started with her lips, caressing them with the pillowy pads of his fingers. Then her neck and the subtle points of her ears. He pressed a kiss to her throat. Languidly, Night touched her breasts. He kissed them in turns over the silk, weighing the supple curves in his palms. She felt each stroke of his fingers, each press of his lips, in a tug between her legs. Her nipples tightened further under his exploration, and her lungs shuddered.

His touch trailed down her stomach to her scarred navel. He dipped a finger inside gently before continuing down and down to the mound of her sex.

"Open for me . . . just like that, sweetheart," he crooned as she spread her thighs. Her hands gripped the front of his shirt uncertainly. He bent his head and kissed her fingers, and her hold loosened.

Night ran his hand down her leg to the knobby curve of her knee, a ghost of a touch leaving gooseflesh in his wake. On the path back up her body, he slid his fingers under the hem of the robe. She swallowed audibly, painfully shy about having no clothing underneath. Rain watched his hand with rapt interest as he pushed up the silk, revealing white curls and pink flesh. He gently thumbed the intimate petals of her sex apart, and she gasped.

Stars, that's where she wanted him most of all, needed him desperately. Had needed him there for much, much too long. Her heart kicked against the cage of her ribs like it wanted out.

He seemed to enjoy every sigh she made. He praised her when she gasped and moaned; even the smallest of sounds earned new encouragement. She melted beside him, feeling wholly relaxed. Pressure climbed deep in her core, and her toes curled into the bedding. Then her hands tightened rhythmically in his shirt. She wanted to investigate his body too, but uncertainty stopped her.

She'd never been explored in such a way before, and she wanted to watch. She was riveted, studying his hands and the gentle path of his fingers, basking in the pleasure he gave her.

His caresses grew more urgent, and her wetness increased, the sound of skin sliding over skin lurid and intoxicating. She released his shirt, fisting the bedding beneath her in its place, opening herself to him. He stroked her faster. She felt herself hurtling toward some unidentifiable thing, desperate for more friction. She pulled her knees up and bit down on her lip.

"Do I have to hold still?" she rasped.

"Move the way your body wants to." Then he lowered his

head and sucked her nipple to a point through the silk, and she felt a delicious pull deep in her core.

Rain's back bowed. Her hips jerked forward, desperate for more touch, more pressure, more of him right on that bud of nerves, right *there*.

"Perfect," he told her. "You're perfect."

Rain's head went back, and she squeezed her eyes shut. She saw sparks pop behind her lids. Absorbing the rapid climb of pleasure, her lips parted around a shallow breath. Intimate muscles quivered and tightened as she found her release.

It was over too soon. She wanted it to last forever.

Her pulse plummeted. A desire to close her eyes and drift washed over her. Night removed his touch and tugged the ends of her robe back down her thighs. His fingers were glossy with her pleasure. He brought them to his mouth and sucked on them.

Rain blinked in surprise.

He met her gaze with a roguish grin. "No offense to your sweet little toes or your dainty knees, but I have a new favorite part of you."

It seemed like such a forbidden thing to taste her there, but it made her curious.

He read her expression and answered her question before she could ask it. "A little metallic, like one of your blades. There's sweetness in your pleasure too, like ripe cantaloupe," he said. "You taste like a sweet dagger."

"Hmm." Her gaze slid down his body to the erection tenting his nightshirt. "Isn't there more to teach me?"

"Not all in one day," he said.

Her release had emboldened her. "But now I think I'd like to know what you taste like."

His head went back with a groan, antlers jabbing the pillows. He carried on like he'd been stabbed. "By the divines, Rain, don't test me . . . It's important to our bond that I treat you gently and teach you slowly, but I've longed for you for what feels like ages now, and I'm a weak bastard. Do you understand?"

"Teach me slowly?" she said, chuckling. "But I really want to know. I've never tasted a duke before. I bet you taste expensive."

"Or I taste like the wine you spat out the other day."

Their joined laughter shook the mattress beneath them.

He rolled onto his back with a sigh and pulled her over his chest, encouraging her head to rest against his heart. "When you're comfortable enough with your body that you'll let me take this robe off you, I'll let you learn what I taste like."

She was too contented now to protest. His pulse was loud, thundering under her ear, a consistent comforting thrum. The bond hummed in her chest, sated. Twined together once more, his soothingly solid form supporting her weight, Rain drifted back to sleep.

* * *

Rain stayed with the duke for fourteen nights. It took three of them to fully adjust to his nocturnal schedule. She slept tangled around his body each day, but he didn't make any more attempts to teach her about pleasure, and she didn't have the courage to insist.

When duty called him away, she and Bernard explored the great house. She had a special fondness for Night's many libraries. While she found old books to read, Bernard exercised his affection for expensive cheeses and crusty bread. He was given generous helpings of both whenever he wanted them, a gift to ease his ongoing frustration about being put to sleep with moon magic.

He'd *almost* forgiven the duke. The cheese was certainly helping.

Rain teased him that he was becoming fat and spoiled, though his trickster shape never actually grew in such a way. She practiced writing in her spare time using modern spellings and the shapes of the newest letters, working old muscles that had gone woefully underused by putting pen to paper.

Bernard played postman in his crow form, delivering her letters to The Red Boot. Penny always wrote her back, letting her know that Margot was well and they were managing fine without her. She complimented the progress Rain was making with her handwriting. Rain knew she was just being kind. Her writing was barely legible, but it made her smile anyway. They were safe and fed. Penny had started selling palm readings topless for tips and had made a tiny profit. Susan was thinking about adding a cheap, unaged alcohol distilled from corn to her stocks at the tavern, a foreign drink growing in popularity. It was cheap to make, but the starting supplies would use up the last of the duke's coin. Rain looked forward to Penny's letters every day.

One of the evenings Night was particularly busy, she helped herself to his bedroom bookshelf, rearranging them into a new order that suited her interests better. Hours later, she returned from tending to the saplings in the courtyard, and the books had returned to their original order. There was a note on the shelf in Night's neat handwriting:

Leave my books alone or suffer my wrath.

Hope you are well.

-Night

The note made her smile.

She helped the staff in the kitchens. The half-fae cook understood the necessity created by the bond, though the human servants found her presence amongst them strange. Rain imagined everything about her was rather strange compared to them: her clothing, her manners, her pronunciation of certain words were all too antiquated for them to always understand. But it satisfied her mating instincts to make Night bread she kneaded herself, so she endured their stares and discomfort. She baked him biscuits and tartlets and chopped vegetables for his soups.

Night made her things as well, trinkets mostly, parchment folded into flowers and birds. He was getting very proficient at it, compared to the wrinkled things he used to give her. Although she cherished those wrinkled things she couldn't always identify, the flowers he made now were growing more elaborate and the birds more complex.

Her favorite was a sparrow folded out of the pages of a fairy story she loved: the tale of *Three Knights* and the nature goddess Rae, a child of the Divine Day. In the story, Rae fought to restore her mate, a Vanir demi-god—one of the Lunar fae's earliest ancestors.

Night baked for her once, but the attempt was disastrous. The bond, however, wouldn't let her *not* eat the biscuits that were somehow both burnt on the outside and doughy in the center . . .

She didn't have the courage to ask him not to cook for her again, so she wrote him a note:

Not even Bernard is willing to eat your baking.

Chapter 14

Her first line was fae-honest, but it also felt like the sort of thing that a mortal or a younger fae influenced by mortal sensibilities might find insulting. He didn't seem like that sort, but just in case, she softened the blow with more fae honesty:

And I think you're beautiful. Other people probably think so too.

-Rain

She left it for him on his nightstand. When she returned from tending to the saplings, he'd folded her note into a tulip and left a return letter on a scrap of paper beneath it.

For you I shall set aside my apron and rolling pin and never don them again. I looked silly in them anyway.

And I know you're beautiful. Other people have undoubtedly noticed, and I'd like to sack all of them.

-Night

Smiling, she traced the letters that formed his name with her fingers, feeling slightly jealous of his ability to turn a phrase in such a charming way.

She kept his gifts in plain sight in the bedroom they now shared, decorating open spaces with his parchment offerings. Rain added the tulip in amongst them.

As the sun rose before bedtime, he tried to engage her in deeper conversation about her life, but she had so little to share with him, convinced that tedious descriptions of surviving in the wild would bore him. She avoided the subject, preferring that he do most of the talking, as was their habit.

He bathed her again. She wasn't willing to allow him to strip her, preferring to get in the tub and under the cover of water and suds before he tended to her. For now, her body and her scars remained her own.

In those two weeks, he didn't once bring up his proposal, but the question loomed big and menacing in her mind, a dark cloud in the distance threatening a storm. He'd promised to be her family and intended for her not to have to fight in a war, but Rain didn't know how to become part of something in half-measures. If she was in it, she'd be *all* in it.

She wanted to help him, but wasn't what he was asking too much? She'd already endured one war. She didn't think she owed the fae provinces another. But this hardly touched on her greatest fear. The duke was attentive now, but what would happen to their connection when their bond settled? Falling in love with him would be so easy, if only he had the capacity to do the same. If only he didn't believe love belonged in fairy stories and not in their relationship.

That evening, she waited on her mate to return from a meeting in the smaller library near the entrance hall. She had a fondness for the various maps and charts that hung on the walls, and many of the books were quite old, written in a language with spellings she recognized. It smelled like her mate: beeswax, vellum, and old leather. She knew immediately it had to be one of his favorites too. The armchairs were worn and well-used. The lighting was gentle on the eyes.

She'd separated her favorite finds into two stacks on an end table near the library entrance. Bernard watched her from the comfort of the nearest chair in his cat form, looking bored. She understood his restlessness. They weren't usually quite so stationary in their day-to-day life. She planned to take him outside the manor on a long walk soon, but the guards Arne and Elayna who watched the entrance in turns had discouraged her earlier. She would allow Night a chance to explain to them that she wasn't a prisoner here. If the guards did it again, she'd enjoy letting Bernard bite them.

After another hour of browsing books and examining

magical charts with illustrations of finger placements for moon magic, Night entered the room in a hurry. When he saw her, he heaved a great sigh.

Rain climbed down from the chair she'd been using as a makeshift step-stool to reach the books that were too high—most of them were too high. She was not vertically endowed.

"Oh?" she said of his pinched expression. "Is everything all right?" Standing near him, she wished she had the chair still. He was brooding and he towered so.

Anxious lines bracketed his mouth. His fingers made fists at his sides. "I was told you asked to go outside. Elayna stopped you, and her request seemed to make you upset, and then I couldn't find you in the courtyard or our room or the other libraries and I thought. . ."

She frowned at him. "You thought I left without a word? No note?"

"I'm glad I was mistaken," he said in a sheepish manner that was very unlike him. He ran an unsteady hand through his midnight hair, ruffling the strands.

Rain stepped up to him, chin tipped back so she could look into his eyes. "It flustered me that your guards seemed to think I needed permission to take a simple walk outside without you, but I was confident you'd clear that up with them once you were free."

"I can do that . . ." He still seemed uneasy, his eyes fixing on an imperfection in the rug by his boot, his jaw set. He wasn't looking at her. He pointedly turned his attention to her stacks of books. "What's this?" He gestured to the smaller pile.

"Old books I plan to read next."

"And the tall stack?"

Her head canted to the side. She smiled up at him. "Newer

books I plan to make you read to me."

His returning grin went lopsided, and some of the distress melted from his features. He crossed to the stack of older books to examine them.

Rain stopped him, placing a hand on his shoulder and squeezing tight. "That stack isn't for you."

His jaw firmed. Worry returned, a line deepening between his brows. "I can't look at the books you intend to read?" His fingers tapped rhythmically against his thumbs, an uneasy staccato at his sides.

"I'd rather you looked at the other ones . . . What have I done wrong?" She wanted to shake the surliness right out of him. "Why are you acting this way? Did your meeting about the railyards not go well?"

A muscle in his cheek flexed. "The meeting went as expected. I didn't know if you had left because I don't know your mind. I don't know your mind because you still won't tell me what you're thinking. Not about anything. You avoid conversations with me like you're avoiding letting me see that stack of books."

"You want to know what I'm thinking?" She pointed at the gathered volumes on the end table, her tone sharpening. "I'm thinking about *reading*. I'm thinking about going for a walk to stretch my legs and to exercise my demon. I'm thinking about visiting with my friends the trees and maybe with the girls at the Boot. I'm *not* thinking about leaving your company without a word."

"That's a start." He shifted toward the short stack of books again. She stopped him, catching his arm and pulling. His eyes narrowed. "And why can't I look at the books you've picked out for yourself? They're my books."

Rain huffed. The second book on the short stack was titled

The Last Night King, and her eyes flitted toward it guiltily. She'd only skimmed it so far to learn Seelie Queen Isla had murdered his uncle, seeking revenge for action taken during the wars. "I was curious, so I selected a few history tomes, but if I were you, I wouldn't want to look at books that reminded me of the family I lost."

His gaze softened subtly. "If you're curious about my family," he said, removing her hand from his arm and briskly kissing the fingers, "then I'd rather you asked me about them. I want you to talk to me, Rain. Do you understand?"

She nodded despite feeling completely uncertain. Did *he* understand that she'd lived alone in the woods for centuries? She didn't know how to do any of this. Words were not her strength. His displeasure stung her deeply, like a pinprick to her heart.

More reasons why she'd make a woefully inadequate duchess . . .

"I'd like to go on my walk now," she said, choking down the new lump in her throat.

"I'll accompany you. I have time."

She shook her head, and his face fell. His hurt expression was another pinprick. "I like being alone with my trees sometimes. They're more themselves then . . ." She tried to think of a better explanation, something to chase away the pain in his eyes, but that was the truth. She wasn't accustomed to being cooped up in a manor full of so many people. She needed to get out and away from all of them.

Including him.

I'm upsetting him, she told Bernard.

Give him cheese, Bernard suggested. *That always cheers me up.*

"But you'll come back," Night said slowly.

"Of course I will."

"And you won't be gone very long?"

She hadn't thought of how long she'd be gone, but she also didn't like the idea of having some sort of curfew. Rain shrugged her shoulders. "I plan to sleep here . . . The freeze has arrived. It's too cold and uncomfortable to stay outside very long." It was the best she could offer.

Night walked her to the door, his steps impatient. He waved off Arne, who hurried away down the hall to avoid the duke's ill temper.

"You will return," he said again, as though he were reassuring himself more than clarifying with her.

Rain hesitated by the doors. It was difficult to leave with him looking so deflated and ill at ease.

"Give me your coat," she said finally.

"My coat?"

She worked the buttons on hers, shouldering out of it, jostling her belt and satchel and the hilts of her daggers. Penny's freshly pressed blouse hung off her frame. "Your coat, please."

With a gesture from Night, a footman fetched it. The duke accepted hers. It looked so much smaller draped over his long arm. Then he helped her into his frock coat. She had to roll the sleeves several times, but the inside was soft and well-lined, the front covered in strokable wolf fur. A fine coat, fit for a lord. She was almost too warm, but it smelled like him: peppery cologne and old books. She lifted the collar and breathed him in.

He caught her enjoying it, and his expression smoothed. His broken smile made her stomach swoop.

Chapter 14

"Now I have to come back," she explained. "I'll want my coat, and I'll need to return yours."

She started for the door, but Night stopped her, catching her shoulder. When she turned to face him, he pulled her against him by the coat's lapel. She came willingly. Bending his head, he touched the curve of his antlers to her brow, then he stole her lips with his. His kiss was full of unspoken longing and deeply-rooted affection. It was embers and ice, a flare of connection that went to her marrow.

He tasted like black tea and honey and passion. His body was a sturdy and unyielding force before her, his arms solid walls that held her tight, and as they kissed, she wondered why they needed words at all. She could feel his desire for her, his worry, his need, in the fingers that fisted in her hair.

Perhaps if they spent more time kissing they'd solve all their problems. The next time he was flustered, she'd just press her lips to his. That would fix it because she was getting the hang of this kissing thing. Proficient, she'd even call herself.

Perhaps she wouldn't make such a terrible duchess after all.

* * *

Rain walked her familiar amongst her trees under a quarter moon in the sky, in the direction of the river Eventide. While they walked, she decided to finally let Bernard in on a little secret.

He did not take it well.

What do you mean no one thinks cats are threatening? Cats are terrifying! The bulgy eyes! The way they just stare at you so unnervingly! He yowled up at her from beside her boot.

"I'm sorry," she said gently, fighting back a smile. "They're just not frightening to most of us."

I've seen women scream in horror over a tiny mouse or jump in fright because there was a spider hanging from a web nearby, a dratted spider *that they could squish beneath a shoe. A cat has teeth and claws, and you mean to tell me they aren't frightening?*

"Not at all." She shook her head. "Haven't you noticed people keep cats as pets?"

Pets, he shouted. *I thought they were servants! Servants they keep to chase away the ugly mice!*

"I'm so sorry, Bernard," she said, choking down her desire to laugh, forcing an appropriately apologetic expression onto her face.

His reply was cut off by rattling branches. The trees were distressed. Rain removed a glove and pressed her palm to the nearest trunk.

And then the trees were screaming. Her head filled with their cries. She had to cover her ears to dampen the shrill sound.

What's happening? Bernard bounced around her feet, frantic, his back arched.

"Giants at the river," Rain whispered. "The girls!"

She sprinted for the tavern as fast as her legs would carry her, Bernard bounding beside her. The frost and dead leaves made the forest floor slick in unexpected places. Rain kept her footing, tearing through brambles and brush.

"Help them!" she begged the trees. "Help!" she screamed.

For the last five hundred and two years, she'd walked the forest. Many of these trees had been saplings in her lifetime. She'd tended to them, protected them, and given them her affection. Now, she was calling them in for every favor, every kind word.

Chapter 14

They responded. She could hear the echo of groaning wood, the snap of massive branches, the whoosh of heavy limbs striking against something solid and hard. The closer they came to the river and to the edges of the Row, the louder the trees were, drowning out the sound of whistles and screams.

She broke through the tree line from between a collection of pines. Two giants were attempting to cross the river to reach the Row. Giants were as big as ten men, with tusks for teeth, thick hides, bald heads, and a hunger for flesh. They were so big they could walk across the bottom of the Eventide and their chests would still be above the water. The two across the way were larger than the trees they fought against, but her trees battled in earnest.

Oaks and pines and maples swung their branches, swatting at the giants. They grew their limbs and trapped them, making nets of vines. Rain peeled her eyes away from the battle and rushed through the front door of The Red Boot.

Susan scrambled toward her. "Oh thank my ancestors!" She embraced her.

"Margot? Penny?" Rain demanded.

"The ferry." Susan released her and pointed out the window toward the Eventide. "It employs street children. They sleep there by the docks. Margot and Penny went to fetch them. The constables are useless. All they're doing is blowing their damn whistles and shouting nonsense. I brought the first batch of littles I could find on the street and tucked them up into the loft. I was about to go and find more and then—"

"We need mages," Rain said. She glanced down at Bernard. "We need the duke."

Bernard hissed up at her. *I don't want to leave you.*

You have to go to Night. He needs to know what's happened

before it's too late. Susan will speak for you, and I'll do what I can while you're gone.

Her familiar had to take her blood, and he did so with a paw laid gently on her leg. He took enough for her to feel it. Her pulse slowed. She was lightheaded, and spots of light popped before her eyes.

I think we should stay together, Bernard said as he broke into a misty shroud that expanded and morphed. Soon, a wolf the size of a small horse shook his shaggy head at her.

Rain caught Susan by the shoulders. "Bernard will take you to the Duke of Night. Keep to the trees and they'll protect you. Tell him what's happened here and be quick." She helped Susan onto Bernard's back, giving her a leg up with her bent knee and cupped hands.

Susan grasped great fistfuls of course black fur at Bernard's neck, her expression resigned. Rain had a moment to reflect that if Susan had been a fae, she'd have made an excellent warrior. She was unflappable.

She caught Susan's wrist, and their eyes met. Rain swallowed. "If something happens to me . . ."

Understanding softened Susan's expression. "I'll tell him," she promised.

Nothing had better happen to you, Bernard groused, and warmth spread through her stomach and chest. His life was tied to hers, but though he'd pretend otherwise, it wasn't his own welfare he was worried about at all. She didn't need him to say what she already knew, however. They'd been together too long to need such reassurances.

I'll be fine, she vowed. *Keep Susan safe. Go to Night as fast as your legs can carry you.*

Rain held open the tavern door, and Bernard barreled

through it. Susan clung to him, her head down near his shoulder blades. They rode off into the trees. Nowhere else was safe. River Row was in chaos.

Rain bolted outside. The walkways were crowded with stampeding humans. Food carts and horses had been abandoned. A constable's whistle shrieked. She sprinted toward it in the direction of the docks.

Frightened mortals ran for their lives, and Rain pushed past them. It wasn't that she didn't care for the other poor sods in the Row who took shelter in alleyways and beneath market stalls. It was just that they weren't *her* girls. She couldn't bear the thought of anything happening to them.

She heard Margot then. The woman shouted curse words at a giant, waving her arms over her head. Penny was beside her, throwing stones at the creature. From Rain's positioning, she could see the ferry workers, some of them human children, stranded on the docks. The girls were trying to draw the giant's eyes away from the young ones and toward the bank so the workers could escape.

And no one was helping them.

Penny hurled a large rock. It struck true, catching the side of the giant's ear. He spun about, bald head gleaming in the moonlight. His tusks were capped in bronze, his large ears pierced with matching heavy metal loops. He lumbered toward the girls with a roar that shook the earth.

Margot turned and fled.

Penny was searching for another rock along the bank to throw.

"No!" Rain screamed.

Penny looked up too late. The giant reached her with his great long limbs. He hauled her up in his fist and shook her hard, his grip much too tight. Her face purpled, her mouth opened, but no sound emerged.

Rain shouldered out of Night's coat, freeing her arms. She let loose a roar of her own and unsheathed her dagger with a rasp of metal on metal. The elven blade was tipped in sharpened steel and made of living tree. Her roar caught the giant's attention, but he had no interest in her. He had the meal he wanted trapped in his thick fingers, and he was slowly squeezing the life out of her.

Margot cursed and shouted and flung rocks. "You great fucking brute! Come over here and try that with me! You whoreson!"

The giant lumbered away, headed back for the waters.

Rain caught up to the creature just as he made it to the edge of the Eventide. The waters were high and moving swiftly. She leapt with all her might, using her dagger to slice through leather clothing and into thick hide. Clutching the hilt and digging deep, she scrambled for purchase on the monster's back.

The giant grumbled, annoyed. Her dagger had barely broken his tough skin. She used the sharp blade to climb the giant, shimmying up his clothing, striking out to create new holds in leather and flesh. He tried to swing her off, swatting at her with big slow limbs. She was faster, swaying side to side, dodging his grasp.

"Let her go!" she grunted. "Drop her or die!"

"Your mother's a dog!" Margot taunted the giant. She chucked another rock. It connected with the side of the creature's head and bounced off. The giant growled. He bent to pick up a projectile along the bank, nearly flinging Rain into the river. Rain dug in and held tight as the creature hefted a boulder big enough to smash a man to mush. He hurled it at Margot, shaking Penny like a rag doll in his other hand.

Margot dodged the boulder with a frightened squeal.

Rain leapt for the giant's exposed armpit, shoving her elven blade into flesh, finding purchase in the softer tissue. "Grow!" she screamed, and the living tree in her blade sprouted deep into the giant's underarm and thickened at the base.

The creature dropped Penny then, flinging her into the river. The rapids carried her off. Rain leapt from the giant toward the bank, landing and rolling forward. She hopped to her feet, searching the edges of the Eventide for Penny's willowy form and her auburn hair. Farther down the bank, a constable hauled the girl out of the icy waters.

"Penny!" Margot fled toward them.

Rain had the briefest moment to feel her relief, to take a quick inhale of cold air, clinging to hope. They would tend to Penny, get her inside and dry, and she would be fine. She was safe now.

Rain was struck hard in the back of the head with a force that would have crushed a mortal's skull. The giant's blow lifted her off her feet and sent her flying into the bank. She protected her face with crossed hands, landing on her belly in frosty grass and frozen dirt, the air knocked from her lungs. Jagged rocks cut at her arms and ripped her blouse.

The giant stomped toward her. She couldn't tell the ground from the sky. Her head swam, but she stumbled to her feet anyway. When knocked down, Rain always got back up again—a dangerous habit. Had she learned to stay down at some point, she'd have significantly fewer scars.

She'd also probably be dead.

"Grow," she coughed. The giant's armpit was rich with veins, and the creature was fading fast, a river of blood coating the side of his leather clothing. "Grow," she said with building strength, and the tip of the living blade burst from the giant's side, running it through.

The giant stumbled on great trembling legs. Then his eyes rolled back into his hairless head, and he collapsed along the bank, nearly crushing Rain. He landed with a great thud, and the earth quaked. On unsteady legs, she ambled closer to him and kicked the side of his face for good measure. The creature remained unmoving. Her ears were ringing, and her skull throbbed. She thought she might vomit.

Then she did vomit. Rain upended her stomach's contents onto the shoulder of the dead giant.

"Loose," she called to her blade, wiping her mouth with the back of her hand. Her dagger made a wet sound as it retracted through the creature. Across the river, the trees continued to battle the other giants. She would join her trees, ensuring the safety of her girls, but first . . .

She tried to lift the dead giant's arm to get at her dagger. Pain flared in her head, and she saw sparks of white.

Darkness engulfed her.

* * *

Rain recognized the voices that whispered over her. Elayna was repeating her name. She blinked her eyes open, staring directly into the guard captain's narrow face and cropped magenta hair. It was surprising to see her so close. Her voice had sounded like it was coming to her from the end of a long tunnel.

At Elayna's back towered a set of long feathery wings, like

the wings of a barn owl the same shade as her vibrant hair. Beside her, Arne had a leathery set, like a bat.

"She's waking up," Elayna said. "Hold her still. I'm going to heal her more . . ."

Elayna made a shape with her fingers to match the quarter moon above. Incense filled Rain's lungs, and the throb of pain slowly subsided. Her nausea left her next. Elayna grasped her forearm and helped her sit up.

Arne had retrieved Night's coat. He draped it over her shoulders. "We saw you from the air," he said, awe in his voice. "You took down that giant all by yourself."

"With one dagger," Elayna added. The corner of her mouth curved upward. "When the time comes, I'll be proud to call you My Lady."

Rain didn't know what to say to that, squinting into the guard's face. Vaguely she remembered why she was there, but it all felt so distant, like she'd been ripped from a dream. None of it seemed entirely real. Her brow knitted.

"Night?" she rasped, trying to get a grasp on her thoughts but finding them coated in smog, polluted and unclear.

Her question was answered by the shadowy figure gliding over the Eventide with great gray wings. Antlers curved back off his head. His cloak billowed around him loosely like the wings had ripped through his clothing. In the distance, the trees continued to battle and bind the giants, branches swaying and twisting, the lumbering creatures swinging and thrashing.

Night landed amongst them, wings stretched wide and glowing silver in the starlight.

Rain tried to stand. He was alone. He shouldn't be alone.

Elayna dropped a firm hand on her shoulder, settling her. "Your mate will be fine. Trust me."

"Just watch," Arne said.

Rain watched with her heart in her throat. "What's he doing?"

"Whispering death to them," Elayna said.

The giants had stopped fighting. Their hands went to cover their ears. Desperate cries rent the air. Then silence. They were dead in moments, in a heap of twined limbs on the forest floor.

Rain's breath misted before her in gulping gusts. The rush of her pulse thundered in her ears. Slowly, the trees fell silent and still like they'd never moved at all.

The peace that followed felt wrong somehow. Haunted.

"He's all right. You see?" Elayna said.

Night turned then, wings retracting behind him. She felt the weight of his eyes from the other side of the river. They'd found each other across the expanse. He lifted a hand to her. She raised hers in salute and reassurance. She was well. She'd be fine. He nodded, a slow dip of his sharp chin.

In one large leap, he launched himself back into the sky and was following the tree line away from her.

Rain worked her throat. "Where's he going?" She wanted him safe and at her side, not going somewhere she couldn't, because . . .

Because she loved him.

Desperately.

The realization caused her pulse to surge. She hadn't meant to fall in love with the duke, not when he so clearly didn't want love in their relationship. He wanted duty and responsibility. He'd promised her family and all the devotion he could spare, not love.

But stars above, she *loved* him. Her toes curled in her boots, and her teeth ached from the force of it.

The end of Arne's leather tail flicked at his side. His wings folded in around him. "He's checking the forest for more giants. We can't go with him. We can't listen when he speaks death to them."

Bernard? Rain glanced about for her familiar.

I'm here. His voice was small. Sad.

Rain climbed to her feet on legs that felt rubbery. Farther down the bank of the river, Margot and Susan held Penny between them. The constable Billingsley looked on at a loss, backlit by a gas lamp.

But why weren't they taking Penny inside? She'd freeze out here. She was all wet . . .

Bernard. She couldn't even think the words she wanted to ask. Her feet propelled her forward without a thought.

Margot and Susan cried, their shoulders shaking, their sobs catching on the cool autumn breeze, turning the cold bitter. It stung Rain's eyes and made them water. Bernard lay at Penny's feet in his large wolf form, his shaggy head hanging. Penny's usually creamy complexion was ash white.

I couldn't fix her . . . Bernard said solemnly.

No! Rain didn't want to hear his words, but they were already in her head. She couldn't un-hear them. Cold, piercing dread spread through her, hardening her stomach.

The giant broke her neck in two places. She was dead before she made it into that water.

"Stars above," Rain cried. Feet catching in the grass, she stopped yards away from her friends. Her arms and legs were trembling, unable to carry her farther. Her eyes burned and welled.

Arne and Elayna had followed her. She hadn't even realized

they were close until Arne's large hand clamped onto the back of her neck, steadying her.

"Your blade, My Lady," Elayna said softly, sliding the elven dagger into its sheath at her belt. It was clean of giant's blood. It had been tended to and cared for. Cleaning another's blade was a sign of great respect amongst warriors. An old gesture she was too miserable to appreciate.

Bernard had always warned her away from loving humans. They were fragile and their lives were too short. She'd known there was wisdom in that, but with the girls she simply couldn't help herself.

It had been Penny who'd invited her inside that first night years ago. The hard freeze was coming. She needed a place indoors to lay her head down. Her elven-fae body was more sensitive to the cold. She had furs to trade for a room, but they weren't worth much.

Penny had brought her inside and spoken with Susan. They'd placed a pallet on the floor of the kitchen by the warm stove for her to sleep on. They wouldn't accept anything in return. Not even chores.

"It was hardly a proper bed we offered you," Penny had said. She'd only been nineteen at the time. She'd had such a charming smile, youthful and sweet and infectious. Rain vowed to come if they needed her, vowed to protect them for their kindness. She had done her best over the years to keep them safe . . .

And now Penny was gone. Her life snuffed out.

Rain had failed her.

Billingsley spoke, his voice low. "The lot of you will freeze out here. Come on now. You're wet, and you'll catch your death. Get inside."

Chapter 14

Margot wailed. Susan pulled her up beside her.

"You go on. I'll get the girl," the constable offered, gesturing at Penny.

"No," Rain said sharply, and Billingsley paused. "I'll tend to her."

Susan nodded, her blue eyes red-rimmed and glassy. Arm in arm, she and Margot walked toward the tavern, the constable at their heels.

Bernard rose to his paws. *Where are we going?*

Rain didn't know yet. "I'll tend to Penny alone," she told the guards. Elayna and Arne had moved to follow her, but they paused then, sharing uneasy glances.

They didn't make her repeat herself. Wise of them. It wouldn't have gone well. She may not know where she was headed, but she knew she wanted to be alone while she got there.

Rain scooped Penny up in her arms, a dripping bundle of long slender limbs, wet auburn hair in tangles around her ashen face. It surprised Rain how cold her skin already was. Bernard followed at her heels. The trees around them clattered their branches together in solemn salute. Tears blurred Rain's vision. Her throat ached.

The skies parted, and rain fell in a gentle patter. It seemed fitting. She wanted the world to stop what it was doing and feel miserable with her. It shouldn't keep going about its business. Not when her Penny was gone. The trees did their best to shield Rain from the wet, but most of them had lost their leaves to the season. Droplets soaked into her hair and bit at her skin.

She carried Penny's body through the woods to the oldest oak tree in the forest, ancient and steady. Rain's favorite tree, the one she'd been lounging in when she met Night. Instinct had brought her this far, and finally she knew what she wanted.

The ground was hard beneath her boots. The freeze had finally arrived. Frost glittered on the edges of the old oak's limbs, casting its bark in silver under a quarter moon.

Rain dropped a kiss on Penny's brow, then laid her at the base of the tree. "I know she's not elven," she said to the oak, wiping her eyes with the sleeve of her coat, "but I swear to you she's worthy. Please old friend," she rasped.

Rain, Bernard cautioned, *she* was *wonderful, but she was only mortal. I'm not even certain the tree can do what you seek . . .*

Rain wasn't sure either, but she had hope.

The ground under her feet shivered, and the roots lifted from the frozen earth like the tentacles of a sea creature. Roots reached and grabbed, wrapping Penny in their embrace, covering her in spindly plant fibers. Carefully, the roots pulled her below the ground, under the ancient tree. More roots pushed fresh earth over the opening they'd created, leaving a dark mound. Then the tree settled with a low groan, and all was still once more.

It was almost too cold to cry. Rain's tears fell hot down her cheeks, then cooled quickly, leaving icy streaks that froze in the bitter wind.

"Thank you," she sobbed, pressing the flat of her hand to the oak's trunk, the bark veined with green and gold that glinted in the night. The tree's essence had changed. It wasn't just warm and ancient now. It was sweet and coltish and full of vibrant life. "Penny," she whispered.

She'd always wanted to take the young girl away from the rough hand life had dealt her, to tuck her someplace safe and soft and warm. This was the best she could do for her now.

Her body would always be safe, always cozy. Her essence would always be at peace here.

The tree's branches stretched toward the sky and sprouted thick auburn leaves, no longer simply living but alive. No longer just an oak but now an immortal tree.

Chapter 15

(Night)

Flying was terrifying. It made Night feel completely out of control, like he was free-falling into a bottomless pit. "A fart in a whirlwind," his guard captain called the sensation. Wings had their uses, however. His mate had summoned him. His throat had tightened the moment the girl mentioned the giants. He hadn't hesitated to make use of the speed of flight.

Rain.

He'd watched her down the giant from the air, too slow to reach her in time. When she'd fallen, he'd roared at the sky. Elayna was ahead of him. She was the faster flyer.

"Heal her and don't leave her side!" he'd screamed.

He'd wanted so badly to ignore duty and go to her first. If her eyes hadn't opened when they did, he would have. The giants could do their worst—he'd have gone to his mate come what may. But Elayna made it to Rain with a speed he couldn't match, and his warrior mate was sitting up soon after.

Then duty called. He couldn't let more giants cross the Eventide to threaten Rain or his court.

Though it had taken hours, he was confident there were no other giants in his province. Because of their size, they were not capable of concealing themselves. He'd scoured the southern borders and found nothing.

Sunrise loomed, turning the sky from an inky black to a rich indigo. He spotted Elayna and Arne waiting for him alone outside the tavern. His hackles rose immediately. Why wasn't Rain with them? They'd been ordered not to leave her side.

He landed stiffly, wings stretching wide before furling behind him with a speed that loosened silver feathers. His guards bowed to their lord.

"Where is she?" he groused.

Arne began to stammer.

Elayna stepped forward, her head bent in deference. "The human called Penny died, My Lord. Distraught, your mate asked to tend to her alone."

Night's nostrils flared. "I told you—"

"—to treat her as my lady," Elayna said. There were times when he appreciated her candor. Now was not one of those times. "I obeyed my lady's orders." Seeing his expression, she gentled her tone. "My Lord," she added.

"It's been hours of freezing rain and bitter cold. Fuck all—she has a head injury, and she's in mourning, for the Moon Mother's sake. Would you have listened to me in that situation? No, you wouldn't have. You'd have argued with me until you were blue in the face and followed anyway."

"She would not have let us follow her," Elayna admitted helplessly.

Ruffling his hair, he snapped, "Which way did she go?"

She pointed south, away from River Row, deeper into the woods. Night turned to squint through the trees. He touched his eyes with his thumbs, borrowing the sight of an owl to further sharpen his senses.

Wings widening with a snap, he leapt into the air and sped off south, using his owl eyes to watch for signs of his mate down below. He spotted boot prints and large wolf paws and sensed he was getting closer. Before long, he was hurtling forward, instinctively certain he knew where she'd taken the girl's body.

By air, it took only a handful of minutes to reach their old meeting place, but it felt like decades. The old oak stood out from the other trees, covered in bright auburn leaves. It was the same oak Rain had been perched in the night he met her, her favorite tree, but it had changed.

The oak no longer appeared so ancient and tired. Green and gold glittered through the bark, and the leaves were lush, new, and seemed impervious to the frost that made the brambles below sparkle. A standing figure of fur rested against its trunk. He glided lower to investigate, wind whipping through his hair and antlers. The scent of sulfur stung his nose. He landed softly on the frosty forest floor, his tall boots crunching glistening grass. "Rain?"

The bundle of furs shivered in the gloaming. The scent of hell was thick in the air. He realized then that what looked like a massive black bear blanket was the demon familiar trying desperately to warm his mistress.

Night ripped the fur back, and his mate stumbled toward him, bleary-eyed and swaying on her feet.

"Divine blood," he cursed, catching her in his arms.

Chapter 15

He cupped her cheek. Her hair was wet, skin ice cold and too pale. Her head lolled. Her words were slurred. Quickly, he grabbed up the fur and laid it back over her. Night forced her limp arms around his neck, covering her with his wings, shielding her from biting wind and stray raindrops blowing off the nearby branches. His borrowed coat hung off her slender frame, damp, dirty, and blood-stained.

"Rain, wrap your legs around me," he demanded, clutching her against his body, desperate to warm her.

"I don't want to leave Penny," she slurred, reaching back for the tree, trying to push her hand through the tangle of his wings. "I don't want her to be alone. It's horrible being alone."

The skin along her cheek was stiff and much too cold. She wasn't talking sense. Her plummeting body temperature had made her delirious.

"She's coming with you," he said, anxiety hurrying his words. He wrapped the fur tightly around her, securing her to him. "You're taking her with you here." He pressed a hand briefly over her heart. "Hold on to me, sweetheart. You aren't alone anymore." He jerked her leg up against his hip. She obeyed, clumsily locking her arms around his neck. Her head tipped onto his shoulder.

She burrowed into his neck. Even her breath was cold. "No one's coming to look for me, are they?" she whispered.

Night squeezed her tight, wings spreading wide at his back. The fur moved, tightening around her and him.

"Keep her close to me," he told Bernard. Then he launched them into the air.

* * *

Night burst through the front doors of his estate, his mate clutched tightly to his chest. In a puff of lavender magic, his wings faded. His shirt and cloak hung off his body, a gaping hole in the back of them letting in the cooler air, pebbling his skin.

The sun kissed the horizon in the distance. A servant was in the process of lighting the incense for the altar of the Divine Day when Night's sudden entrance startled the match out of his hand. Bernard dropped from around Rain's shoulders, transforming from a fur blanket to a shadowy smog. The smog became a cat at his feet. The demon scrambled to hover by the doors, keeping out of the way.

Night barked orders, and the foyer swarmed with servants coming to see what the commotion was about. "Send for a physician immediately. Draw a bath in my room. Luke warm water," he stressed, "not hot. Bring towels, blankets, and fresh linens, and add more logs to my fire."

He ran Rain up the stairs, taking the steps two at a time. Maids sprang into action, rushing ahead of him to tend to their work.

A copper tub was carried into his bedroom by three footmen. Servants dragged pails of temperate water filled from the tap in the lavatory across the hall. They emptied them into the tub. At his command, the pitcher was filled with steaming hot water and set on the stand beside the tub. The fire was stoked and fed, and the temperature quickly rose. Sunlight filtered in through the velvet curtains as Night removed Rain's filthy borrowed coat, letting it fall to the floor.

"The maids will help you undress," he told her. "I'll be just outside until you're in the tub."

"No!" she clung to him, her grip weak, body shivering. "I

don't know them."

"We have to get the wet clothes off you. They're half frozen."

"I can do it." With trembling fingers, she tugged at the buttons of her trousers.

But she couldn't do it. She could barely stand. When the tub was filled, he ordered the servants out of the room.

"All of you is beautiful to me," he said hurriedly, helping her with her buttons, his movements frantic. "Do you hear me, Rain? All of you. Every follicle. Every pore. Let me help you."

She leaned into him then, pressing her brow to his sternum. If she took a moment longer to think, he was going to haul her into the tub fully clothed and strip her there. His pulse pumped panic through his veins, surging loudly in his ears.

"Don't ask me about the scars," she muttered into his torn cloak. "I don't remember how I got most of them anyway."

Night stripped her hastily, jerking off her boots and tossing them aside. He peeled down her wet trousers and drawers, earning no complaint, but she protested when he started on the blouse.

"It's Penny's," she said, chin trembling.

"You can keep hold of it," he promised. The sorrow in her gaze put a dull ache in his chest.

He unbuttoned the blouse and helped her out of the sleeves, but then he draped the garment around her neck like a scarf. She worried the edges of the linen with shaking fingers, her eyes fixed on the ceiling as he removed the band of boned cotton and linen she wore to cover her breasts. A thin white scar curved over the top of her left breast. Her slender belly was scarred too, the navel torn open and healed back together unevenly, the shape jagged like a bolt of lightning.

Evidence of her bravery.

Seeing the wounds his fierce mate shouldn't have survived, he felt only admiration and surprise. He'd known she had an impressive will, but this . . . this was no less than legendary.

Night kicked his boots off and shucked his torn cloak. He brought her to the copper bath. It wasn't big enough for two, but Rain was slight. He lifted her in his arms and stepped into the tub clothed. He lowered them into the temperate water together, causing it to overflow. Water sloshed against the sides and dribbled onto the carpet.

Rain hissed, the water a shock to her senses. After several long moments, she sighed, slipping under the waves to her chin. He worked off his torn shirt and laid it over the edge of the tub with a wet splat. He took her back in his arms, pressing her bare chest against his, sharing his heat. He flattened his hands along her back, testing the warmth of her skin, finding many scars with the pads of his fingers and instinctively tracing them. Knife wounds. Cuts, gouges, and various injuries he couldn't identify.

He didn't ask about them, but curiosity burned within him.

Rain rested against him, but he wouldn't let her fall asleep, worried she'd lose consciousness or worse. He checked her fingers and toes next. If she was bothered by his lack of 'please' and 'may I,' she didn't comment. Her hand movements were stiff, fingertips pale with signs of frostbite. He healed them with his connection to the Divine Night. In his distress, he called so much moon magic to him that furniture rattled in the room. Towels and blankets floated off his bed, lifting into the air. Droplets of water left the tub, floating around them like iridescent bubbles. Carefully he added hot water to the mixture, raising the temperature of the water and her by gentle degrees.

Chapter 15

When she was restored and her body had stopped shivering, she buried her face in the crook of his neck. “I’m going to marry you,” she whispered.

Night’s heart stuttered. He’d felt the movement of her lips against his flesh as her mouth formed the words. Water droplets plopped back into the tub. The furniture stopped rattling. His grip around her tightened. “You might still be delirious from the cold.”

“I’m going to marry you,” she said more firmly, “and while you’re trying to prevent a war, I’m going to start one.”

Night caught her chin between his fingers, and he lifted her eyes to his. An undeniable fire burned in those amber depths. “You wish to avenge Penny.”

Her jaw set. “There haven’t been giants this far north since the first war. We both know they didn’t wander up here by accident.”

“The dragon king received news of our engagement and sent us an early wedding present,” Night said evenly. “A warning for refusing his kin and the offer of alliance that would kill us all.”

“I want the dragon king’s *head* as a wedding present.” Her hands lifted, disturbing the water. She held his face between her palms, slicking his cheeks, but he felt more captured by her eyes than her touch. “Do you understand me, Ardis? I’m going to marry you, but I’m not the harbinger of peace you hoped for.”

Ardis. The word made his soul sing and the bond thrum, even as it was spoken in bloodlust. *Husband mate,* an old elegant word. As for peace, he’d always known war was coming. Stalling would only get him so far. It was one of many reasons why he needed her so. Marriage to his true mate gave him time. Time he desperately needed.

Marriage to her would help him find victory.

"I understand who you are. I've known it since I first laid eyes on you." His thumb trailed along her chin. Her slight breasts pillowed against his chest, accenting the curved scar there. He released her chin, and with his thumb, he followed the broken flesh. Her skin pebbled. "We have a *lot* to discuss about where and when you'll be starting this war of yours, but first say that old word to me again."

* * *

Night wanted his mate to *want* to marry him. It was a foolish wish, one he tried all week to banish from his thoughts. He had wisely offered her a marriage of convenience, and yet here he was, craving a marriage full of flighty affection instead.

The persistent bond growing between them was largely responsible, he was sure. When it settled, keeping his priorities straight would become significantly easier. He needed a partner. An ally.

Not a fairy story.

A week flew by at his estate. No other giant or troll sightings were made. He expanded patrols to be sure. Rain wanted her hands in all of his duties that involved war and rumors of war. She kept to the bonding rituals with great attention, committed to completing their mating.

He gave her a generous allowance because a future duchess should have spending money. Rain asked what she was to buy. He listed off clothing items a gentry woman might favor. She'd stared at his coins crossly for a moment, but then accepted them. It pleased him to give her things, even though he was fairly certain she would send most of the money to the remaining women at The Red Boot.

She'd left during the day while he slept and returned later with fabrics and a new set of boots she'd purchased. She spent the next evening fashioning new clothing for herself. She dressed like a soldier: long tunics, thick belts, woolen trousers, shirts made of broadcloth, jackets with a high collar. Efficient, practical clothing.

Penny's blouse had been folded sweetly and given a place of honor tucked under a pillow Rain never used, like she wanted it close but could no longer bear to look at it.

She slept on him every night. He'd grown so accustomed to the weight of her, nothing else would do. When she ran an errand or went for walks during the day, he tried stacking several blankets and pillows on top of himself to mimic the pressure of her, but nothing worked. He ended up dozing fitfully until she returned.

It was more than the weight of her. It was her presence: sweet and uncertain, analytical and thoughtful. The gentle sounds of her deep exhales, the patter of her heart pressed against his, the humidity of her breath on his cheek—he needed all of it. All of her.

That week she attended every meeting with him. Usually she kept quiet, but if she had questions, she voiced them to him in a surprisingly crisp and direct fashion, especially when it came to guards and mages—the majority of their force. The Lunar Court's militia was laughably small and existed only in secret. When they weren't together, separated by his need to make appearances at functions or clubs, she studied in his front library, old history books mostly. She claimed there was little she remembered, and she needed to know her enemy better.

That evening they shared the midnight meal in his bedroom. Rain wasn't comfortable eating with an audience, even Bernard, the act of feeding each other too intimate to share, and he agreed with her, but it cut down on the amount of work he could attend to during the night. Usually, he'd share his meals with accountants, advisors, and the business owners he needed to speak with.

Preserving meals for her required adjustments. Adjustments he was eager to make. He was coming to crave her in such a way he couldn't tell what parts of his desire were born of the bond and which parts were his entirely.

Rain surprised him then. After making a small plate of shepherd's pie from the cart of food and refreshments next to his armchair, she came and sat on his lap instead of next to him, disrupting his thoughts and sending them scattering. Balancing the plate in her hand, she tested the crispy potato crust with her finger, then the meaty insides, making sure it wasn't too hot. The bond liked when they didn't use utensils, so she ignored the forks and spoons.

"You've been deep in the history books again," he said, noting the impressive stack on the nightstand, aware of how his voice had gone rough. They shared a bed every day, though he knew she sometimes left it to take walks with Bernard and her trees, to gather supplies, to experience sunlight, to pick wild herbs she wanted to add to the food she helped make him.

To mourn poor Penny.

"I have been, and I have questions for you." She took a roll of bread from the cart, using the edges to scoop up bits of shepherd pie.

He opened his mouth and let her feed him, chewing and

swallowing before responding. "I was hoping you wouldn't just leave it all to the books . . . Did you make the bread? It's excellent."

She blushed and nodded. He had grown fond of the stain of color that showed high in her cheeks when she was delighted. It reminded him of the time he'd brought her to release, a moment he relived in his dreams with great regularity. She'd flushed beautifully for him then. He planned to do it again and soon, but she'd been in mourning.

But now she was sitting in his lap . . .

Rain mulled her words over, tasting a bit of the crust. "At the end of the last conflict, the Lunar Court was called in to serve as a mediator between the Seelie and the Unseelie." She shifted her weight, rubbing herself against him. He couldn't tell if it had been intentional or not. His body responded anyway.

Night swallowed hard, his throat suddenly dry. "Hostages were entrusted to the Lunar Province for safekeeping during peace negotiations. The peace talks took more than a century, and they weren't all that peaceful. My parents died in a border skirmish during that time."

Rain scooped up more of the meaty mixture with a pinch of the roll and placed it in his mouth. Then she licked her fingers clean. He studied her while she did so, oddly fascinated by the movement of her pink tongue. It did more than inspire lust in him. Lust he expected. He understood lust . . . This other feeling, this fixation, puzzled him.

"The Seelie queen . . ." Rain said, lapping the last of the gravy off the side of her finger. She licked her lips. "She demanded King Yaga's daughter Sora be given to the Lunar Province. According to my research, the witch had turned spy against her father during the war. Do you think Queen Isla chose Sora to preserve her?"

Reflexively, Night ground his teeth. "Don't make the mistake of assuming the queen had noble intentions. She isn't the sort to be altruistic unless she has something to gain."

Rain's gaze lowered to the roll she was pulling apart between her fingers. "I know what she did to your uncle, a man you cared for and respected. The man who raised you with kindness. If talking about this is painful for you, I—"

He waved her words away. "I'm well. Go on. Ask your questions."

"I just need to be sure I understand it all . . . There's so much I don't remember about that time. The books help. Talking to you will help more." She chewed her cheek, uncertain, breaking the pieces of bread into finer bits.

He laid a hand on her knee and steadied his voice. "Keep talking to me. I promise you aren't hurting me."

"Or at least not too deeply, I hope." She popped a corner of bread into his mouth, watching him chew. "But you won't convince me it doesn't hurt at all."

He parted his lips for another serving of meat pie, then spoke with his mouth full. "You're picking at a well-healed scab. It has to come off eventually."

She leaned her shoulder against his chest, resigned. "The Seelie hostage is unnamed. The way they described him in the books, though, he was some sort of strategist, I think. He's repeatedly referred to as 'the Seelie queen's favored.'"

"They called him Row. Otherwise, all I know about him is written in the same books you've read. His deeds were before my time, but according to rumor, he was the reason the Seelie started to win the war against the Unseelie and finally the dragon king had no choice but to come to the negotiation table." Night touched the scarred side of his mouth reflexively. "The hostages were never supposed to be harmed . . ."

"Was Row her mate? Queen Isla never married. It's helpful to understand what motivates your enemy. Love lost is certainly a strong motivation for vengeance . . ."

"Or family lost. The Seelie cherish their blood lines deeply," he offered. "Rest assured, harming Row was not the intention when the last King of Night became involved."

She pushed the bread around her plate, letting it soak up the gravy. She fed a soggy piece to Night. "Sora still lives."

"The food is excellent," he told her, eager to see her blush again. "As a part of the treaty, the chosen hostages were required to swear fealty to the opposing ruler and to live out their days in the neutral lands of the Lunar Province. Row wouldn't bow to the dragon king. Per the peace agreement, he had to die. At his request, my uncle gave him a warrior's death and then offered him to the trees."

"An elven death," Rain said thoughtfully.

"A noble end." He took another large bite of the offered pie, swallowing it down.

"The queen disagreed." Rain fed herself next, staring off through the balcony doors. The moon was high, the night too cloudy to see the stars.

"Isla fiercely disagreed," he said. "However, she could do nothing at the time. The treaty required that the Seelie and Unseelie not venture outside their court for two hundred and fifty years, monarchs included. The peace agreement was sealed by bargain magic."

"Then after those years, she came to the Lunar Court, killed your uncle, and stripped the province of its king . . ."

Night's chin dropped, guilt and shame twisting his insides.

His uncle had been a good and kind man. A dutiful ruler, loved by all who knew him. He'd had no children. His mate had been unable to carry an heir to term, a common fae difficulty. Night had been like a son to him.

Rain touched his cheek, the brush of her flesh so light he barely felt it, but it pulled him from his revelry. "Why didn't you take the empty throne?"

He couldn't meet her inquisitive eyes. Instinctively, he touched the scarring at his mouth. "Because the queen didn't murder my uncle."

Rain studied him, brow furrowed.

"*I* murdered him."

Chapter 16

(Rain)

Rain thought she'd misheard her mate—hoped she'd misheard him. "How could that be?"

He pinched a piece of the bread off her plate and placed it in her mouth. She sensed it was to give himself time to prepare his words, or to avoid the question entirely. His fingers kept traveling to the scars at the corner of his mouth, aimlessly grazing the jagged tissue, then pulling sheepishly at his lip.

When he finally spoke again, his voice was devoid of emotion, his face blank. He stared off at a corner of wall between two hangings. "The queen came unannounced and demanded an audience. Night . . . my uncle at the time was the Night . . . He knew why Queen Isla was there when she arrived. It had been two hundred and fifty years to the day since the treaty was struck and he'd had to take Row's life. He never spoke of the man except to name this city River Row. I believe he respected him deeply. It wasn't fear I sensed in my uncle that day, but pain for what he'd had to do. He wanted to make it better when he let Isla inside. He wanted to pay penance."

Rain laid a hand on his chest, a gentle encouragement. Then she set aside the plate of food and poured him a cup of tea. He accepted the cup, balancing it on the arm of the chair without drinking it.

"I didn't realize the Seelie queen was a witch," Rain confessed. "Or I didn't remember it."

"Her familiar is a fairy, and their combined powers are god-like," Night said, his fingers straining around the cup in his hand. "It's those god-like powers that make King Yaga incapable of keeping to himself. He always has to have more, has to be the strongest. It's the dragon way. Queen Isla used her fairy powers that day to bend my mind . . ."

Rain's eyes went round. The urge to soothe him was overwhelming. At a loss as to how to do that, she sat there gifting him with her silent company, feeling woefully inadequate. How terrible to be manipulated in such a fashion. A spark of fury ignited inside her, burning low in her gut.

How dare the queen do that to her mate?

He continued softly, "My uncle used his dying breath to try to rid me of my guilt. He told me he didn't blame me. Told me it wasn't my fault. Demanded I see to his mate. Protect her . . ." Night lifted his cup and took a heavy swallow. "They were true-mated. My aunt died within days of him. There was absolutely nothing I could do. Not for either of them."

She added honey to his tea because she couldn't think of a gesture good enough to console him. Using a small spoon, she stirred the honey and encouraged him to lift it to his lips.

Briefly she touched the scar at his mouth. "And how did you get these?"

"Queen Isla forced me to run my uncle through with the dagger I carried . . ." He sipped his tea and then set it aside. His eyes were red-rimmed and hollow. "It was dreadful, not being able to control my own body, horrible in a way I'll never be able to describe. I tried to turn my blade on her for what she'd done—what she'd made me do."

"Stars, I'm so sorry . . ." She was sorry for all of it. For the weight he carried, the pain he'd endured, and for making him talk about it now. She hated words. This would have been a torture for her.

But now that the floodgates were opened, he didn't appear to be closing them. He continued unabated. "The queen stopped me with her fairy magic, handed me her iron-tipped dagger, and compelled me to take it to the side of my mouth. Something to always remind me of what she was capable of, she said. Then she just left. And my choices were to take the crown and start a new war or choose peace. My uncle fought hard for that peace. The Lunar Court needed leadership, its mages needed guidance, but we didn't need a king to lead us back into war. I became Lord of the Lunar Court and allowed the Seelie and Unseelie to impose their tariffs all in the name of that peace. The tariffs were supposed to break us."

"But you didn't let them," she said admiringly. She stroked the scar at his mouth, drawing his eyes. "The queen did this to you—to my mate." Not a question.

He nodded, his gaze silver pools in the twilight. "Sora believes that the magic of a true mate bond will prevent the queen from being able to compel me ever again. In a way, my will belongs to you now. She won't be able to turn it against me."

"Hmm. Good to know." Rain brushed blue-black hair off his brow. "For hurting my king—"

"I'm no one's king, Rain," he said somberly.

"You're my king. As far as I'm concerned, I died in that first war, as did whatever loyalties I had that I no longer remember. Fuck the other courts." At her crass words, he coughed a laugh. She pressed on, "I choose to bow before the man who sacrificed all for the sake of peace, who made his province a safe place for people with less power to call home. My king and my mate," she cooed, "for hurting you so gravely, I'll have to take the Seelie queen's head one day soon. My wedding present to you."

His eyes lit. Instead of being tired and melancholy, they softened into something dreamy and heavy-lidded. He gripped the nape of her neck with a pressure that was both unyielding and tender. He kissed her before she could finish deciphering the flood of emotions streaming through his gaze. Hot and hard, his lips took hers.

He'd kissed her before, but this was something different. She felt consumed, feasted upon, and the bond reveled in it. Pleasant heat pooled low in her belly. Sensitive muscles clenched. In his lap, she felt the growing length and weight of his desire prod at her thigh. She leaned into that firm pressure, and it twitched under her. Curiosity burned through her gut.

Tipping her back in his arms, he lowered his head and kissed her scarred navel. "My brave mate," he said, his voice husky.

Rain quivered in his arms. He was everything her dreams promised he'd be. Tender and generous, able to teach her so many things . . .

"You don't believe in love," she said, breathless.

Chapter 16

Night groaned. "Whenever we talk about this, I always end up accidentally insulting you somehow. Could we skip it?" He nuzzled her neck, then gently caught the shell of her ear playfully between his teeth.

"Yes," she said, chuckling, "but I just thought I should warn you. It seemed polite to do so."

"Warn me about what?" He undid the top buttons of her woolen shirt, slipping a hand inside the opening he made. She watched intently as he fingered the curved scar high on her chest. She liked how he explored her with no hesitation, touching her old wounds without discomfort, treating her injuries with the same unadulterated boldness he displayed toward his own. When he touched her in such a way, she felt cherished.

"I no longer care that you don't believe in love," she said quickly, remembering she'd been trying to say something important. Then his hand slipped lower, shoving down one side of the band of fabric she wore in place of a corset. Her breasts were small and didn't require much in the way of support.

He arched a brow at her. "You don't?"

"I'm going to make you fall in love with me ev—" She sucked in a breath. He'd rolled her nipple between his fingers, a gentle tease that made it stiffen. She worked her throat. "Even though you don't believe that's possible." He'd put a catch in her voice. "Even though that's not something you want in our partnership. I believe in love enough for both of us."

For a moment, his expression was completely unreadable. Then his gaze flooded with feeling, too many to differentiate all of them, but she did her best: passion, fear, worry, longing, panic . . . Hope. A line deepened between his brows, and his lips parted like he wanted to say something.

She freed him from that burden, sealing his mouth with hers. He responded to her kiss, clutching her close like he just couldn't get her near enough, couldn't hold her hard enough. She teased his lips apart with her own, then she sucked gently on his tongue. He moaned low in his throat, a sound that sent a desperate thrill through her.

Night removed his hand from her shirt, then fisted the fabric. "I want to take these off you."

"All of them?" She regretted the worry in her voice. She wanted to be braver around him about such things. Shyness was her reflex, however.

He started to withdraw politely. He'd never push her on this, and for that she loved him with a passion that would find no equal in the world.

"Yes," she said suddenly, catching his retreating hand and bringing it back to her shirt. "Remove them. All of them."

Night touched his brow to hers, a display of fae deference that made her throat and eyes sting with emotion. "You're sure?"

"*All* of them," she said with an unshakable certainty. Stars above, she wanted this man in every way possible. Didn't he understand? Wasn't it all over her face? Couldn't he see it in her eyes, feel it in her fingers? Surely her want of him was seeping from her very pores?

He stood then and brought her with him, lifting her easily. She clung to his neck, her legs wrapping his waist. It took only two of his long strides to reach their bed. He tossed her onto it with a playfulness that left her giggling.

He lifted her foot first, removing her boots and socks one after the other. She wiggled her toes, feeling the cooler air on her skin. She started to scoot farther up the bed to make room for him, but he caught her by the ankles and dragged her back down so she was seated near the edge, jarring another laugh from her.

His broken smile was painfully beautiful. Candlelight made silver diamonds of his eyes. She sat up, bracing herself on her arms, resisting the urge to look up at the ceiling as he thumbed open the last of the buttons on her shirt. She shouldered out of it, heat flooding her cheeks.

She started to help with the strapless band of fabric that secured her breasts, but he stopped her, briefly trapping her wrist, speaking words with his gaze in that way of his. He needed to do this for her, he told her with his eyes. She raised her arms over her head instead, and he slid the band up and off her body, tossing it to the side.

His gaze flittered to the scar at her belly, to all of the scars and scrapes on her stomach, but never lingered. Never prodded. Never made demands. His eyes were dark and dilated. His cock stretched the front of his trousers. The longer she stared at the bulge, the fuller it seemed to grow.

Her timidity returned, and her throat bobbed. She knew intimacy could hurt the first time. She didn't look forward to that part. Night chucked her chin until her lashes lifted. Apparently her eyes had done some talking of their own.

"Pleasure is all you'll feel tonight." His honey-rich voice was thick and sweet. The hair on her arms rose.

"Because of your magic?" she guessed.

His smirk went crooked. "I don't need moon magic for that."

Rain reached for her belt, but he stopped her again, gently pushing her hands away and working the fastening himself. He brought her trousers and drawers down slowly. She helped, lifting her hips.

Then he lowered to his knees before her and encouraged her thighs apart with his hands. Rain blinked at him. Surely, he didn't plan to . . .

"You're a duke . . ." she said sheepishly. "I assumed . . ."

His smile was wolfish. "You thought I'd pleasure you like a gentleman?"

Rain scoffed. "I wouldn't know what a gentleman does in bed, I suppose, but this . . . I just assumed . . ." It seemed like the most forbidden thing. A wild and depraved thing. A thing she wanted desperately, remembering what his fingers had done to her, the pleasure they'd wrought. Stars, what could he do with his tongue?

He kissed her knee, then shouldered between her legs, trailing his lips farther up her thigh. Her breaths came in short bursts. His fingers tested her intimate white curls, then the furrow of her sex. She was already wet.

He spread her folds with his fingers and kissed her. Right *there*, and her head went back. "Stars, you are no gentleman." She swallowed, her lungs catching. Rain spread her thighs farther apart. His tongue lapped at her, a quick testing swipe. "Wicked," she said admiringly. "You're absolutely wicked."

Her hands burrowed into his hair, clutching her to him. His lashes lifted, lips curling upward, watching her. He'd told her once before that she should move the way her body wanted. When he pressed the flat of his tongue against that bud of nerves, her hips jerked. She allowed the rhythmic movement to continue, rolling into the caress of his lips and tongue, letting go of bashfulness.

"My king," she gasped, fingers moving to the base of his antlers, grasping hard. "My wicked king."

Chapter 16

His eyes met hers again, gazing up her body from between her legs. He puckered his lips and sucked on her sex, and Rain's spine arched like a pulled bowstring. Her release consumed her, stealing the air from her lungs. She dropped to her back on the mattress.

He licked her through her climax until the clenching and pulsing subsided. Then he entered her with his finger. Her body was ready for the invasion, and it gloried in it.

Slowly Rain sat back up, wanting to watch as he pressed into her, working the digit deeper. She felt fullness and pressure, but no pain, not even as he attempted to slip a second long finger inside. There was more fullness, and then her body resisted him. He was gentle. The second finger retreated.

Emboldened, she brushed blue-black hair off his forehead. His skin was sweltering. "Take off your clothes."

His laugh was breathy, a look of rapture softening his features. "The barrier of my clothing is helping me stay patient, darling. I need most of them for now."

"Your shirt?" she begged.

He removed his fingers and wiped them clean on the bedding. She helped with his buttons. When his shirt was open and his chest was bare, he lowered himself over her, pressing her body into the mattress. He was careful, letting her grow accustomed to his weight, holding himself up on his elbows. Experimentally, she wrapped her legs around him, squeezing his waist between her thighs, longing for more of his bare skin. He moved over her, rubbing his straining erection against her through his trousers, caressing the neediest part of her body with his.

He buried his head in her neck, dropping sucking kisses along her throat and jaw. "Do you feel me now?"

"Yes," she moaned. Stars, how could she not? He was hot and so very hard, his shaft thick and heavy. The curved bulge glided over the furrow between her legs. Muscles low in her belly tightened. She rolled her hips to meet his, surprised as pleasure built anew. It seemed greedy to be on her way to another finish when he'd had none. His body rocked hers, the motion sending pleasurable pulses through her core.

When he paused, a whimper of disappointment escaped her. His lips quirked. He reached down between them, opening his trousers, freeing his length from the confining wool.

He gave her a moment to inspect the shaft with her fingers, her touch tentative. The skin was slate gray and surprisingly silky. The head of his cock leaked a clear fluid. He swiped a drop of his essence onto his finger and lifted it to her lips. She opened her mouth, and he placed it on her tongue, a question in his raised brow.

She tasted him, licking her lips. "Salty," she said. Then she grinned. "Definitely expensive."

Chuckling, he rolled onto his back, taking her with him. With his help, she straddled his thighs, his cock jutting upward toward his exposed belly. The sides of his shirt fell open, revealing an expanse of smooth gray skin, dark nipples, a shallow belly button, and a lean stomach. A tuft of dark hair started below his navel, trailing down to his sex.

Rain explored him, first the head of his cock, then the thick vein that ran down his shaft. Very gently she cupped his balls, his sack satiny and full. His pleased sigh delighted her.

"Do you want to make me come, Lausat?" His eyes had dilated to near black. He fisted his shaft and pumped it once. Her head tipped to the side, absorbing the movement.

She nodded. "You . . . want inside me now?" Nerves had

her body clenching tight.

"You're not ready for that, sweetheart," he said, smiling broadly. Rain exhaled, relieved and disappointed at the same time. He grabbed a pillow and slid it under his head, propping himself up. "We'll get you there, just not tonight."

"But isn't that what you need now?"

"You're small, darling. I'm not, and I don't need to be inside you to spend. Let me take care of your body. Let me show you how good it can be." He gripped her waist, scooting her forward. Then he sat her down against the shaft of his cock, flattening it against his belly. More liquid pearled on the tip, leaking onto his stomach.

Rain hesitated.

"You're not hurting me," he soothed. "Fuck, Rain. You're wet and so damned hot. I'm going to try to bring you to release, but you feel so perfect I can't promise I'll make it."

She smiled down at him, feeling powerful. His face contorted with restraint, then his fingers firmed along her waist, and he moved her. She rocked forward slowly, gratified by the whoosh of his breath, the pink color blooming in his cheeks. When she increased her pace, rubbing sensitive flesh deliciously along his shaft, his nostrils flared, and he bit his lip. The bond loved that.

She loved that.

Pressure building in her sex, she rolled her hips with growing urgency. She was going to come again. It made her feel wanton and greedy and incredibly alive. Her nerve endings thrummed. Seeking balance, she placed the flat of her hands against his chest and worked his cock until her thighs burned. He helped her when her energy waned, pulling her forward and back. She was so wet, the slippery sounds both excited and embarrassed her.

"You beautiful creature," he panted. His murmured encouragements chased away her worries. "Gods, yes, Rain. You're a piece of the divine, a drop of starlight . . ."

His words pulled her farther up that mountain, bringing her to a peak. "Keep talking," she breathed.

"Come, Rain," he begged. "I want your pleasure, sweetheart. Gods, do it now."

She was so deliriously close, and the sight of him grimacing to hold back his release only nudged her farther toward the brink. A sheen of sweat coated her scarred body. Her golden skin glowed dimly in the gloaming.

"*Ardis*!" As her climax crashed over her, her eyes rolled back in her head. Night bucked his hips and pressed her down, lacing his abdomen with his spend.

In the stillness after, Rain ran a finger through his release, curious. She lifted it for closer inspection.

"Rain," he said warningly. "Don't you dare taste me like that. Not tonight. Certainly not with that look on your face."

Her grin felt wanton. "Why not?"

"You're not ready for me to take you yet, you wicked girl. Don't tease me." He swatted her ass, a playful admonishment that startled laughter out of her.

"But we'll get there?" she said hopefully.

"We *will* get you there."

* * *

Rain tended to her saplings at dusk the next evening, Bernard curling and unfurling around her ankle in his cat form. The courtyard's old oak began to rattle its branches at her. She removed her gloves, new ones made of kidskin, and pressed her palm to its bark.

Margot and Susan came to her mind. They both appeared sad in a way that put a lump in her throat. They were asking after her, hopeful she'd come for a visit.

Night was busy. She wasn't certain when she'd see him next, so she left a note, letting him know she planned to go to the tavern. Bernard was excited to get out again.

Along the way, he jabbered about human jokes he'd overheard the kitchen staff sharing. Rain wasn't sure she understood them, but she smiled encouragingly all the same.

The Boot was closed up and empty when she arrived, very unusual given the time of day. Susan and Margot came out to greet her.

"Thanks to the coin you sent us, we're taking a brief holiday to shop for distillery supplies," Susan explained.

Margot appeared several years older than the last time Rain had seen her, but the lively glint in her hazel eyes was still there. Dimmer than before perhaps, but there. She pulled out a leather bracelet with a wooden charm on its end, and she handed it to Rain. Engraved in the center of the round charm were Penny's initials.

"Do you know what that is?" Margot asked.

"A charm?" Rain guessed.

Margot and Susan shared a smile. "Of a sort," Susan said. "It's called a memory flat. Mortals like us use them as a reminder to pray to all of our ancestors. It can get challenging remembering them all. The flats help."

"Oh?" Rain looked it over with new understanding, a fondness spearing through her. "I assumed such things required blood relations."

Margot shrugged. "I've never been blood-related to any of my family," she said, staring pointedly between Susan and Rain.

Rain blinked at her for a time, letting her words take root and grow. Then she hugged her so tightly she made the girl cough. Susan chuckled at the two of them.

"You like it?" Margot guessed.

"I will cherish it," Rain said, voice thick. "Thank you for being my family."

Bernard kept oddly quiet after that. He'd been fond of Penny and had taken her loss as hard as the rest, Rain reasoned.

"Your ancestors are made stronger by your thoughts about them," Susan explained, "and the stronger they are, the more they are able to protect and assist you. When you have something you're thankful for, you squeeze the charm and thank Penny. When you have bad luck, you hold the charm and ask for her to intervene. Just talk to her, Rain. Make her strong enough to help you."

There was something beautiful about that. She rubbed the smooth charm between her fingers and took a moment to thank Penny for her friends. Rain visited with them for a time, sharing about life living with the duke. There was laughter and tears and more talk of Penny. Susan took Rain upstairs, offering for her to take one of Penny's things as a memento.

Rain stared at Penny's unmade bed, her stack of books, the little knickknacks on her nightstand, and she couldn't bear the thought of disturbing any of them. It looked like she'd just left the bed that morning. Like she might walk back into the loft again soon and need all of her things right where they were. There was soul-ache in the realization that she never would, but there was peace in allowing her presence to continue to haunt that space a while longer too.

Penny was safe and warm and cozy now and would be always.

Rain assured them the charm was all she needed. She hugged them in turns, the mortal way. Then she laid her forehead against theirs in the fae way. Before she left, she tied the leather band around her wrist so the charm could rest easily in her palm.

* * *

Bernard remained distant during the walk back, leading the way instead of padding at her side.

Are you all right? she prodded.

Bernard didn't answer immediately. *You called them your family . . . but you haven't known them as long as you've known me . . .*

Rain jogged up to him and scooped him into her arms.

Oh no, Bernard groused.

Rain nuzzled his fur, ignoring how strongly his sulfur scent burned her nose. *Of course you're my family.*

You've never said before, is all, he noted glumly.

Carrying him in the crook of her arm, she scratched behind his ears until he was purring. "Well, of course I didn't. It never occurred to me I've had family all along. I guess it's the Seelie in me. They don't have unconventional families, but I do. No brothers and sisters and cousins. I've got prostitutes and a demon and a duke . . ."

Not very conventional at all, Bernard agreed. *Now unhand me.*

Instead, Rain kissed the top of his head. "You're not any less of a powerful and majestic demon just 'cause you like affection,

Bernard."

I don't like affection.

"Sure you do." She stroked his neck, eliciting more purrs.

He leaned into her touch. *Maybe a little. In moderation.*

Rain headed for the meadow favored by the dragon princess. Cutting through it shortened the distance to Night's estate.

Her home.

Rain! Bernard's shouted warning came too late. The dragae brute was on her in seconds, leaping out from the tall grass, brandishing a dagger. Dusan. That bastard. When he lunged at her, Rain moved her arms instinctively to protect Bernard, giving her attacker a clean shot at her exposed side.

His blade ripped through her traveling cloak, burying itself in her flesh. Rain froze. She knew it had entered her body, but the shock kept the pain at bay.

"Bernard," she gasped. Hot agony scorched through her.

Gnashing her teeth, she recognized that hideous burn. The blade was tipped in iron.

More dragae sprang from the grass and stepped out from the trees. Her familiar burst into a dark cloud and fell over her. Bernard pushed the blade out of her side. The searing pain brought her to her knees.

They're surrounding you. You have to run. Bernard's voice was sure and demanding. It cleared the chaotic thoughts pulsing through her mind.

I . . . I can't just yet.

Yes, you can.

"Oh gods," Rain moaned, climbing back to her feet with sheer will.

Dusan was instantly recognizable, the same bastard who'd imprisoned the girls at the Boot for two days, the one she'd bargained with. Her lip curled back in a grimace.

That one's the least of your worries, Bernard said. *Stay away from the blood mage.*

Nine soldiers circled her. She spotted the blood mage instantly. He was smaller, thinner, and covered in self-induced scars. He had a tail that whipped sided to side, a long scaled one, and he wielded a little penknife, a short folding blade he'd use to carve his flesh, draw his blood in a pattern that called magic to him.

I need your help, Rain whimpered.

I am helping you, Bernard said. *I'm holding your lacerated insides together.*

"Oh fuck," Rain gasped.

Sora, Bernard said. *She owes you a boon, and she'll have no love for these dragae. Get to Sora.*

Rain craned her neck. She couldn't see the hut, not from her position. Rain dropped to her knee again, pretending to be in too much pain—an easy feat given the circumstances. She took hold of the hilt of the dagger in her right boot. When Dusan moved in closer, she pulled the blade and buried it in his thigh. He screamed at the sky.

Run, Bernard shouted.

Rain leapt up and sprinted for her life. Her side screamed at her. She lowered her chin, gritted her teeth, and pressed on. Lunar butterflies shot into the air. The soldiers were fast, the thump of their boots thundering behind her. They jeered and cursed at her, their presence looming closer.

The arm of the Eventide wasn't far now, and Sora's crooked hut came into view.

"Sora!" she screamed. "You owe me a boon!"

The hut rose up on great chicken legs. One swipe of its

massive claws and it threw a clod of dirt as big as a boulder, downing one of her pursuers. Then Rain was tackled to the ground. She scratched and punched and fought. Old and new, her wounds protested. Gritting her teeth, she shoved her thumb toward Dusan's eyes, but the body pinning her into the grass was heavy and strong. He knocked her arms away.

In her peripheral, the great bird legs swiped and stomped and a dragae was crushed into the dirt. Rain reached for her elven blade, but the soldier brought the flat of his head down hard against the soft side of hers. The first time dazed her. The next hit connected, sparks popped behind her eyes, and the world went black.

* * *

Rain came back to herself propped against something moist and unyielding, unsure if she was awake or dreaming.

Thank the blazing stars, Bernard gasped. *Rain? Open your eyes.*

Her lashes lifted. The darkness around her was absolute, save for a distant torch on the cave wall yards away. Her head throbbed. Nausea turned her stomach. Her mouth was too dry, and the air around her was dank with little movement. She had a crick in her neck she wanted to rub out, but when she tried to lift her arm, the pain in her side stole her breath.

Whispering voices drew her attention. Her vision swam, then slowly solidified. The blood mage with the bald head and scars argued with Dusan. Dusan's leg was bandaged with a band of cloth stained crimson.

Can you heal me? Rain asked.

Yes, but you've lost so much blood I'm scared to do anything more than what I've done already.

Rain stretched her arms out behind her, feeling cold stone. The rush of falling water echoed somewhere in the cavernous space. Her hands and feet were frigid. She'd lost feeling in her extremities. The two dragae hadn't yet realized she was awake. They argued.

"I can't guarantee there won't be consequences," the blood mage grumbled.

"King Yaga was clear. If the true mate bond isn't complete, we kill her now and dispose of her."

"Yes," the mage groused, "but the king doesn't wish the Duke of Night to be harmed. I sense their bond isn't complete, but it's very, very strong. I can't guarantee that killing her won't also kill her mate."

Limping, Dusan drew a blade from his side, a curved piece tipped in iron. "Doing anything less than exactly what King Yaga tells you to do is a good way to end up dead. No true mate bond, the witch dies. Those were his orders."

Rain had just enough time to feel panic as Dusan limped toward her, stained dagger in hand, ignoring the blood mage's protests. She raised her arms, shielding her face. He batted her limbs away easily. She kicked out at him, her legs heavy as lead, her pulse slow and sluggish. He dodged it.

With a flick of his wrist, Dusan jerked the end of the blade across Rain's throat. The iron burned like hellfire. She tried to cry out but choked, her throat filling with blood, fingers dragging uselessly over hot wet skin.

I have you, Bernard soothed, his voice small.

Don't let me drown! She could think of no worse way to die, panic gripping her in ice, but Bernard worked quickly, sealing her wound. Her fingers went to the gash in her throat. The skin closed up to form a jagged scar across her windpipe. She choked and swallowed mouthfuls of copper and salt.

"There. She's dead," Dusan said.

The blood mage shook his head. "Her familiar heals her."

"But at what cost?" Dusan looked her over and shrugged. "She's dying."

Bernard, you have to leave me. You have to go get Night. Her breaths came in small gasps, her throat full of poison. She coughed and swallowed. Her heartbeat slowed painfully. Her eyes wanted to close, her vision tunneling and growing hazy around the edges. She was so very cold.

I can't, he said solemnly. *You've lost too much blood. If I leave you now, you'll succumb. I'd die on the way to your mate . . . I'd rather die with you.*

I . . . I'm trying to hold on, she said. Her legs dragged against the cave floor, fighting futilely to get her feet under her. She braced herself, and that little effort brought her so much pain and exhausted her so thoroughly it nearly sent her under. Darkness loomed at the edges of her vision. Her hearing sharpened. The flow of water was loud in her ears, the voices of the dragae arguing louder still.

I know you are, Bernard told her gently.

Tears pricked Rain's eyes. *You don't have to die too. Demons can be reborn, reforged. You can go on. I want you to.*

Bernard's chuckle was low and thoughtful. *That's not for me. I'd rather cling to the piece of soul you gave me and cross over with you, my dear family. I want to walk with you through the stars for the rest of forever.*

I love you, Bernard. Rain sniffled. Her strength was failing. It took every last ounce of will she possessed just to remain upright against the slab of damp stone at her back. She found the charm on her wrist with her fingers and squeezed it. The Penny charm. It was flat and smooth and warm in her clammy palm. She let Penny know she'd see her again soon, then she asked her to look out for their girls.

She thought of her mate, and she begged Penny to make sure that what the blood mage had said wasn't true. When she died, she wanted Night to carry on. She wanted him to fight and win and thrive. She didn't want their growing bond to choke the life out of him.

She wanted him to know how very much she loved him. She'd never have the right words to tell him so. They'd fall from her lips bumbling and stammered, but she'd give them to him anyway.

"This is taking too long," Dusan grumbled. He rounded on her and kicked her, his boot connecting with her shoulder and knocking her to the gravel. Tiny rocks bit at her palms. Splayed out on the cavern floor, her side throbbed and her throat burned. Her breath stirred up a cloud of grit and dirt. Blood coated her tongue.

She was furious, and she was tired. Her body was wracked with shivers, the charm the only source of heat in her hand. *Penny, help me.*

She wanted to live. She wanted to make them pay, make them hurt. Rain gritted her teeth. She wanted to see Night's broken smile again.

Damn it all. She wanted a chance to make him fall in love with her.

Her fingers tightened into trembling fists. Kicking her over was the worst thing Dusan could have done for himself because Rain had a terrible habit. After years of battling as a warrior and a survivalist, she had a will that was unmatched by death.

When knocked down, Rain always got back up again.

* * *

King of Tricksters is available now.